After the Devil

Kayla Frederick

This is a work of fiction. All the characters and events portrayed in this novel are either products of the author's imagination or are used fictitiously.

After the Devil

Story was previously published by Crazy Ink Publishing in 2020

Cover by betibup33
Edited by Samantha Talarico
Library of Congress Control Number: 2024933530
ISBN: 9781950530243
First Edition March 2024

Prologue

OOKS HAD ALWAYS been a huge part of Jamie's life, his favorite escape from reality. He inhaled literature with a speed that shocked his friends. Every break he had, and each moment of restlessness was greeted with a book in his hands. It had been that way since middle school. Instead of dealing with the struggles of cliques and popularity, like other boys his age, he would hole up in the library, losing himself in endless stories.

That was how he found *her,* Alex Alpine.

It was a unique name, the alliteration intriguing him before he read the summary of her book. He clicked on the cover, skimming the first page.

It's our darkest parts that know us best, she had written. *Those parts of us that we're scared to reveal to the light of day. Those are the pieces that make us who and what we are.*

Impressed, he continued to read. At the end of the first chapter, the sample was complete, and he'd have to buy the book to read more. He wasn't a fan of ebooks, but Alex's words had stirred something in him, the very dark parts she mentioned. He hit *buy.*

The clock on the wall told him it was time for work, but he paid it little mind as he settled in to read. *I'll head out after a few chapters,* he told himself. When he looked up again, an entire hour had gone by. Already late, he called off work, ready to finish her every word. His vision started to blur from staring at the screen, but he stayed in the seat until the words *The End* appeared.

The story wasn't over so soon, was it? He wasn't ready. Frantically, he clicked a few keys, trying to conjure a few more pages into existence, but there was no more to read. The clicks took him to the landing page to buy a physical copy, and he didn't second guess himself as he clicked the buy button on that too.

The order confirmation popped up, and that was when he saw her picture. An author photo next to her one-line biography. Time stopped, and suddenly, everything had a new meaning.

That had been the beginning of the rabbit hole.

Love was a concept Jamie had always struggled to understand. He wasn't a psychopath or a sociopath or any of those fancy terms that essentially meant "dead inside," but his feelings for life, and the world around him, were dulled. Numbed by trauma and hardship. The rush of feelings inside him every time he thought of Alex, however, was something, and he considered that something to be close to love.

When her book came in the mail, he hardly wanted to unwrap it from its packaging, worried about damaging it. That same picture of Alex from the website was on the back cover, and it was because of that that he started to carry it around with him everywhere.

It didn't take long for him to discover that Alex had other works. Two in particular, and he went through the same process of reading and buying them that he had done with the first. He scoured the internet, desperate for more, but there were no other pieces by Alex on the market.

Part of Jamie dimmed. Of course he could reread her books, but that wouldn't hit him the way reading something new would.

I need more.

And that was how he began the process of finding her across several social media platforms. Who better to tell him about her writing journey than the author herself?

A year passed, and his adoration of Alex Alpine grew deeper. The intrigue he had first felt at discovering her was blossoming into a very real obsession. There were a lot of people who didn't believe someone could love someone they didn't know. Someone they had never met. Jamie himself used to believe that too, but now, every time he got a notification that Alex had posted something new, existential nervousness worked its way into his stomach. He was a believer now, and no one could tell him otherwise.

The longer he watched her, the more a new urge grew. He yearned to talk to her. The thought that she was potentially one message away never left his mind. He drafted conversations in his head, scrapping every one. Cold words sent through the binary web of the internet would never be enough for her to understand how much she meant to him, and the last thing he wanted was for her to mistake him for a creep and block him.

So, he kept watching, trying to get to the bottom of the mystery of who she was. Her posts often varied from book quotes, to books she was currently reading, and sometimes memes. From her social media, he learned that she was only two or three years younger than he was. She didn't post like other girls their age, barely any selfies and the ones she did take didn't have those god-awful duck lips. In fact, there were hardly any posts about her private life at all, but when they did pop up, they were his favorite.

From what he could gather, she was reserved and quiet—a personality in direct contrast to her looks. She was pretty, face angular with bright blue eyes similar to his own. Her hair was light brown, and her entire persona looked mousy. He could imagine her speaking only in whispers.

Can't wait to dive into this, she had written, and beneath that was a picture of a book.

"*East of Eden*, huh?" he said. "Interesting."

He hadn't known she was a fan of classics, but that particular book happened to be one of the ones on his to-be-read list too. He bought the book with one day shipping.

Chapter One

THE BEEP OF the register was like a metronome, the driving force of Alex's day to day. She heard it so much that the sound blended into the background, fading with the rest of the chatter of the customers and associates around her. The only way she knew the items had scanned was the flicker of red numbers on the black screen before her.

She moved one item after the other on autopilot. It was the best way to get through the day. Otherwise, the boredom threatened to consume her. It wasn't often that the trance was broken, usually only by her breaks and the end of her shift, but the occasional odd item tucked into the groceries did the trick too. This time, it was a book. Subtly, she turned it over, pretending to have a hard time scanning it so she could read the summary. She didn't recognize the author, but the blurb had her attention, and she mentally added it to her to-read list.

The slightest hint of a smile touched her lips as she slipped it into a bag with the rest of the groceries. Alex had always loved books. She used to think she could be an author. She'd written a few books and invested money in self-publishing them. It had been a hopeful time in her life. One where she believed in dreams. A few years down the road, and reality came calling.

In the time since she'd hit *publish,* only a handful of copies had sold. The family and friends who had been supportive at the idea hadn't bothered to buy one to placate her. After admitting her failure, she'd had no choice but to take this job where, day in and day out, she wasted her life away to keep the lights on at home without the promise of her dream to comfort her.

Her lip quivered, but she hid it by saying, "Your total will be $133.72."

The lady on the other side of the register pulled out two hundred-dollar bills, and Alex envied her. She wondered what it would be like to open her wallet and actually see money inside it. Every check Alex got was snatched away by a long list of never-ending bills that always exceeded her meager income.

As Alex cashed the order and counted out the woman's change, her zombie mode reached up to claim her again.

Beep. Beep. The register cooed as she scanned.

On the checkout lane next to hers, two of her coworkers talked a snort of laughter coming her away. She resisted the urge to look, always doing her best not to engage with the others. It wasn't that she thought herself to be better than them; she was simply mindful of the fact her friendship had nothing to offer them.

When she had no customers, she contented herself by cleaning up her area and getting ready to clock out. There would be more work to do when her shift ended, after all. There always was.

When three o'clock came, she called goodbye to her manager and went out the door, her steps on a timed routine. She hopped into her S.U.V. tossing her nametag and vest into the passenger seat beside her and breathed deeply. The alone time was a welcome relief after eight hours of forced socialization. Alex longed to curl up with her daughter, Katrina, and watch a movie. To her, that was the end of a perfect day. As she drove to the daycare to get her, she sang along to the music coming out of her stereo. She couldn't carry a tune to save her life, but something about the act let out all of the stress from her day.

At the daycare, Alex spoke little to the woman she followed one down the long hallway to the yard out back. Katrina was one of many kids streaking across the green grass, caught up in a game of tag. Alex watched her with a small smile as she chased her friend, almost catching her before the girl zigzagged away at the last second. Lately, her daughter was the only thing that could bring that expression to her face.

"Mommy!" the little girl cheered when she noticed Alex.

"Hi, baby," Alex said and hugged her.

"Bye!" Katrina called to her friend and slipped her hand in her mother's.

Alex savored the warm feeling of her skin, her tiny fingers, as they walked back down the hall to the car. "You have a good day?"

Katrina skipped beside her, a smudge of dirt on her face a badge she wore proudly. "Uh-huh. We played hide and seek and watched a movie and had applesauce!"

She chattered away, and Alex offered her a small smile as she worked to buckle her complicated car seat. "That sounds like a fantastic day," she said, wishing she sounded a fraction as amused as her child did.

Katrina didn't notice her sour mood and continued on during the drive. Alex let the chatter soothe her, a melody for her stressed out heart and mind. As they closed in on the apartment complex they called home, her hands tightened on the wheel. She wished they could drive forever, right out of town and into a home full of love and warmth.

But some things weren't meant to be.

They pulled into the parking lot and right into her assigned spot. The building had three stories with people crammed so tightly together that Alex imagined it to be the human equivalent of an ant colony.

Katrina got herself out of the seat, and Alex held her hand as they walked up two flights of stairs to their apartment. At the door, Alex fumbled with her keys, frustrated when the right one didn't open it. Her husband, Peter, must've turned the deadbolt again.

Groaning, Alex pounded on the door with her palm, hoping he would be able to hear her. The last thing she needed was to be locked out of the house for half the day. It had happened before. Peter had, of course, pretended it was an accident, but Alex wasn't so sure.

Frustrated, Alex looked around, eyeing the nearest window, when the door suddenly popped open. Peter stared at her with his usual expression—the one that made him look irritated when he wasn't. As if he were annoyed she wanted to be let inside her own home.

"Thanks," she said, ignoring the look, and pushed her way inside.

Katrina didn't notice the tension. She squealed at her toys and dove to them. Peter scoffed at Alex and went down the hall, to their bedroom. Alex didn't follow him. She knew that to do so would only elicit a fight. Instead, she glanced toward the kitchen. From where she stood, she could see the dirty dishes piled in the sink, waiting for her, and the tiniest twinge of bitterness crawled into her stomach. It had been a good month since Peter had worked, and he'd assured her time and time again that he would be the perfect househusband until another job came through.

So far, Alex hadn't seen it.

Alex looked down at her daughter, who was still young enough to be brimming with the life that had been beaten out of her. "Hungry, sweetie?"

"Yeah," she said, putting a hand to her stomach for added effect.

Alex moved to the tiny kitchen, rummaging through their meager supplies. She couldn't remember the last time they'd had a good grocery run. Food prices got higher, and her check only seemed to get smaller.

Defeated, Alex settled on making the easiest thing she could think of: grilled cheese. She made one for Katrina and one for herself, purposely not thinking about Peter. Plopping the sandwich onto a pink plate, she handed it to her daughter. Katrina had already turned on the television and DVD player, booting up *Frozen* for what had to be the hundredth time since Alex had bought her the movie.

Alex took a bite of the sandwich, but her stomach wasn't interested in the food. It was upset with the knowledge that she had something to do before she could truly get settled for the day. "I'm gonna go talk to your daddy, okay?" she told Katrina.

"Mmhmm," Katrina replied through a mouthful of gooey cheese, eyes glued to the screen.

Clutching her plate, Alex moved down the hall. Peter sat at the edge of their bed, watching TV.

"What? Nothing for me?" He gestured to her plate.

"You're in a mood," she said, purposefully pausing to take a bite of her sandwich.

"I was having a good dream," he replied, yawning. "And you woke me up."

"I take it that means no luck on the job front then," Alex said, hesitantly sitting on the mattress beside him.

He picked up his phone, fingers flying across the keyboard. "I haven't really had time."

Alex lifted her hand to press against her forehead. Pain steadily blossomed there. From Alex's point of view, he'd had nothing *but* time.

Peter looked up, watching her movements with a frown. "What is it now?"

"I don't understand why we pay for daycare if you're gonna be home all day anyway. It was your idea to sign her up so you'd be able to go job hunting, remember?" she said. "That was a month ago. We don't have the money to keep going like this."

"It's *always* something with you, isn't it?" His voice nearly dripped venom as he picked up the remote to increase the volume on the television.

Alex didn't want to be in the room with him, so she got up and went to the living room, each step heavier than the last.

Hollow. She was hollow inside. The way she usually felt after any extended interaction with Peter. A long time ago, his coldness would've hurt, the unprecedented anger a sting, but now, it felt like she deserved it. After all, she was a nobody. She'd only had one real dream in her life, and that had been a failure. Alex had a book still in the works, she added bits to it on her lunch breaks, but it seemed pointless.

Everything did.

If Peter wouldn't get a job, she'd have to find a second one. Otherwise, they were in serious danger. Food was already a rarity. If rent increased like the rumors she'd heard around the complex suggested they might, they would face the possibility of losing their home.

Alex wondered how Peter care so little for her. For his child. *Why did he marry me?* she wondered, not for the first time in her life.

As Alex stepped into the front room, Katrina turned to look up at her, cheese and crumbs around her mouth from her already devoured lunch. Alex slid her mostly uneaten sandwich onto Katrina's plate and turned to go to her tiny computer desk in the corner of the room. She sat in the stiff chair, staring at the black screen.

Autopilot mode kicked on as she pulled up her social media, staring at the little cursor encouraging her to spill her guts. Her eyes welled with tears. Writing had been nothing but a waste of time, energy, and hope that she should've been using to get her family out of this situation. She'd spent enough time hoping her dream would flourish into something. It was time to put an end to it and funnel her skills and effort into something lucrative. Something that could support them.

She started to type: In a Dark Place *was officially my last book. As of today, I am resigning from my writing career to pursue other interests. Thank you for your support. I love you all.*

She read it over, unsure if anyone else would care, and hit *post* before she could change her mind.

Chapter Two

I N A DARK Place *was officially my last book. As of today, I am resigning from my writing career to pursue other interests. Thank you for your support. I love you all.*

No matter how many times Jamie read those words, he couldn't make sense of them. He sat back in his seat, shoving his fingers through his hair without moving his eyes off the post. This couldn't be happening. Jamie tapped his finger on the desk, trying to center himself, but it didn't work.

Automatically, his eyes went back to the computer screen, to the words he wished would change, but they didn't. She *couldn't* quit writing. Her words, her thoughts, were like a drug, and he was addicted. The scars in the crook of his arm itched. He knew from experience that the worst thing a person could do was cut an addiction cold turkey.

But for all his wishing, the post stayed the same.

Jamie stood up so fast he knocked his chair over. Anger bubbling inside him, he reached out, ready to knock all the books and papers to the floor when he restrained himself. Having a mess to clean up wouldn't help the situation any.

Breathe, he told himself, holding his hands in midair where they couldn't do anything destructive.

This wasn't the morning he had been hoping for, not at all. The alarm on his phone started to beep, and he turned it off. It was time for work, but he *didn't want to go.* Not with this news at the front of his mind.

How could he be expected to focus on anything else?

He hit the mouse on accident, the cursor hovering above the comment button. He stared at it. That temptation to message Alex was there again, loud and proud. Usually, he kept it at bay, but it was strong. Stronger than he was used to, and he wasn't sure he had the strength to fight it.

Calmly, he sat back down and picked up his headset, positioning everything before he went to his profile. He didn't have much on it. Not even a profile picture. It had been his way of keeping up with her, and that was it. Outside of that, he had no desire to connect with the world. He stared at the white and gray anonymous picture and wondered if she would be more or less likely to respond if he put an actual picture of himself.

No time, he thought and did the one thing he had wanted to do since he'd discovered her. He hit the *call* button.

Heart thudding against his ribs, he listened while it rang and rang and rang. The longer the moment dragged on, the more he panicked. If she answered, he had no idea what he was going to say. By the fifth ring, he felt as if his head were about to explode, and he hit *end call* before tossing the headset across the room.

Instantly, he regretted it. Regretted doing anything to make him stand out. What if she blocked him for the attempt? Leaning his elbows on the desk, he buried his face in his hands, trying to get himself to calm down. He wanted to tell her everything he felt, that her words were too precious to keep from the world, but he couldn't do it like this.

She would never listen to him. Never *understand.*

The alarm on his phone chimed again, reminding him he had other places to be. *Duty calls.* He grimaced at the unpleasant noise as he fumbled to turn it off.

He dusted himself off and got ready for work, but the panic didn't dissolve. Not that he had expected it to. The entire drive to work, he contented himself by brainstorming possible ways to get Alex to change her mind and write another book. All of them involved getting in direct contact. When he remembered how nervous the failed phone call had made him, he groaned. How could he pull off his important mission if he couldn't talk to her?

It was insanity.

By the time Jamie parked at work, he was shaking. He had the urge to try calling her again, but he didn't want to repeat the ugly emotions the first attempt had flooded him with. He peeked at the chat log long enough to guarantee she hadn't blocked him before he clicked his phone off.

Slowly, he got out of the car, gathering his uniform and doing his best to take his mind off his stress. As he entered the restaurant, he pushed any hint of ugly emotions off his face, forcing a smile to go in their place. It was the same carefree expression he always wore in public, but today it felt fake.

Well, faker than usual at least.

Wherever Alex was in the world, she was hurting, and he couldn't do a thing to comfort her. Instead, he had to waste his life toiling in this place of minimum wage misery. Jamie walked through the dining room, earning a few greetings from the other waiters. He responded politely, always with a smile. As much as the act wore on him, it was important.

None of them suspected the darkness in his head. They had no idea that if he had his way, he would set this place on fire to get out of work for the day. When Jamie pushed his way into the kitchen, his friend and temporary manager of the restaurant, Damien, patted him on the back.

"Good to see you," he said.

Jamie returned the sentiment. Being nice to him was the only thing he didn't have to fake. Damien had been cool to him long before he'd had to step up and fill in for his father when he'd had to step away for medical reasons. The job hadn't gone to his head, and he treated Jamie the same now as he always had.

Jamie looked around the kitchen as a way of getting caught up with the current happenings of the restaurant. From what he could tell, it was a slow time of day. Two tables had customers and neither were in his section. Usually, Jamie adored the downtime, but today, it only made him feel worse. Jamie tied his apron behind his back, checking his pocket for his notepad. He pulled it out, opening it to a blank page. There were no distractions, nothing to keep his hands busy and his mind off Alex. All he wanted to do was check her social media again, to refresh it over and over to see if she was joking. For all he knew, she had deleted the post, and he was worrying over nothing. He found himself writing her name over and over again.

"Jamie. Are you okay?" Damien asked.

Jamie slammed the notepad shut. "Yeah," he said, tucking it away before Damien could see his literal insanity.

With a breath, he put his fake expression back into place and went out to the dining area before Damien could ask any follow up questions. Fidgeting with the black ring on his right hand, Jamie approached a couple seated at one of the tables in his section. "Hi, my name is Jamie, and I'll be your waiter today. What can I get you to drink?"

"Water for me," the woman said, smiling up at him.

"Unsweet tea for me," the man said.

"Coming right up," Jamie said and made his way back to the kitchen. He gathered the drinks and went to the table, setting them down as he retrieved his notepad from its tiny pocket. He flipped past the page he'd filled with Alex's name, trying not to focus on it as he said, "Are you ready to order?"

The man took a sip of his tea and winced. "I said I wanted *unsweet* tea," he complained and set the cup down with such force Jamie thought he'd cracked it.

"Oh, I apologize. I'll get you another one. Be right back," Jamie said and picked up the cup.

When he turned away, he heard the man mumble, "Honestly, how hard is it to get a drink order right?"

On any other day, it would've been easy to brush off the comment. In fact, Jamie considered a large part of his job to be the verbal abuse he suffered from self-entitled people, but today, he was in no mood. Not when his nerves were already on edge.

"I guess as hard as it is to be polite to other people," he retorted, turning back to him.

The man held up his hand, palm out, and refused to look at Jamie as if he were a bothersome fly. Jamie saw red. Before he could stop himself, he launched the full cup of tea at him.

"What the hell?" the man roared, tea dripping from his face to soak into his white shirt. He hopped to his feet to size Jamie up, but Jamie was a good foot taller.

Jamie copied the man's gesture, chin high. He smiled, baiting without words. This balding man and his attitude didn't scare him. Not in the least. "Karma, dear friend," Jamie whispered.

By then, the restaurant had gone silent, the other waiters and customers watching the show. The man pulled back his arm as if he were about to hit Jamie when Damien intervened. He stepped between them, glancing to the man first. "I'm so sorry, sir. Please, your meal will be on us today. I'll see to it that you're attended to by another member of my staff. Melanie!"

As soon as Melanie trotted over, Damien grabbed Jamie's shoulder, pulling him into the kitchen where he would be out of sight of the eyes that still clung to him. The eyes that dared him to do something else.

"Dude, what the hell was that about?" Damien asked as soon as the door closed, separating them from the main room.

Jamie swiped his fingers over his forehead, wiping away the bit of sweat that had gathered. "It's been a rough day."

Damien looked Jamie over. What he was looking for, Jamie wasn't sure. "We all have our rough days, but you can't go taking it out on the customers."

"He started it," Jamie said.

"They pretty much *always* do, but if we attacked every customer who pissed us off, we'd be out of business in a week."

Jamie frowned and folded his arms over his chest.

Damien's took in a deep breath. "Look, chill here for a minute. I gotta go handle that, okay?"

"Thanks, man," Jamie said.

As soon as Damien went back out, Jamie stared down at the floor. Alone with his thoughts, the shame came. Had he really lost his cool so easily? And in front of everyone at that. If his boss wasn't his friend, there was a good chance he could've been fired.

I can't live like this.

Alex had gotten under his skin. He breathed her words, and without them, he felt as if he were suffocating. While he waited for Damien to return, he pulled his phone out, checking her page. There was no sign that she had messaged him after the call. No way to tell if she had noticed he'd done so. At the top of her page, that terrible post was still there. Still taunting him to do something about it.

"Can I trust you to go back out there?" Damien asked as he came back into the kitchen.

Jamie hurried to tuck the phone away. "Yes, you can."

"I'm going to hold you to that," Damien said. "Arden is late, so make yourself useful and clean up a couple of tables for me."

Jamie grabbed the bus-bucket, tucking it under his arm as he went back out to the dining room. The man he'd nearly gotten into a fistfight with glared at him, but Jamie kept his back to him. Like that, it was easy to block out the rest of the world.

The next few hours drifted by in an uncertain fog. Jamie wasn't sure of much besides Damien watching over him as if he expected Jamie to break down again at any moment. Jamie somehow kept himself together. At the very least, he didn't throw any more drinks. When his lunch came, he let out the first real breath he'd taken since the altercation at the beginning of his shift. He dug a pack of cigarettes out of his locker and saw the book nestled among his apron and notepad.

In a Dark Place. It was Alex's final book.

He pulled it out and ran his fingers over the cover before he closed the door. Tucking the book against his body, he moved through the restaurant. This time, any greetings called to him were ignored. Only when he was alone in his car did he give himself permission to pore over the book. He stared at her picture on the back cover. She was smiling, the sunlight sparkling her light brown hair with blonde highlights, and suddenly, he could picture himself there beside her.

His hand started to shake and all his earlier fears melted away. Phone calls weren't for him. They never had been, but that was okay. It wasn't the only way he could get in contact with Alex. Maybe, just maybe, he could *find* her. Track her down and tell her the error of her ways. Surely he'd be able to get his point across in person.

Jamie adjusted himself in the seat. He imagined Alex's blue eyes staring at him, waiting to speak, and nervousness came over him again. He'd be just as tongue-tied in person, he was sure.

Like a bolt from the blue, a new plan emerged. Maybe instead of talking her down, he could persuade her to see things from his perspective. He could show her the effect her words had on people, and for that reason, she couldn't give up on her gift. She couldn't give up on *him.* His spirits lifted. All the uneasiness, the uncertainty, the *weight* that he had carried the entire day vanished in a wisp of smoke.

All Alex needed was some guidance, and clearly, she wasn't getting it from the people around her. He could offer that and so much more. Jamie's heart swelled at the idea of having her all to himself, and he stared down at the picture with a brand-new level of intensity.

I'm coming for you.

Chapter Three

USUALLY, THE FIRST thing Alex did in the morning was check her sales. It was an app on her phone that took forever to load, and then the disappointment would crush her when she'd see one, maybe two sales tops. Then, she remembered the night before and her decision to quit writing forever. She hadn't actually delisted her works yet, but the resolve made her not want to check.

She wanted to forget everything about her dream, cut it off like a dead hand, and turn to something more productive. Something she could cling to that would help her support her family. Logically, she told herself it was the best move she could make, but inside, she was hollow. Writing had been her therapy for so long, she wasn't sure what to do without it. She'd never really had many friends, and writing let her get out the thoughts that had no other place to go.

Rubbing her eyes, she sat up. Peter was asleep beside her, and she did what she could to get up without waking him. Katrina was asleep too, nestled into the soft pink blankets on her tiny bed, and Alex let herself breathe. The apartment was quiet. She made a cup of coffee, enjoying the moment of peace and turned on her phone.

A tiny *one* sat next to her messaging app. Alex clicked on it. She had a missed call from a *Jamie* with no profile picture.

"Ugh, scammers," she murmured and turned her phone off.

She drained the last sip of coffee and decided that since she had no work for the day, she would make productive use of her time and clean the apartment.

By the time she finished, Katrina was awake, and Alex made breakfast for her and her daughter. Peter was still asleep, mouth wide open and drool covering his chin. Alex sat with Katrina, balancing her plate of food on her lap as she watched cartoons. When Peter finally woke up, their breakfast was long gone and the dishes washed. Alex was at her desk, searching through a list of local job listings.

Peter stood at the end of the hall, staring at her. Alex didn't know he was there until he said, "No work today?"

She bobbed her head, clicking on a potentially promising link before looking at him. "It's my day off."

Peter huffed and crossed the room to the kitchen. He plucked the gallon of milk out of the fridge and sipped from it. "I thought you just had an off day."

Alex turned to look at him full on. "No, I haven't."

Peter made a face and turned his back to her to try to hide it.

Alex's skin crawled with intuition. "Why? You expecting company or something?"

"No," he said and went back to the room.

Forgetting her task, Alex followed him. "Is everything okay?"

"Yeah, yeah," Peter said without looking up from his phone. "I have…an interview today."

"Oh, where at?"

Peter pretended he didn't hear her, tucking the phone into his pocket as he changed shirts. Alex went to ask him again when he shouldered his way past her and went into the bathroom, closing the door. The faint murmuring of his voice through the wall was clear. He was on the phone with someone.

Who?

A bad feeling crawled into the pit of Alex's stomach as she waited for him to emerge. It niggled at her, like a tick burrowing under her skin.

It's a woman, she somehow knew.

Peter came out a few minutes later, hair combed and cologne on in such a cloud that she could smell it before he opened the door fully. His eyes widened when he realized how close she was, but he said nothing as he pushed past her.

"Who were you talking to?" she called after him.

"Huh?"

"In the bathroom? I could hear you on the phone with someone."

"I think you're imagining things," he said, pulling on his sneakers.

"I don't think I am," she replied, folding her arms over her chest as she studied him. There was a twitch in his jaw, and his shoulders were tense. There was definitely *something* he wasn't telling her.

Peter glanced up at her as he tied the laces. "What are you implying?"

"I don't think you're going to a job interview."

Peter rolled his eyes and stood up, glaring at her. "Don't

start this again."

Alex opened her mouth, but she couldn't think of a thing to say. Peter grabbed his keys and slipped out into the world, not bothering to say goodbye as he went.

Katrina looked up with wide eyes. "Is Daddy mad at you, Mommy?"

"No, baby, it's okay," Alex said. "Watch your cartoons."

"Okay," she said chipper as ever and grabbed one of her stuffed animals, holding it as she plopped in her little pink chair.

Alex watched her for as long as she could before she hurried to the bedroom, barely making it before the dam inside her broke. She leapt onto the bed, screaming into the pillow. Peter was cheating on her. She was sure of that.

Her life had officially hit rock bottom.

Alex felt a thousand things at once and then nothing. She was small, useless, and replaceable. For everything she did, she simply wasn't enough. Her insides felt as if they were drawing inward, taking her with them. Alex's palms itched for the familiar feeling of a blade, and she sat up, glancing at the scars all varied in color and healing down her arms.

Before she knew it, she was in the bathroom, her trusty pocketknife in her hand. The silver sliced across her skin, the pain hardly registering over the sadness. Four more slashes and the blade came away red, a metallic smell flooding her nostrils.

The knife clattered into the sink, and she watched with morbid curiosity as her blood began to flow. Crimson streams dripped against the porcelain. She imagined all her pain and rage leaking free with it. The cuts were deeper than she usual, and a swell of fatigue swept over her as her body tried to compensate for the loss.

When the blood on her cuts clotted, she was calm inside. The storm had passed. Every emotion she had felt only a few minutes prior no longer existed. No longer mattered. She stared off into space, a kind of high produced by the spike of her adrenaline.

"Mommy?" Katrina called.

Her tiny fist banged on the door, and Alex came back to herself as quickly as she had left, staring at her pitiful expression in the mirror with disgust. "One minute, baby," she said and went to work cleaning up all traces of her own blood.

Chapter Four

B Y DEFAULT, JAMIE was a private person, but he loved social media. It was so easy to exploit it. People often put more about themselves online than they realized. In spite of Alex's privacy settings, it wasn't hard to use the information she'd provided to find the town she lived in. She was four hours away somewhere in Louisiana. He couldn't believe his luck. If he did everything smoothly, he could nab her and be across state lines before anyone was any the wiser.

As he planned out his trip, he was careful to consider all possibilities. He could try to slip the trip in on his next day off, but he didn't want to do that. Didn't want to feel pressured. A week off should be more than enough time to stake out the place, grab her, and make it home. As he pulled out his phone, he was glad to be friends with his boss. Damien wasn't happy about the request, but after the incident with the man and the drink, it was easier to negotiate the time off.

It would be their little secret why.

Jamie was on cloud nine as he drifted around his house, packing clothes and other essentials in a black duffel bag. The first book he had bought of Alex's was tucked right at the top where he'd be able to see her picture without having to open the bag all the way.

On his way to the door, he stopped in the kitchen and grabbed a can of soda. The less stops he'd have to make on the drive, the better his nerves would hold up. The chances would be low, but he didn't want anyone to report seeing him traveling to or from Alex's town. For that same reason he had three canisters full of gasoline in his trunk.

Hand on the doorknob, he stopped and surveyed his living room one more time. Inside his head, he ran through a final checklist of everything and stepped outside, locking the door behind him.

***

FOUR HOURS LATER, he found himself in Ponchatoula. It wasn't much different from his own town, perhaps a little bit bigger. It was small enough to maneuver without getting lost, but big enough that he didn't have to worry about standing out. The hotel he'd planned to stay at was right on the outskirts of town, and he parked, grabbing his bag from the backseat. He slung it over his shoulder and went into the lobby.

There was a woman maybe a few years older than him at the reception desk. She smiled at him wide enough to show her teeth, but he didn't return the look. He was used to women looking at him like that, hoping they could get something from him. At one time, he tried to feed those desires, but the truth was that they did nothing for him. He didn't have those tendencies, those urges. Couldn't understand why anyone else did either.

He downplayed those thoughts, returning the woman's smile as he reached the counter. "Hi, I called and made a reservation. Jamie Knox."

"Alright, let me pull up your info. Got your driver's license?"

"Yep," he said, setting it on the counter.

She studied it over. "From Texas, huh? What brings you to Louisiana? Business or pleasure?"

Jamie tapped his fingers on the counter, eyeing a plant in the corner beyond the desk. "Let's say both."

"Sounds like you've got yourself a week planned out." A giggle that Jamie wished would end and then, "Here's your key. Have a nice stay."

"Thanks," Jamie said, scooping it up before she could say anything else. Their two-minute interaction had been draining enough.

His room was on the second floor, beside the staircase and a door that led out to the parking lot. It would be easier for him to get in and out without being seen. Better for him. Jamie slid the key into the door and opened it to a tiny room. It smelt of cleaners and disinfectant, and he crossed through the tiny kitchen to the king-sized bed. Jamie tossed his bag onto the red comforter and sat beside it, going to work spreading out the contents across the bedspread. There were some ropes, a tiny bottle of chloroform he had bought from a sleazy guy behind a gas station on the way, and a couple changes of clothes.

It was clear what he was here to do. Staring at his items together should've made him rethink his plan, but he didn't. Instead, he found himself wondering what it would be like to bring Alex back here. He couldn't risk that, but it didn't stop the thoughts. Focusing on the last item in the bag, the copy of

Alex's book, he turned it over to see her picture again before he hugged it to his chest. Being in the same city as her brought out new feelings in him that he hadn't anticipated. His skin nearly crackled with intensity, with the desire to see her. To *touch* her.

That was probably the strangest part of it all.

Now that he was settled, it was time to scope out the town and find where she worked. With another scan of his room, he grabbed the list he had created of stores that could fit the description, along with her book, and went back out to his car, glad to have the side door available to avoid another interaction with the receptionist.

As Jamie started up his car, he thought about what he knew of this place. Alex had never posted much about her day job. A few little stories here and there, sometimes selfies, but nothing concrete. A year of following her had given him time to gather enough hints to piece it together. She was at a grocery store of some sort. There were maybe a handful of those in this town, but based on color schemes in her pictures, it was easy to rule out a majority of them. That still left a list longer than he was happy with, and he was glad he'd had the foresight to get an entire week off. It might take that long to find the right place. Pumping himself up, he exited the parking lot of the hotel.

The first store he decided to check was the one directly across the street. It was a gas station/convenience store, and as soon as he entered it, he knew it wasn't the place. It didn't match any of Alex's pictures.

Happy to already be making progress, he crossed it off and went to the next one on the list. It was more promising, but after a walk around the place, he was confident in crossing it off as well. That accomplished feeling turned to dejection and then disdain once ten of the names were scribbled through, and he was no closer to finding her. This town was bigger than he had hoped it'd be. Not to mention the fact that he had no idea what Alex's daily schedule was like. Here he was checking out late evening shifts when she could be a morning shift worker.

His head started to feel spacey, the first feeling of dissociation, and he considered calling it a night. A good night's rest would fix him, but he planned the route back to the hotel in a way that would allow him to hit one more store before turning in. When he pulled into the parking lot, his eyelids drooped, and he nearly slammed his forehead to the steering wheel. Shocked, he jolted awake, glad he had already parked.

I need an energy drink.

He had been sitting most of the day. It was reasonable to assume that some exercise would do him good. Maybe it would help him perk up. His legs were rubbery when he climbed out and stretched. The inside of the store was bright, his head aching with the sensation. Jamie tried to keep the light from his eyes as much as possible as he traveled to one of the drink coolers near the front of the store. He snagged an energy drink and got in line when he saw the cashier at the register.

She smiled at her customer and turned to glance to the next person in line. Jamie's breathing was rough, and it took control to even it out, to keep himself from getting light-headed. It was *her*. Alex Alpine. In the flesh. In person, she was much smaller than he'd guessed, and that only made her more adorable. The line ahead of him moved, but he was petrified. A sharp jab came from behind, and he turned to see an elderly woman glaring at him.

"Sorry," he said and slid out of place.

He used the nearby self-checkout, studying Alex over the top of the machine. She didn't notice. Her head was down, her mousy hair framing her face as she focused on the task before her. After Jamie paid, he lingered at the Coke machine beside the door, risking a glance over his shoulder. She looked up at the same moment, catching his eye. A bolt of electricity zapped through him, staying with him during his jog to his car.

He sat in the driver's seat, downing half his drink in one go as he thought about their moment of eye contact. Jamie had planned to spend the night in the hotel and continue scoping in the morning, but if things worked out, he could catch her when she got out of work. Right here and now.

Jamie tingled all over with the possible plan. He edged his car to a spot closer to the front of the store and waited. By the time she came out, Jamie finished his drink and contemplated running back inside to use the bathroom. His heart skipped a beat as soon as he saw her. She stepped into the parking lot, the silver light of the moon reflecting off her hair. Jamie licked his lips, prepared to head toward her when a car beat him to it, pulling up beside her.

He halted, watching as she opened the back door. There was a miniature version of her in the backseat, and Alex greeted her. Jamie leaned back in his seat. He knew she had a family, but he hadn't wanted to *see* any of them. The moral part of his conscience wanted to nag at him, to tell him that stealing her from them was wrong, but he didn't want to hear it.

He tried to move himself back to anger. Anger was what he *should* feel. After all, it had almost been the perfect moment to put his plan into action.

Was it though? he asked himself.

There were too many witnesses here, too many people who could've stopped him or gotten his license plate number. No, this was a beginning. A point he could start from to craft a smarter, steadier plan.

Soon, he thought, watching Alex climb into the passenger seat.

The unknown driver pulled out of the parking lot, never suspecting Jamie following in close pursuit.

Chapter Five

THE NEXT MORNING started off the way Alex's nearly constant anxiety warned her it could. During the night, her phone died and her alarm went with it. She woke on her own, and when she realized what time it was, she jumped up and got ready in a panic. Her heart felt as if it had climbed up into her throat and decided to take permanent residence there.

Alex breezed out the door in such a hurry she didn't bother to brush her hair. When she made it to work, she was disheveled and breathing hard. Inside the store, a rush of customers clattered around her as she hurried to the time clock, trying to shave off any minutes she could. At last she punched in, finally getting hold of herself. Alex made a move to head to her register when she bumped into someone.

The last person she wanted to see. Kyle Miller. Her boss.

Arms folded across his chest, he glared at her. "You just get here, Alex?"

Alex considered lying, but there'd be no use. He already knew.

"Can I see you in my office, please?"

There was a bad feeling in the pit of Alex's stomach, but she followed him anyway. The office felt ridiculously small when he closed the door, taking his seat behind the desk. Alex eyed the chair beside her before at last convincing herself to use it.

"Do you know why I called you in here?" he asked, leaning on his elbows to peer at her.

"Cuz I was late?"

"You were late *again*," he emphasized, tapping his fingers on the desk. "There's been a decline in your work ethic, and it's garnered a few customer complaints. I don't know what's happened to you, Alex, but this is not acceptable behavior."

Alex breathed out, sitting up a little straighter. "I'm sorry, really. My phone died this morning and—"

He held up his hand. "To be frank, I'm a little tired of hearing your excuses. It's always something with you."

Peter's words. Those were *Peter's* favorite words, and the sentence hit her like a kick to the abdomen. "It won't happen again," she squeaked, trying to keep the tremor out of her voice.

"You're right, it won't," he said, reclining in his chair before he added, "You're fired."

"Wait. You can't do this," Alex said, gripping onto the edge of the table until her fingers hurt, and the skin turned white. "I'm sorry, I'll do better!"

"I'm sorry, Alex. It's nothing personal, but I've given you so many chances, and you've let me down every time," he said, getting up to go to the door. He held it open, staring at her expectantly.

Alex's bottom lip trembled, and it didn't matter that she told herself not to cry because she did it anyway. She hurried past him, shielding her face as she rushed through the throngs of customers with tears streaking her cheeks. Once her car door closed behind her, she let it out, the sobs wracking her body as she hid her face in her hands.

When she looked up, there was a man a few cars down peering at her, and she sniffled, thinking how foolish she must look. It wasn't often that she let her emotions show, fearing others would see her as weak, but in the moment, she hadn't realized how many people there were to witness her spiral. Wiping her eyes with the back of her hand, she turned the engine on, pulling out of the parking lot. Silent tears rolled down her cheeks as she made the drive home, but no more sobs accompanied them. Instead, there was a pit in her stomach. Peter already thought she was less than useless. What would he think when she told him what had happened?

He'll blame you, that tiny voice in her head. *He'll say you did this on purpose.*

As she turned off the car and started to trudge up the stairs to her apartment, she found no way to disagree. Her stomach sloshed when her foot hit the top step. She tried to push everything into that dark place in her stomach, wishing the butterflies would digest so she could face this head on. The door opened easily to her key, and that left her wondering if Peter had woken up to bolt it behind her. Inside, Katrina was seated on her blanket on the floor, her huge eyes watching television.

"Hi, Mommy," she said without looking away.

"Hi, baby. Is Daddy in the room?"

"Yes."

Alex was still unsure what she would say as she traveled

to the bedroom. For all the tension in her spine, she could've been walking to her own execution. She stood in the doorway, peering at her husband. Part of her hoped he'd be asleep, but that hope was dashed when she realized he was awake, watching TV. He looked peaceful, and Alex took a step forward, feeling weird with the knowledge that she could, and would, destroy his peace of mind with only a few words.

"Hi," she said at last.

He turned to look at her, eyebrows drawing together as he sat up, like he wasn't sure he was really seeing her. "What are you doing home so early?"

Her feet felt like lead as she moved to sit on the edge of the bed, staring down at her hands. "I uh…I have some bad news."

"Oh?"

"I got fired," she said, quickly, maybe too quickly, but that was the best way to rip off the band-aid.

"You *what*?"

Alex worked up the nerve to look at him. Every feature on his face was twisted into something fierce. He glared, and Alex squirmed in her skin, suddenly wishing she wouldn't have said anything at all. She could've spent the rest of the day job-hunting. Who knew, maybe she could've gotten a new job without Peter realizing what had happened.

Too late now.

"I-I got fired," she repeated, voice low. Pathetic. At that point, she was almost like a submissive animal, waiting on the mercy of her dominant pack leader to decide her fate.

"You've got to be kidding me."

"I didn't mean for this to happen," Alex said, trying to keep the tears in her eyes like she'd done in Kyle's office. "My phone died, and I didn't wake up in time. I left as soon as I could, but my boss said he wasn't going to give me anymore chances."

"Is this because of yesterday?"

"What?" she asked, confused. Then, "No."

"It seems funny you were so dead set on the idea that I wasn't really going to a job interview, and now you're fired?" He rolled his eyes as if it was obvious. "If you're trying to prove a point, it's not a good one."

"How did it go?" Alex asked softly, eyes on the ground.

"What? The interview?" Peter laughed. "I didn't get the job so you should've thought twice before losing yours."

"I didn't *want* to get fired," she tried to protest, but her voice was soft and weak.

Peter waved his hand. "Save it. Leave me alone. I can't deal with this right now."

The tears started to spill down her cheeks, and Peter watched her, grinning, before turning back to the television. Alex hurried into the bathroom, palms tingling with the urge to hold her pocketknife again. She leaned over the sink, staring at her reflection in the mirror. The air felt too thick to breathe. She was on the verge of having a panic attack, far worse than any she'd had in a while.

I need fresh air, she thought, knowing the last thing she wanted was for Katrina to see her like this.

Alex nearly flew through the living room and out the front door, sure not to slam it behind her. The neighbors didn't need to be let it on the fact that they were having problems.

Everything was too much. She hurried down to her car, with no idea where she was going to go. Besides work, she didn't go out. She had no friends, and she'd never had much of a family either, but she was desperate to get away.

Where do other sad people go?

The idea of bars made her skin crawl. Her father had been so heavily dependent on alcohol after the death of her mother that Alex had seen the ugliness it could present in a person firsthand. Long ago, she'd vowed to never be anything like her father, but right then, she couldn't deny that the idea of losing herself in alcohol seemed a far better alternative to being sober.

Chapter Six

TWO DAYS OF following Alex in person taught Jamie more about her than the year of following her on social media. There were still plenty of things he didn't know. Things he wondered about—what she smelt like, the sound of her voice, and maybe more importantly, how she'd react to seeing him.

Jamie didn't know how much longer he'd be able to wait to get close to her. Based on what he had seen of her routine, it might be a while. She didn't seem to leave her house much, and when she did, it was usually with the little one in tow.

He idled in the parking lot of her apartment complex, hood pulled up to shadow his eyes as he reclined in his seat, waiting for the first bit of movement. Alex went flying down the stairs, hair sticking up on one side as if she hadn't bothered to brush it after getting out of bed. There was a nametag pinned hastily to her shirt, but the rest of her work uniform was gone.

Her driving was reckless, and Jamie had to tell himself several times not to copy her as he followed close behind. She would notice him then. *Everyone* would notice him if he drove like that. Alex got several honks, but her erratic driving didn't cease. Running a red light didn't bother her.

At last, they made it to the grocery store he had seen her at on that first day. Her car barely slowed before she threw herself out of it, rushing through the door. Jamie inched into a spot a few spaces down, a tiny smile on his face.

From her pictures, she always looked clean and put together. He wouldn't have taken her for the type to be late for anything. Figuring she would be here for a few hours, Jamie thought of going back to the hotel and taking a nap. He started the car up, ready to back out of the spot when Alex reappeared outside the door. Her nametag was gone, her red face hidden under her hair.

From across the lot, he could tell she was crying, and he wondered what had happened. Had she gotten fired? His lip quirked upward. If that was the case, it would certainly make things easier. After all, there would be less people to notice she was gone.

Excitement buzzing through him, he followed her back to her apartment, pulling into his usual spot beneath an oak tree, the shade ensuring his dark car didn't stand out. He ducked down in his seat, peering at the driver's side mirror to make sure he was inconspicuous as she got out of her car. For a minute, she stood there, not moving as she looked up at the building.

He couldn't imagine what she was thinking. Her gaze fell to her feet, and she crossed the parking lot. Jamie's sat up, watching her go. This might be the last he saw of her for the day, and the look on her face had been heartbreaking.

He contemplated what he would do next, when Alex made *another* appearance, face much redder than earlier. Jamie's fingers gripped around the steering wheel as he watched her.

Alex was in her own little world. She sat in the driver's

seat of her S.U.V., not bothering to turn the engine over. Her arms were laced over the steering wheel, face pressed to them as she cried.

His heart hurt. All he wanted to do was go over there and comfort her, to tell her it was alright. That things would get better. Jamie's fingers inched to grab the handle of his car door, and he had to take a full minute to chastise himself. It didn't matter how well *he* knew *her*, he was a stranger to her.

As if she had heard his thoughts, Alex finally lifted her head, wiping her face with the back of her hand before she turned her car on. She plucked out her phone, its light streaming through the window, and then she started to drive. Jamie trailed her, staying closer to her bumper than he had over the course of the past two days, but the change in her routine was too intriguing to lose her.

Where could she possibly be going?

His question was answered a minute later when she pulled into a bar. Jamie had to stomp his brake to avoid ramming her. In the best way he could manage, he slowed down in front of the next building and made a careful U-turn, easing his way into the original parking lot. He parked in the closest open space to the exit and peered through the cars, picking out her slight form. She had stopped crying, her mousy hair knotted together and thrown over one shoulder. As he watched her, he convinced himself she wouldn't go inside.

Alex seemed to wage the same war inside of herself. For a minute, she stood outside the door. Someone came out, holding the door open for her as he left, and she plastered a fake smile on, disappearing inside. Jamie's mouth went dry, feet itching to chase after her. All that separated him from his favorite author was about a hundred steps.

He unbuckled his seat and looked at the supplies tucked under his passenger seat. Everything had fallen into place so far. This was the last step he had to take. Yet, he couldn't move.

Going inside is the worst thing you could do, he told himself.

He thought about everything he had seen, and his brain turned against him, warning him that this was the opportunity he had been waiting for, and he was letting it slip through his fingers.

He argued back for a little while until his brain wandered to the fact that there were *other* men inside the bar. Men with the real potential to bring harm to a delicate human like Alex. The idea of anyone else approaching her had him moving through the door before he could tell himself again how bad of an idea it was.

I need to keep her safe, he told himself, wiping his sweaty palms on his jeans.

The dim lights inside the bar made everything a bit disorienting. His eyes adjusted, and he slipped into a seat at the table nearest to the door. There were two other tables in the place, but Alex wasn't at either of them. His eyes roamed, gauging everyone. Paranoid, he was sure that they would see him for what he was and would call him out on his plan. A couple sat with their heads bowed closely together at a nearby table and there was a man in a suit drinking at the bar.

When he finally found Alex, she was nestled into a seat at the end of the bar, a large colorful drink in front of her. Jamie relaxed, keeping his head down as he watched her. He wanted to order himself a drink, knowing that the longer he didn't, the more he'd stand out, but he didn't want to risk her seeing him before he was ready.

Alex went through one drink and then another. Her sips started to slow, and he thought she'd call it quits when the bartender placed a third drink in front of her.

Jamie wouldn't have taken her for a drinker, but she had to have somewhat of a tolerance to keep drinking at her size.

Now or never.

Swallowing down the butterflies in his stomach, he rose from the table. On shaky legs, he approached the bar, hoping no one could see how out of his element he was. Leaning on the counter close to Alex, he waved down the bartender. "Get me a beer."

The bartender nodded, and at last, he turned to look directly at Alex. The low light sparkled in her blue eyes, and she gazed up at him through full eyelashes. He almost choked on his tongue as he added, "And another round for the lovely lady over here."

Alex smiled at him then looked down at her cup shyly, grasping it with long pale fingers to swirl the remaining contents around.

Encouraged, Jamie sat on the stool beside her, resting his elbows on the bar. "Never too early in the day for a good drink, right?"

"Yeah," she murmured, and her sip disappeared.

"There you are," the bartender said, placing a drink in front of each of them.

"Thanks, man," Jamie said then turned back to Alex as he tilted the bottle back. Now that the moment had come, he didn't know what to say. What he *could* say. He had been so focused on how he would approach her, he hadn't brainstormed what would come after. He wanted to tell her how much he loved her books, how much he loved *her,* but that would scare her. Everything that wanted to spill out of him was inappropriate.

Jamie took a deep swig from his bottle, glad for the tiny buzz of alcohol coursing through his veins. He needed the liquid courage.

"Thanks for this," she said, softly, almost as if she were speaking to herself. "I had…kind of a rough day today."

"Explains why you're in a bar at one in the afternoon," he said with a tiny chuckle. When he caught sight of the red streaks on her cheeks again, it caught in his throat. "But really, I'm sorry to hear that. Hopefully this makes it better."

She swirled the tiny black straw. "It does a little, I suppose. I got fired today, so blowing my money on alcohol probably isn't the smartest thing I've ever done."

"Guess it's a good thing I'm here to pick up the tab then," he said with a careful smile. Then, more seriously he added, "Was it a customer's fault? I'll tell you, I had a little altercation at my job last week. Threw a drink at the guy. Needless to say, my boss was *not* happy at all."

Alex chuckled. "Bet not."

Jamie took another sip. "So, sounds as if your day is wide open. Any plans?"

"I'm most likely going to hang out for a while. I thought about job hunting, but I don't think I'm in the head space for it. And things aren't so great at home right now either so…I don't know why I'm telling you this," she said with a nervous laugh.

"Well, alcohol is good for the soul," Jamie said, taking another swig for emphasis.

She picked up her glass, holding it out to him. "To new friends."

He clinked his bottle. "To new friends."

They fell silent, but Jamie kept a careful eye on Alex's movements. As the alcohol took over, she started to slump in her seat. Before she faceplanted the bar, Jamie threw some money beside her cup and slung his arm over her shoulders. The bartender didn't notice, but he would in a minute.

Alex was light and delicate, the smell of her perfume reminding him of a field of flowers. Briefly, she looked up at him, eyelids fluttering, and he thought she'd tell him to back off. She said nothing, letting out a strong breath that reeked of alcohol before she rested her cheek against his chest. He glanced around, but no one was paying them any attention.

He slipped Alex off the stool, expecting to have to nearly carry her. Alex's steps were shaky, but she managed to walk on her own. Jamie counted his blessings and nearly buzzed with energy as he led the way to his car. She leaned into him as he reached out to open the passenger door, easing her into the seat.

Head resting on the leather behind her, she peered up at him and asked, "Where…are we going?"

"Home," he said, reaching over her to buckle her in.

He expected some protest, some fight, but got none and suspected she was too drunk to fully process what was happening. Closing the door, he surveyed the parking lot. After ensuring that no one watched them, he opened his trunk, rummaging for the needed supplies. He crouched down behind Alex's bumper and popped off the license plate, replacing it with a fake one before he hurried back to the safety of his car.

As he started the engine, Alex didn't stir. He waited until they were out of the parking lot to glance over at her, worried what he would see when he did. She was curled into the seat, her cheek resting beneath the window.

It looked as if she were asleep, nothing more and nothing less.

Chapter Seven

JAMIE'S FOOT FELT as if it were made of lead. It took effort to take it off the gas pedal, to slow the car down every time he came to a red light and to keep under the speed limit. He wanted to blast out of the county and out of the entire state of Louisiana without stopping. He couldn't believe that his plan had worked. Couldn't believe that Alex Alpine was really two feet from him in the same car. Heart still thudding erratically, he had to put work into getting himself under control to focus on what would come next.

Warily, he pulled into the parking lot of the hotel, making sure to park in a spot at the back of the lot, far from any prying eyes. He turned off the engine and glanced over at her. The drive had jostled her around, and she slouched at an angle that was guaranteed to leave her with a neck ache when she woke up.

As gently as he could, he reached over her, reclining the seat so that Alex was out of sight, and anyone who got too curious might think she was napping. Taking in a breath to compose himself, he hopped out of the car and hurried inside the hotel.

Jamie kept his head down as he went through the side door and up to his room. There wasn't anyone in the hall, and he was grateful. Part of him was sure they would see the utter panic on his face, and he didn't have time to worry about lasting impressions. Jamie breezed around the room in such a hurry that he hardly remembered packing everything back into his bag. Before he knew it, he was moving to the lobby, bag slung as casually over his shoulder as he could manage.

He tried to keep his face warm as he approached the desk. Like someone normal. Not like someone who was in the process of kidnapping a woman. The receptionist was the same one who had checked him in a few days prior. As soon as she saw him, she perked up, and Jamie felt himself wilt a little inside with the knowledge that she was about to make their interaction harder than it needed to be.

"I'd like to check out," he said, digging into his pocket for the key.

"Aww, so soon?" she asked, typing something into her computer. "You still have a few days on your reservation."

"Yep. Things are about wrapped up here," he said and set the key card onto the desk, sliding it toward her to emphasize his point. "I'm ready to get back home."

"That's too bad," she said, picking up the key and twirling it in her fingers. "If you've got the time, I would really love to take you out for a coffee."

"Yeah, no thank you," he said, thrumming his fingers on the counter in annoyance. "I'm sorry."

Her face fell, and Jamie knew he was a terrible person for the fact that he was glad to see some of that hope dim away. "It doesn't have to be coffee. It can be—"

"Look, are we done here?"

Her mouth opened into a little *O,* before she frowned and typed something into the computer. "You're all set."

Jamie rapped his knuckles on the counter once before turning away. "Great."

He hurried out of the lobby, feeling her eyes on him the entire way. She would remember him.

So much for not leaving an impression.

When he returned to the car, Alex was still in the same place. With a relieved breath, he eased her seat back into a sitting position and started the car again. He emptied one of the gas cans into his tank and started to drive. Jamie willed himself to keep his eyes on the road, but that only lasted until they were out of the parking lot. No matter how many times he told himself to focus, he was awestruck by how close she was.

Jamie merged onto the highway leading out of town. In the back of his mind, he wondered who the first person would be to notice Alex was gone. Who would raise the red flags? She didn't have a job expecting her so it would likely be her family. They probably wouldn't notice she was gone until that night when she never returned from the bar.

Best case scenario he had until tomorrow before someone noticed. There was a possibility that people had already noticed. That someone thought it was funny that he walked her out of the bar when she had been almost unconscious.

I should've worn a disguise, I should've... His mind was an endless whirlwind of potential mistakes.

To break himself out of it, he glanced at Alex again, at the peace in her features as she slumbered on. She'd adjusted her position, tucking herself as tightly into a ball as she could manage in the tiny space offered to her between the seat and the seatbelt.

Jamie forced his eyes back to the road, knowing that if he didn't, he would stare at her until they crashed.

"Mmm," Alex mumbled in her throat.

She was starting to stir, and he hated the thought of her waking up before they made it back home. No doubt she would panic and try to break her way free. He could always lie and tell her that he was taking her home, but as soon as she saw the unfamiliar scenes out the window, she would know the truth. He didn't want her to do anything that could compromise either of their safety.

The next exit advertised a gas station, and he pulled off the highway to find it. As the car rocked to a halt beside a gas pump, he looked over at her again. She looked so content that he wondered how bad the contrast of expression would be when she woke up and realized what had happened. In the bar, her gaze had held nothing but warmth, and he ached knowing it would be a very long time before he'd see anything remotely similar again.

Jamie bent toward her, reaching to recline the seat. He paused over her form, staring into her sleeping face. With shaking fingers, he tucked a lock of hair behind her ear. Her skin was soft, and her hair felt silky. He wanted to kiss her, to hold her close and breathe in her scent until he fell asleep.

A car honked nearby, and he was brought back from his trance. He remembered who he was and what he had done. What he still needed to do. He pulled away from her and grabbed an almost completely empty water bottle from the middle console. There were a few gulps of liquid left in the bottom. Rummaging through the glovebox, he retrieved his bottle of sleeping pills and poured three of them out.

He crushed them up to a powdery mist and dumped them in the water, swirling it until the white dust was all but gone. In a swift motion, he brought the bottle to Alex's lips and pinched her nose with the other hand, forcing her to swallow the concoction.

Alex spluttered, and Jamie pulled the bottle away, sitting her up to ensure she didn't choke. A second later, she relaxed, and he did too. From the corner of his eye, he surveyed the parking lot. No one paid him any particular attention, but he was still uneasy.

For the time being at least, he had gotten away with it.

***

JAMIE WAS RELIEVED to see Warren, the laid-back people and roads. It wasn't long before pavement turned to dirt roads, buildings into trees. There were no streetlights beyond a certain point, but he had driven this way so many times that he didn't need them. His headlights guided him easily along the winding road, the occasional *ting* of pebbles hitting the side of his car the only sound. At last, he recognized his mailbox at the rise in the road before it dipped down onto his property.

The sun had already disappeared beneath the horizon, leaving the world in dark purples and blues. Alex started to stir again, and he was quick to pull the car into its spot in the driveway. He climbed out and eased the passenger side door open. Out here, he didn't have to worry about the possibility of being seen. There were no neighbors within a five-mile radius. With dangerous wild boar and snakes living in the nearby forest, whatever neighbors he did have weren't foolish enough to go traipsing around on foot.

What he didn't want was for Alex to wake up yet and bolt away into the woods on her own. Jamie tucked his arms under Alex before she could topple out of the car, bringing her close. She was so light, a doll designed to look like a human. He hurried inside, closing the door behind him before he looked down into her unconscious face. That thrill of being close to her ran through him again.

It had worked. His plan had really *worked*.

Jamie nearly cheered inside his head until a new thought had him frowning. He'd been so preoccupied with getting her home that he hadn't spent much time planning what he would do once she was here. Jamie tucked his lip in his teeth, and his eyes went straight to the door of his basement.

It wasn't ideal, but it would be enough to hold her until a viable plan emerged.

Chapter Eight

BEFORE ALEX OPENED her eyes, she was aware of the pain at the front of her brain. It was quickly followed by swirling nausea in the pit of her stomach, and she had the very real fear that she would puke all over herself. This was why she didn't like to drink. The hangover was worse now that she was older. Even when she'd been younger, she couldn't understand why people thought this was fun.

Smacking her lips, she desired the biggest glass of water she could drink. Groaning, she tried to situate herself, but her joints ached. It felt as if she were sitting on something hard and stiff. Slowly, her eyes fluttered open, and gray flooded her world. She tried to move her hand to wipe her eyes but couldn't budge. Her other hand didn't either. Her vision cleared, and with the haziness gone, the memories started to come back.

A bar. A handsome man. *A lot* of alcohol.

Then nothing.

She was bound to a chair, hands behind her back. Across from her was another chair, and someone sat on it. The chair was backward so that the man seated on it straddled it, his elbows resting on the backrest as he watched her. There was a black ring around the middle finger of his right hand that he twirled absently as if he were nervous.

Her eyes drifted to his face. His jaw was sharp, face pale, and eyes the bluest she had ever seen on a human. He had a thin nose and full lips. Shaggy layered black hair cast a shadow over his face as he peered back at her. In any other situation, she would've considered him to be attractive. When she had first seen him at the bar, she had thought exactly that.

"Good morning," he said.

Alex's breath caught in her throat. His words carried no malice, voice sweet and syrupy as if they were old friends. "Wh-what's going on?" she rasped, wincing at the pain in her head again. "Where am I?"

The man's face twisted into a grimace as he stood from the chair. He took two steps forward, crouching down before her. "Whoa, there. Take it easy," he said, maintaining eye contact no matter how Alex tilted her face away. "Your head might hurt for a little while, and for that, I apologize, but some of it is probably your own fault. Alcohol can do that."

Alex narrowed her eyes, flinching backward in her seat as he rose to his feet. He was taller than she remembered or maybe that was because she was stuck sitting down. She stared up at him, tugging her wrists against her binds again. When she made no progress she said, "Please take me back to the bar."

"You are where you need to be."

"I *need* to be back home with my husband, my daughter," she said. In her wallet, there was a picture of Katrina, and she wished she could pull it out to show it to him.

Humanize yourself.

The man shrugged, face not changing expression. "You didn't seem worried about that earlier. You said you'd spend the entire day at the bar."

Alex paused, mouth dry as if it were stuffed with cotton. "You spiked my drink, didn't you?"

"No," he said, lifting his eyebrows as if he couldn't believe she'd ask such a thing. "Didn't have to. Seems someone isn't very good at handling her liquor."

"You knew that, didn't you?" she asked, mind racing. That was why he had insisted on buying her another drink when she was already at her limit. He must've been watching her, keeping tabs on how many she'd downed. "W-who are you, really? Did Peter send you? Is this some kind of test?"

The man laughed into his hand before he looked down at her. "No, my dear. It's not a test, it's…oh, my. How to put this into words that won't scare you. Not to sound too *Misery* or anything, but I'm your biggest fan."

Alex swallowed, the pain in her throat once again making her wince. "My biggest…fan?"

She tried the words out, but they didn't feel right coming out of her mouth. She was thrown for a loop, and her expression must've shown that because his eyes glowed as he ducked down, hands on her thighs. He brought his face an inch away from hers as he said, "I've read all your books, your social media posts. I've listened to all the songs you've recommended and laughed at all your memes. You've been my drug for the past year. I can't get enough of you."

Alex was taken aback. He stared into her eyes with a twinkle as if he hoped she'd be thrilled to learn that information.

She remembered the strange anonymous profile that had tried to call her less than a week prior and didn't know what to say. A stalker? This entire time she'd had a *stalker*? Alex always believed she blended in to every room she entered like a shadow or another piece of furniture. To think someone had seen her and *sought her out* was hard to process.

"T-thank you?" she said, wishing he would put some space between the two of them.

He didn't back away. His eyes dropped to her lips before he reached out, fingers touching her softly beneath the chin. "God, I can't get over how pretty you are. Those author photos don't do you justice."

She looked up at him, and an alarm blared inside her head; one she recognized too well. It was the feeling of danger deep in her gut. From the moment he walked up to her in the bar, it had been there, but the alcohol had dulled the sensation, making it easy to ignore. "What do you want from me? I-I don't have any money if that's what this is about. I used to work as a cashier for crying out loud, and I couldn't manage that."

The man licked his bottom lip and pulled his hand away. He stood straight up, looking at her with eyes so watery she wondered if he was about to *cry*. He lifted both hands to his temples and shook his head from side to side like a child refusing to eat his vegetables. "No, no, no, you've got the wrong impression of me."

Alex was unsure what to think. He had stalked her and now she was tied up in his basement. How could she be *wrong*? She thought about his *Misery* reference, imagining her legs broken, and shivered.

"Don't look at me like that," he said, holding his palms

out. He paused as if he were considering something before he stuck his hand into his pocket, retrieving a knife.

Alex tried to pull away, but the ropes still held her in place. In the dim light of the basement, it was clear the blade was sharp. Alex's wrist burned with the memory of what a knife like that could do.

The man hardly noticed as he reached forward to slit the ropes. As soon as they thumped to the floor, Alex tried to jump up. He had anticipated the move and wrapped an arm around her waist, pulling her to him. Alex struggled, but the man didn't give in. He was strong, and she tried to shove away the fear. Being closer to him made her privy to details she hadn't noticed before. He smelled clean, the crisp scent of his cologne flooding her nostrils. And he *was* tall. At her full height, her head barely came up to his collarbone.

There was a crooked smile on his face, revealing mostly white teeth with a visible cavity toward the front of his mouth. He either didn't notice her stares or didn't care as he moved her across the basement. Alex gave up fighting, deciding to save her strength for a more opportune moment as he hoisted her up the stairs.

"Where are we going?" she managed to choke out.

"I wanna show you something," he said as they touched down on the landing.

Beyond the door to the basement was a hallway. Alex's head swiveled left and right as she studied the details, looking for ways to escape. It looked normal, beige walls and a burgundy carpet. There was a picture on the wall of a man and woman, but the man who was dragging her down the hall wasn't in it. Alex tried to spot him in any of the pictures, but he didn't make an appearance.

Was this his house?

A brand new fear overcame her. Had he *killed* the real owners and was hiding her here? She shivered, hoping he didn't notice as they came to the end of the hall. There was a bookshelf there with glass doors over it. Beneath it was a drawer. The man stopped her in front of it.

"Look," he said, gesturing to the eye-level shelf.

She did and froze. Those were *her* books on the other side of the glass, all three of them. No other books around. "You…you were the one who bought my books."

"Told you I'm your biggest fan."

"I see."

"Am I the only one who bought them?"

Slowly she forced her chin to move up and down, not taking her eyes off the tiny bit of familiarity.

"That's a damn shame," he said, features dipping away from the excitement they had showed only moments prior.

In another situation, she would've agreed, but she was preoccupied. From the corner of her eye, Alex could see the front door, and in her head, she calculated the time it would take to make it. Five, maybe seven seconds if she could get out of the man's arms. She licked her lips, knowing her best bet to get that chance would be to distract him first.

His arm tightened around her waist as if she had spoken the words out loud, and she was aware of how close to her he was. The warmth of his skin, how little control she had over what happened, and the danger of her entire predicament.

Lip trembling, she tried to sound friendly as she asked, "D-do you want me to sign them?"

He craned his neck to look her in the face, eyes sparkling as if his biggest wish were coming true. "Would you really do that for me?"

"Uh-huh," she said, trying to keep the fear from showing. To act perfectly normal. "Got a pen?"

She expected him to let her go to search, but he didn't. He whisked her with him easily, grabbing a pen from the nearby coffee table. The plastic slid into her hand, and he closed her fist in his.

"Thanks," she said, staring at it, considering how valuable a weapon it could be. Could a cheap pen do any damage?

His arm slowly snaked off her as he reached for one of the books, thrusting it into her hands. From the corner of her eye, she gauged the distance to the door as she cracked open the cover, pen hovering over the white space on the title page.

He watched her hesitation and asked, "What's wrong?"

"You uh…you never told me your name."

"I'm Jamie," he said, nearly purring it in her ear.

She shivered and tried to imagine what an author would write in a normal situation. If she wrote something nasty, it would backfire on her, she was sure. Holding her breath, she forced herself to write, *I've always wanted to meet my number one fan. With love, Alex Alpine.*

Jamie watched over her shoulder as if he didn't quite trust her. The second she finished writing, he slipped it from her fingers, reading what she'd written. When his eyes weren't on her, she elbowed him as hard she could in the ribs and bolted toward the door.

Chapter Nine

"WHA...HEY!" JAMIE yelled, sure to set the book down where it would be safe, and hurtled after her.

Before Alex touched the door, he slid a taser out of his pocket and pulled the trigger. The coils emerged, embedding themselves in Alex's back. She quivered and spasmed, the electricity seemingly all that held her up for a minute before she collapsed to the floor, shaking uncontrollably.

Jamie grimaced and turned off the taser.

Alex's body trembled with the aftereffects then stopped. A pool of urine seeped out from beneath her, but Alex didn't move. She stared up at the ceiling, face blank as if she were trying to come to terms with what had happened.

Jamie drew his eyebrows together and knelt beside her. Her blue eyes moved to him, drops of water clinging to her lashes. "Shh, it's okay," he said, wrapping an arm around her shoulders to ease her up off the floor.

"No," she whispered and tried to twist away, but she had no strength to do so.

"Come on," Jamie said, gently, soothingly. "Let's get you cleaned up."

Alex's face went red with what he guessed was embarrassment, but she didn't fight again. She stood on shaky legs, looking to the floor so that her brown hair formed a veil around her face. He couldn't tell if she was looking at her mess or not, but either way, she wouldn't make eye contact. He scooped her up and carried her into the bathroom.

He closed the toilet lid and sat her on it. "I didn't want to have to do that, you know. I want you to like it here, but I suppose it's human nature to resist change so I can't really blame you for trying to escape."

He turned toward the bathtub and put the stopper in, testing the temperature of the water. Ears alert for the slightest sound of movement, he readied himself for another sudden burst of defiance, but Alex didn't move. She stared down at the floor, emotionless. A wax statue of grief.

He would've given away everything he owned to know what she was thinking in that moment.

Silent tears ran down her face, and when she peeked up and caught his eyes on her, she folded her arms over her chest. When their gazes met, the look she returned was unflinching, heartbreaking. He didn't speak as he reached forward, grasping the edge of her shirt. Her eyes didn't leave his as he tried to pull it up. Lip trembling, Alex screamed out, smacking his hand away. The fit was so sudden that she nearly slid off the toilet seat trying to free herself.

"Get away from me!" she yowled, bringing her knees to her chest.

Her eyes were huge. Too huge. Jamie didn't like this part. Didn't like it at all. There was murder in those sapphire eyes. He wanted her to adore him like he adored her, but those eyes spoke of hate and loathing. It would only get worse, he knew, and wondered if he had made a mistake bringing her here.

Too late now, he chastised himself.

"I'm not going to hurt you," he assured her, voice as gentle as he could make it. He was nearly whispering, fearful that anything louder would come out crass. "I'm sorry about what happened, but you must understand that I can't have you running away. Now that we've got some ground rules laid out, I need to clean you up. You've had an accident."

"I'm not getting in the tub," she said, drawing herself into a tighter ball to prove her point.

Jamie mentally weighed his options. Hypothetically, it wouldn't be hard to get her stripped down, and in the tub, but the more brutal of an approach he took, the longer it would take for her to forgive him in the end.

If she ever did.

"Don't you want to be clean? You've got to be uncomfortable."

She turned her face away.

Jamie almost pouted, feeling as if he were dealing with a sullen child rather than a grown woman. He couldn't say he blamed her. If their roles were reversed, he wouldn't want to cooperate either. "Look, bottom line? Those clothes will make you sick if you stay in them," he began and set his hand to her knee, trying to push her feet to the floor. She held them stubbornly in place. "I'm not a rapist, if that's what you're worried about. I'm the farthest thing from it. All I'm trying to do is help you."

Silence.

"Don't you think it's gross sitting in your own pee?"

Still no answer.

Jamie flared his nostrils. "You're going to get in the tub one way or another. Don't make this harder than it has to be."

She squeezed her eyes shut and at last let her feet touch the floor. Uncertainly, Jamie reached toward her, keeping his eyes on her face as he grasped the bottom of her shirt. He paused, waiting for another strike, but it didn't come. The fabric eased over her head, and she didn't fight it. She gave in easily, too easily as if part of her was *used* to being beaten down on a regular basis. When her shirt was off, he stopped, gazing at the faded scars over her stomach and tops of her arms.

They were everywhere.

He tried to count them, but older scars faded into newer ones making it impossible to guess how many there were. Alex opened her eyes as if to check if he was still there. She followed his gaze to her stomach and turned her head away, tears brimming in her eyes. It hurt him to see her like this. It was so…*unexpected.* Had someone *done* this to her, or had she done this to *herself?*

He didn't know which angered him more.

Alex reached down, unbuttoning her pants and blocking the patch of scars on her stomach that Jamie had been in the process of counting. He watched her sit up, pulling the fabric down to reveal her milky white thighs and flowered panties. There were scars there too.

The wounds embarrassed her. He could tell that much. As respectfully as he could, he turned his attention to pulling the soiled jeans off Alex's ankles, avoiding the spots soaked in urine. When she was in only her bra and panties, he eased her up and into the tub. As she sunk beneath the surface of the bubbly water, he watched the scars disappear.

Leaning his elbows on the smooth edge of the bathtub, Jamie said, "Take off the rest."

Alex didn't move, eyes on the wall straight ahead.

"Please don't make me act out of character again," Jamie said, but he didn't know how he'd punish her if he had to. He hated what the taser had done, but what other options were there? Hobbling her would undoubtedly hurt him as much.

Alex sighed as if she could hear him sorting through punishments, and a second later, she shuffled, pulling off her remaining pieces of clothes. She tossed them to the floor with a wet *splat* and sank down until all Jamie could see of her was from her collarbone up. Alex stared at the rippling surface of the water, and Jamie stared at the top of her head, hating that he had no idea what she was thinking. He couldn't begin to guess.

The fear she had shown when she had first woken up wasn't there. Nothing was. It was as if she weren't in her own body anymore, and he wondered where she was at. Dissociation was something he was familiar with, and he wondered if she suffered from bouts of it like he did.

"Why are you doing this?" she asked at last, turning her head only slightly to peer at him from the corner of her eye.

"It's a...long story," Jamie said as he handed her the bodywash.

"Look, if I said something at the bar that angered you,

I—"

"No," he said, reaching for the shampoo. "I…it's not that. I have plans for you."

"What does that mean?" she asked, hesitantly clasping the bodywash in both hands as if she considered throwing it at him.

"You'll have to see, I guess, to really understand," he replied, running a glop of shampoo into her hair. It was as soft wet as it had been dry, and his fingers easily ran through the strands.

"Whatever you have planned, you don't have to do," she said, pulling away to look at him. "You could let me go back home, and I won't say anything. No one would know we ever met. You have my word."

Jamie eased a few handfuls of water through her hair, watching the white clumps of bubbles disappear. "*I'll* know. I'll know that I could've helped you and didn't. That would weigh on me."

She slammed the bodywash onto the edge of the tub with a *thump*. "Wait…*help* me? You think this is…that you're *helping* me?"

"Not yet," he said, reaching his hand into the water to pull the stopper from the drain. "But we've got a long way to go."

Alex scrambled away from his hand. "How long are you planning on keeping me here?"

"I'd rather not answer that," he said, hoisting her out of the tub by her elbows.

Alex started to shiver, wrapping her arms around her midsection to protect whatever bits of herself she could. Jamie handed her a fluffy blue towel, and Alex snagged it, wrapping it firmly around herself.

"I don't…I don't think I can accept your answer," she said softly. "You didn't have to *kidnap* me to ask me about my books or get me to sign them or be your friend or whatever. You could've just *talked* to me. We-we got along at the bar. I actually kind of liked you."

Jamie clicked his tongue as he ran a small rag over her hair, pulling out the excess water. "I couldn't do that. What we did…that left the possibility of rejection, and for this plan to work, you need to be on board. It seemed like things were going well, but I didn't know how long that would last when you weren't sad and drunk. But *this*? You have no choice, no *chance* to say no. Even if you do, it doesn't matter because you're here. It's simple. Straightforward."

Alex stared at the wall, speechless. Jamie wrapped an arm around her, leading her out of the bathroom and into the hallway. Her eyes were frantic, moving around the space as if she were trying to come up with another plan to escape. Jamie walked her to the basement door, and she went rigid, looking at him through wide eyes.

"I don't want to go back down there," she said, digging her nails into his chest.

"For now, this is the way it's going to have to be," Jamie said as he opened the door. "Until I can trust you, you need to learn that your actions have consequences."

The fight came back. She growled and slapped, but between the hold he already had on her, and the desire to keep her towel in place, her attacks were limited. It wasn't hard for him to get her down the stairs. The chair was still there, but he pushed it out of the way, revealing a pile of comforters and blankets in the corner. Beside that was a water pipe, and he walked over to it, pushing her to sit down. She bared her teeth at him as he hooked a handcuff around her ankle, connecting it to a chain that had been secured around the pipe. Jamie tested the chain, pulling on it with all his might, but the pipe and the chain held tight.

Confident in his decision, he stood up. "Goodnight," he told her and moved to go back up the stairs.

"Wait!" Her eyes sparkled again, but not in the way they had in the bar. This was a sad sparkle, a fearful one. "Please don't leave me down here."

"I'm sorry," he said. She had no idea how much he meant it.

Chapter Ten

LEX SCREAMED UNTIL her throat was raw. With only the towel around her, she felt more vulnerable than she had when she'd first woken up in binds.

"Help me!" she cried, pulling her ankle against the chain. She pulled until the skin was red and raw and the metal started to cut into her leg. "Please! Somebody!"

There were no windows in Jamie's basement, not even the tiny ground-level ones most basements had. The more she looked around, the more claustrophobic she became. The door at the top of the stairs was the only way in and out. Most likely, her screams wouldn't make it upstairs let alone to people outside.

Pulling herself into a tiny ball, she stopped screaming. Goosebumps broke out across her arms, and she rubbed the skin, trying to soothe them away. She was cold. In her experience, basements were always cold. She closed her eyes, trying not to see it, not to feel it. To block it all out and pretend she was somewhere else.

For as long as she could remember, her imagination had been her best friend. It was always capable of taking her places that the real world could not. She needed that magic now, that temporary escape, if for nothing more than to save her sanity.

It didn't work.

She was still afraid and not because of the dark. Basements were always a trigger for her. Most of her teenage life had been spent in her dad's basement. Days without food, sitting in her own urine and feces-stained clothes while she waited for him to finally let her out. How many days had she sat thinking she would die in a basement like this one?

Alex screamed, loud and long, trying to get her mind out of her memories, but it didn't help. The sound faded, mixing with all the screams of her past, and the feeling of the stone wall beneath her cheek. Heart thudding, she found it difficult to breathe and backed up against the wall, trying to use the cold stones to center herself. Flashes of dizziness rolled through her, and the world around her started to close in. Before her panic attack could claim her, the door at the top of the stairs clicked open. She tried to wipe the tears off her face, desperate to hide all signs of weakness. Her eyes were on Jamie as he descended. He had taken off his shirt, his black jeans hanging low on his hips.

Dread welled up, but in the wake of what her mind had put her through, it was dulled. She looked down to the floor, wary of making eye contact. In most predators, it was a trigger to fight, and she was in no way, shape, or form ready for another struggle tonight.

"I got you some clothes," he said, extending a black nightgown to her.

Alex stared at it. On the surface, it seemed like a kind gesture, but she was sure there were strings attached. She caught it before the cloth could smack her in the face.

"You've got to be freezing."

She was. Every pore in her skin felt as if it had a tiny ice cube in it, but she didn't want him to know how grateful she was for this favor.

"Look, it's been a long day, and I'm exhausted. Seems you feel the same, so get some sleep. I'll be back in the morning to check on you. Hopefully, you'll feel better after a good night's rest, and we can talk."

He turned to start walking back toward the stairs, and Alex dropped the nightgown, hurrying toward him on her hands and knees. "Please don't leave me down here!" she said, trying to grab any part of him she could reach. She didn't know why she hadn't thought about the possibility of him leaving her again. Some stupid part of her brain assumed he'd bring her back upstairs to the warmth and sunshine.

Stupid, stupid girl, she chastised herself, but she wasn't prepared to accept it.

"I'm sorry," Jamie said.

Alex tried to grab him again, but he dodged her every attempt. Desperate, she grabbed her chain and thrust it out, hooking Jamie's ankle. He fell to the ground, elbows smacking the concrete with a resounding crunch. Alex pounced, straining to hold him down while at the same time seeking out the key to her shackle. She couldn't hold him long, and he easily rolled to the side, sending her flying back onto her blankets. Before she recovered, he pinned her down.

With his figure looming over her, and his breathing rugged in her ear, she could feel how heavy he was, how *muscular.* She wished she would've put the nightgown on because she was very aware of the fact that the only thing separating them was a towel. He dipped his face toward her, his lips trailing softly over the skin on her throat.

Alex sobbed, trying to turn her face to the side to gasp for air. "Please, don't."

"Oh, you don't like that, huh?" he asked, fingers digging into her skin. "Kind of funny that you would invade my space when you think it's particularly unpleasant to have it happen to you."

She closed her eyes, bracing herself for what would come next when he pulled away. Cursing under his breath, he stood up and brushed himself off, glaring at her before he backed away, careful eye on the chains.

"I'm sorry," she said. "I...I don't want to be alone. Please."

"This has to be done," he said, voice cold as he turned to resume his journey up the stairs.

"Don't leave me," Alex tried to scream, but it was only a soft whisper. He wouldn't hear her, and if he did, it was clear he didn't care.

Once the click of the door announced she was alone again, Alex deflated, eying the cloth he had given her. The nightgown was soft and warm, and she caved, pulling it on. With some cover, she kicked the damp towel away, feeling a little better. Jamie hadn't given her any underwear, so she was still uncomfortable.

But she could make do.

The thought of him had her shivering all over again, and she lifted the top blanket, curling up to preserve warmth. It smelt like fabric softener and cologne. As much as she didn't want to admit it, Jamie had been right in a way. This could be worse. A lot worse. She could be tortured. She could be killed.

She could do this. She'd done it before and survived. This time, at least she had blankets.

Alex stared up at the top of the staircase. She didn't bother to scream again, because it was clear Jamie was the only one who could hear her. She would save her strength and put her wits into forming a plan.

I'm okay, she told herself and tried to find a distraction by studying her surroundings. There was a bucket and a roll of toilet paper, but there was nothing else in reach.

She eyed the rack on the other side of the room. Most likely the things she'd need to break the chain were on it, but it hardly mattered because there was no way she could reach it.

Alex gave up, thinking about what he'd told her. He wasn't going to hurt her; he wanted to help her. Or so he said. If he was true to his word, he wouldn't kill her if she kept calm and obeyed him. If she did that long enough, she was sure the opportunity to escape would present itself.

She wiped her face with the back of her hand and settled in to sleep. It was surprisingly easy, and she wondered if that was from everything that had happened or the drugs he had used to knock her out.

As soon as unconsciousness claimed her, her brain started to flicker with memories. It had been four years ago, but she could still remember Katrina's birth as if it had been yesterday.

Peter had been there, holding her hand despite her squeezing hard enough to risk breaking his.

When Katrina reached the birth canal, Alex felt as if she was being torn in half. She hadn't had an epidural and regretted it, but it was too late to go back now.

"I can't do this!" she screamed.

"You've got this, mama," the nurse at the foot of her bed said.

Alex almost didn't hear her over her own screams. She pushed with everything in her then her baby was there. Her screams started when Alex's stopped. When she saw the tiny bundle in the doctor's arms, she forgot about all the pain, the sweat clinging to her temples, and every bad thing that had happened in her life. Eagerly, she reached out to accept the baby.

Katrina's eyes were huge, and the moment their gazes met, Alex's heart melted. She had never felt love like this before. Love that was pure and powerful and unconditional. Love that gave her life some meaning. She bent forward to press a kiss to her daughter's soft forehead.

"I'll never leave you," she whispered.

ALEX WAS WOKEN up by the sound of her own sobs. She had only made one promise to her daughter and being here meant she had broken it. She couldn't remember the last thing she had said to her on the way out the door. Had she said anything at all? The only thing she was sure of was that it wasn't

I love you, and for that, she would hate herself forever.

Chapter Eleven

JAMIE HALTED BY the door, keeping careful track of the minutes it took for Alex to be quiet. To his surprise, she stopped before the door closed all the way. He tried to take that as a good sign, but he couldn't be sure. After everything that had happened, she was most likely so exhausted she had fallen asleep.

In a desperate attempt to distract himself from the desire to go back down into the basement, Jamie went out to the living room and plopped down on the couch. Turning on the television, he tried to relax, but he was uneasy, positive that at any moment he would see the broadcast about Alex's disappearance. He saw other news stories from her county all the time. After an hour, there was nothing, and he was dumbfounded. He changed stations, thinking maybe it was a fluke, but none of them said anything about her.

How could this be?

Frowning, Jamie got up and went to his office. The familiar picture of Alex on his monitor made him smile as he sat down, but it eased away as he pulled up the web browser. He went to his social media and searched through Alex's page. It wasn't hard to get to her husband's page from there. He scrolled, but there was nothing about Alex. No desperate pleas for information. Not even a post asking if anyone had seen her.

They haven't noticed yet, he told himself.

It hadn't been a full day yet so most likely, people wouldn't start to notice until tomorrow. His phone chirped from his pocket, and Jamie jumped. Annoyed with himself, he scooped up the device, staring at the message from Damien.

Man, you doing better today?

Yeah, Jamie texted back.

As far as he was concerned, everything was perfect. He had passed the riskiest part of his plan, and he liked to think that it would get better from here. That made him think of something that he hadn't considered so far—he had no supplies for taking care of a woman. No hygiene products or clothes besides the few spare pieces of his mother's things that he'd found around the house.

The drive into town was easy with him so lost in his thoughts. Warren wasn't like other towns that he had been to. It was small, so small that nearly everyone knew everyone else. It made it hard for new people to move in, and even harder for people to mind their own business. His favorite part of the town was the fact that many houses, like his father's, were on a backroad. The town was surrounded with so many woods that it was easy to disappear. In town, however, all he could do was be seen.

Those were the thoughts that clogged Jamie's brain as he drove to the main store. There was only one grocery store in town, a handful of restaurants, and the rest were gas stations. They all knew his face. He'd gone to school with these people, grown up in these streets. Jamie got his groceries here, and he had never shopped for a woman before. They would notice what he was buying, and that would lead to questions.

I can't afford that. He left the parking lot.

Raking his fingers through his hair, he told himself to calm down and drove over to the next town. It was a small town too, but not as small as Warren, and the best part? People around here didn't know who he was. He felt a little bit better as he pulled up in the parking lot, staring into the lit windows of the tiny store. He knew the likelihood of him being recognized here was slim to none, but he was still hesitant as he got out of the car. It was paranoid thinking, but he couldn't stop worrying that they would know what he had done and who he was shopping for.

You're being ridiculous, he told himself.

Somehow, he managed to keep his face wiped of emotion and the worst of his paranoia under control as he went inside. He got a cart, gaining some looks from the woman behind the counter. She smiled at him in the flirty way he'd come to expect from women, and he forced himself to smile back before rushing down the nearest aisle to compose himself.

Besides the clerk, the rest of the store was thankfully empty. That gave him the ease to breathe as he wove up and down the aisles. He found his way to the toiletries and picked out a deodorant and shampoo he thought Alex might like. In the bar, she'd smelt like jasmine. The scent tickled his nose, and he tried to pick out the soaps that would complement that smell. Thinking of her brought him a sudden surge of warmth.

He rounded the corner and realized the rack of clothes was in the clerk's eyeline. She had her back to him, messing with the supplies behind the counter, but Jamie felt a flush creep up his cheeks as he looked over the women's underwear.

Jamie made sure not to look up and see anyone who could potentially be watching him. If he focused only on his mission, it would be easier to forget the world around him. Sweat clung to his temples as he looked at the options before him. He had no idea what he was looking for, and his anxiety was exaggerating the difficulty of the task. Partly, he wondered why he hadn't tried to disguise his appearance. They might not know who he was, but he was sure that people could see someone acting erratically.

The clerk turned and offered him another smile. The flush crept back into his cheeks, and he wanted to disappear. This entire thing was ridiculous. He was a grown man. What was so hard about picking out ladies' intimates? Husbands and boyfriends did it all the time.

"Need help picking something out?" the clerk called at last.

"No, thank you," Jamie said.

He snagged the nearest camisole bra and pack of underwear. He had no idea about Alex's measurements and had to pray they would fit. Once the packets landed in his cart, he turned toward the rack of shirts and pants. From the corner of his eye, he watched the clerk again. She wasn't looking at him, but she had the smallest hint of a smile on her face.

Jamie wondered what it meant.

Focus, he told himself again.

His eyes scanned the shirts, but he didn't know if Alex would like any of them. It was then that he realized how little he knew about her. He thought he had a good grasp on who she was as a person, but that lent nothing to the things she liked. He snagged a few shirts and matching pajama pants. They weren't anything fancy, but they didn't need to be. It would be a long time until she'd leave his house. If ever.

At last, he got everything on his checklist and stood in the middle of the aisle, waiting. What he was waiting for, he wasn't entirely sure. Part of him dreaded the encounter that had to come next, and he wondered if he waited long enough if someone else would take the clerk's place. After five minutes of pretending to browse, he forced himself to approach the scanner.

"Got everything you needed?" she asked, a warm smile on her face again as she started to drag his items across the counter.

"Yes," he said, fumbling with his wallet to avoid making eye contact.

She said nothing as she bagged his stuff, at last totaling it on the screen. Jamie handed her a couple bills, and she passed him back the change. As he gathered the bags, she said, "She's a very lucky girl."

"Huh?" he asked.

"The girl you're shoppin' for."

He relaxed a little and let out a soft chuckle. "Thanks."

He couldn't get out of the store fast enough.

In the parking lot, he still felt as if the walls were still closing in. Only when he was inside his car, away from the prying eyes of the public, did he feel as if he could truly breathe.

He wondered if the girl would still think Alex was lucky after news got out of what had happened to her.

He shivered and tossed the bags into the passenger seat. It looked as if he had gotten a good amount of stuff, but he wished he would've stuck it out long enough to grab a little more. He didn't know if he'd be able to go shopping like this again once Alex's disappearance was reported.

Someone's gonna know your face, a little voice told him. *You looked right at that bartender.*

Jamie's fingers tightened around the steering wheel until his knuckles were white. He needed to see Alex again. It would be easy to remember *why* he was doing this. When he made it back to the edge of Warren, the town was already on the cusp of shutdown for the night. It wasn't a place big on late nights. Jamie used to hate that, used to hate how boring it was, but now he appreciated it. There would be no prying eyes. It would be him, the shadows, and the trees.

Relief washed through him as he eased his car up the curvy road that led to his house. Jamie sat in the car for a long minute after he turned off the engine. He wanted to go inside and check on Alex, but he waited. Before he knew it, he found himself doing another quick survey of her social media.

Nothing had changed.

There were no posts calling him out for being a monster. Not one mention of the fact she was missing. Jamie felt as if a weight had been lifted off his shoulders as he gathered his bags and went inside. In the living room, he sorted Alex's things across his sofa into three piles: bathroom stuff, bedroom stuff, and other.

Then he went to work putting them where they belonged. Something about her deodorant and underwear next to his warmed him. It drilled in the reality that she was here, that he had really followed through with his plan, and that he was no longer alone.

The urge to see her was nearly overwhelming as he put the last of her new things in place. Snagging a pair of underwear, he approached the basement door, pressing his ear to the wood. He couldn't hear anything from the other side. Confident, he popped the door open and crept down the stairs.

Alex was asleep, curled up among the blankets and sheets. The nightgown he'd given her was loose on her frame, and he crouched beside her, taking a minute to study her over with adoration before he pulled the key from his pocket and undid the chain on her ankle. He was gentle as he moved her body, slowly easing the new underwear under her nightgown. Jamie held his breath, fearing she would wake up and think he was doing something else, but she didn't. Once the elastic snapped into place, he let go of her and reached out to stroke her cheek.

In his mind's eye came the image of another girl, a younger one, with mousy brown hair.

She was eight or nine, and Jamie himself had only been a few years older. They were outside, the sky above purple with the oncoming night. Inside the house, his foster parents were screaming at one another, but out in the yard, it was him and his foster sister, Lana.

She was watching him with big eyes as he held out a jar, tongue stuck in the corner of his mouth as he concentrated. The tiny light flashed by, and he jerked the container, slamming the lid into place to seal the firefly's fate. He smiled and held it up.

Lana clapped excitedly, bending her head to see the little bug as it flashed a blast of fluorescent lights, a little S.O.S. to its friends. "It's so pretty!"

"It really is," Jamie said, setting the makeshift cage on the grass.

The bug inside started to thrash, its light growing brighter before it spluttered out.

Lana picked up the jar, frowning. "Why'd it stop making light?"

"Well, it's scared," Jamie replied. "It knows it's trapped."

Lana blinked, the frown deep-set in her little face as she adjusted her grip to unscrew the lid. The bug clicked against the glass as it bounced around, sensing its freedom. Lana watched it gain its bearings and fly out into the sky, the light on its lower half flashing twice before it disappeared. "No one should be trapped somewhere that scares them."

"No, they shouldn't," Jamie said, but he wasn't thinking of the firefly, and he doubted she was either.

"I don't want to go back inside," she said, eyes on the spot in the sky where the firefly had disappeared.

"Me either," Jamie said and opened his arms.

Lana cuddled up to him, her tiny body so thin and wiry that her bones jutted into his skin. She was asleep almost at once, and Jamie held her tight, savoring the bit of light his life had provided as the sound of his dueling foster parents echoed in the background.

Chapter Twelve

ALEX COULD'VE BELIEVED the last day had all been a strange, crazy dream until she opened her eyes, and the gray wall was there to greet her. The cold stone beneath the blanket hurt her hip, but she didn't bother trying to get comfortable as she stared at the dirt crusted in the crack where the wall met the floor. The only comfortable part about this was her pillow.

She didn't know how long she had been asleep, or how long she had been in Jamie's basement, but everything was starting to hurt. Her leg was the worst from the awkward angle she had to keep it in. Fingers disappearing beneath the blanket, she prodded at the metal band, trying to swish it around to give her aching skin some sort of relief. Then she paused as a new realization swept over her. She was wearing *underwear.*

He was in here when I was asleep, she realized and started to pat herself down, checking for any damage.

Besides the usual ache of a too-hard rest, she seemed otherwise okay. When she heard the click of the door at the top of the stairs, she clutched the blanket tighter but didn't turn over. Part of her was curious to see what he would do if he thought she was still asleep.

Alex held her breath and continued to stare at the wall, listening as his footsteps drew closer. They stopped beside her, and she coaxed herself to not tense, knowing his eyes were on her, studying each and every movement.

"Good morning," he said.

Alex didn't look away from the wall.

"You know I can tell you're awake, right? No one holds their breath when they're sleeping."

Damn, she cursed inside her head.

"Come on, get up. It's morning," he urged.

"Not a good one," she assured him. "If it was, you would be letting me go."

Jamie nudged her with his foot, and at last Alex turned over to look at him, fearing a kick to the ribs if she didn't. Like the night before, he was shirtless, pajama pants hanging low on his hips and hair a mess of black strands. Creases on his face made it apparent he had woken up a few minutes prior.

There was a bowl in one hand and a cigarette in the other. He dropped the latter to the floor and crushed it beneath the heel of his foot. Alex couldn't tear her eyes away. She'd imagine that would hurt, but his face showed no sign of pain.

"How'd you sleep?" he asked and extended the bowl as he crouched beside her.

"Like I'm chained in someone's basement."

Jamie pushed his lips together into a hard line, unamused. "I was really hoping you'd be in better spirits today."

"I'm sorry. When I'm kidnapped, I tend to take it hard," she said and sat up, folding her arms over her chest.

"Fine. That's fine, because you'll get used to it," he said, plopping down on the blanket beside her before he offered the bowl again. "Want some breakfast?"

She peered at the eggs inside, stomach growling. She didn't know how long it had been since she'd last eaten, and her body rioted, demanding she devour them, but she wouldn't give Jamie the satisfaction.

"I can hear your stomach." He set the bowl on her lap. "Come on, it's not poisoned. I promise. Some food will make you feel better."

"I'd rather go home and eat."

"And you know you can't do that," he said. "Besides, I don't think that's what you really want."

Despite herself, a flare of anger ignited in Alex's chest. "How would you know what I want? You don't know a thing about me. You might've made your own image of me in your head when you were stalking me, but I promise you, I'm not her."

"Maybe not yet, but in time," he said.

Alex went quiet, staring across the basement in the hope he would get bored and leave her alone.

"Your words... resonant with me. I haven't made up a mystical woman in my head. All I did was compile what I know about you from information that *you* put out into the world. Whatever image I may have is a direct product of yourself."

Alex's glared into the bowl. How could she argue that? Everyone knew the dangers of social media. Whatever you put out there was there for *anyone* to see forever.

This is all my fault.

"Eat. I'll be back for the bowl later," he said and made a move to stand.

She reached out to set a hand on his wrist, stopping him. As soon as the heat of his skin reached her, she jolted her hand away as if his arm was made of fire. "Can I ask you a question?"

"Anything," he said. "If it's about the underwear, they're clean and new. Picked them out myself."

Alex's eyes half-closed. Not what she was going to ask, but good to at least have an idea of something that was going on. "You keep saying you're going to help me. How in the *hell* are you going to do that if you're not gonna let me go home?"

"You're special, but I don't think you understand how special you are. You were…ready to throw in the towel on your work, on yourself, but I can't accept that. Your thoughts, your words, they're important, but the problem is they're not reaching the people who need them. People like me. I can get your work seen. I can help you be the person you've always wanted to be.

"Are you kidding? You did all this…for my *books*? You could've asked, and I would've given you the rights to any that you want."

Jamie huffed, not amused. "That's not the point. I don't want the rights. I want *new* books. And I want *you* to write them.

"I'm done with that part of my life. I mean it. Yes, at one point in time, it was my dream to be a bestselling author, but I tried it and failed. Clearly, it's not in the stars for me."

"I don't believe that," he said. "Once a writer, always a writer."

Alex flared her nostrils. "Who cares what you think?"

"You will in time," he said. "You'll see what I can do

for you, and why it's in your best interest."

Alex collapsed against the wall, fight gone. "How long have I been down here? Hours? Days? My daughter must miss me like crazy. She's only *four* years old. I've never been away from her for this long before." Something about this man made her doubt he had kids of his own, but she hoped he could understand her need to be with her child again.

Jamie's lip quirked upward. Alex didn't like the look. "You think people miss you? Okay." He pulled a key from his pocket and undid the shackle, hoisting her to her feet.

"Where are we going?" she demanded, struggling in his grip. She felt weaker, her struggles having seemingly no effect.

"I didn't want to do this to you, but you're not giving me much of a choice," he said, wrapping his arm around her tiny waist to haul her up the stairs.

She tried to break free as he dragged her down the hall and was unsuccessful until he dropped her on the couch. One hand stayed on her shoulder, keeping her in place while he picked up the remote and turned on the television.

She watched the news, confused. "Wh-what am I supposed to be seeing?"

Jamie sat down beside her, arm slung over her shoulders to hold her in place. "You've been in my home for twenty-four hours now, and in that time, no one has reported you missing."

Alex's heart skipped a beat. A few hours she could understand, but a full day? How could she be gone that long, and Peter not report it? *He's tricking you.* "You're lying."

"It's not, I'm afraid," he said and pulled out his phone.

For good measure, he showed her Peter's social media as well as her own. "No one's looking for you."

Tears started to course down her face, and she didn't try to hold them in. She scrolled down his page and hers, looking for some sign that things were amiss. She had spent her time in the basement thinking of Peter and Katrina. Sure, her life had never been perfect, but it was *her* life, one built of *her* choices, her blood, her sweat, her tears.

And it meant nothing to anyone.

Jamie's eyebrows drew together in concern, and he held his arms out as if he were about to hug her, but she wasn't having it. Alex jumped up and made a bolt for the door. Thoughts of the shock from her first attempt didn't come to her. She needed to get home, see her family again and prove that Jamie was a liar, that they cared about her and missed her dearly.

She had lived her whole life in Ponchatoula. Surely *someone* must miss her.

Jamie tackled her to the carpet. With his chest to her back, she could feel the intensity of his muscles and knew all her struggling wouldn't be enough to break free. She gave up, cheek pressing to the carpet as her body went slack. She was stuck, and no one cared enough to come find her.

Why bother fighting?

Chapter Thirteen

ALEX WENT SLACK beneath him, and Jamie held tight, expecting a trick of some kind. After a full minute, she didn't get up, and he sat up without letting go, peering at her face. Her eyes were closed, but the glint of tears running down her face was unmistakable.

"Come on. Get up off the floor," he said, hoisting her to a standing position.

She was like a ragdoll. With the willpower gone, she moved anywhere he posed her. Somehow, that made him more uneasy than when she fought. When she tried to escape, at least he could understand what was going through her head. Like this? He was clueless.

"Hey," he said, turning her toward him. Her eyes were trained on the floor, and he reached out, setting his fingers beneath her chin. "Look at me."

She obeyed only after he forced her to do so. "They don't deserve you."

Another tear streaked down Alex's cheek then the absence of emotion turned into something deadly. Her eyes hardened to cold blue pieces of flint, and she raised her fists, striking him in the chest once then twice before he was able to get her under control again. She howled like a wildcat, twisting this way and that to try and land any blow she could. Jamie took everything she gave him. A few of them were pretty good, but for the most part they were weak. He let her do it, let her get out her rage and her sorrow.

When she collapsed into a sobbing mess, he hoisted her into his arms, carrying her bridal style down the hallway.

"No more basement," she said as he eased the door open.

He pretended he hadn't heard her as he began the descent down the stairs, Alex fighting every step of the way. Somehow, Jamie managed to get her back to her spot, chained to the pipe, but she spit curses at him the entire time. His heart shattered all over again, but he did it and left the basement, leaning against the door for balance.

She did this to herself, he told himself.

The look on her face, the betrayal in her eyes, stayed with him after he closed the door. He hated it. Hated himself for being this person, but he got past the feeling by reminding himself that this wasn't permanent. Eventually, she would learn her place. Eventually, things would get better.

They had to.

In his head, he took a mental note to look into Stockholm Syndrome. How long did it take to kick in? Were there ways of speeding up the process?

He was about to go to his office when scuffling from the front door caught his attention. Jamie froze, heart thudding as it flew open, crashing against the wall from the force. Glass shards rained to the floor, and Jamie hurried from view, pressing himself into the shadows against the wall. He couldn't see whoever it was, but their audacity boiled his blood. This was *his* home, and someone wanted to challenge him for it?

Perfect. He'd been itching for a fight, a way to unleash his frustrations, and the opportunity seemed to have found him.

Jamie pulled his pocketknife from its safe place and flicked out the blade. Creeping down the hall, he peered into the living room, seeing the suspect. His back was to Jamie as he knocked the knickknacks off the shelf by the door. He was tall and muscular, though his baggy clothes made it hard to tell. Not to mention the fact they were dirty and torn. Long, deep orange hair was pulled into a ponytail, and when he turned, similar colored hair covered the bottom of his face. He didn't notice Jamie as he worked around the room, destroying everything in his path.

Jamie recognized him, and that only made the situation so much worse. When he'd thought it was a stranger, it was all a matter of getting the upper hand. But now that he knew who it was, it would take more finesse, more of a plan, to get him to leave.

Flaring his nostrils, Jamie made sure his knife was visible as he said, "What are you doing here, Zack?"

"Looking through this stuff," Zack said, picking up a vase. He rolled it in his hands before he smiled at Jamie and let it smash to the floor. "You never told me you had such nice things."

"You never asked," Jamie said patiently.

A grin spread across Zack's face. "Kind of hard to ask you anything when you up and disappear on me."

"No news is good news, right? You should've taken the hint," Jamie said, holding up his knife.

Zack smiled wider as looked from the weapon back to Jamie's eyes. "Guess we're on the same page. We always did share a brain."

"I used to think so," Jamie agreed. "But we went our separate ways for a reason. That life's not for me. Not anymore."

"Look at you. Got all Daddy's worldly goods and suddenly you're better than the rest of us." Zack scoffed. "I'd be clean too if I had a house to call my own."

"That's the problem with you. Always the victim, never the problem. You could have a home, a life, if you would've listened to me, but you didn't want to do that."

"And *you* should've listened to me. I told you I'd come after you. You really thought you could split after everything. I did so much for you, and you abandoned me. Well, I have my own debts to pay, and happy day! It seems you're gonna help me do it." He reached into his pocket and pulled out a gun. The black surface shone in the light of Jamie's lamp, but his eyes were drawn to the darkness inside the barrel.

Of all the months waiting to hear from Zack, this was the worst time for him to come back. If something happened to Jamie, there would be no one to take care of Alex. She'd be trapped in his basement. Would most likely starve to death if dehydration didn't claim her first. Thinking of her terrified and slowly withering away gave him the strength, the motivation, to face this head on. After all, this wasn't the first time he'd had a gun pointed at him. He'd won before, and he would now.

"How'd you find this place?" Jamie asked, clutching tighter onto his knife as the two of them circled one another like alley cats.

"Wasn't hard. Public records and all that."

"Fine," Jamie said. "I commend you on your journey. You want money? I'll give you money, but you have to promise your sorry ass is never going to show up on my doorstep again."

"No, man. See it's not that easy anymore. In the beginning, that would've worked, but now?" He laughed. "Now, I want the satisfaction of watching you bleed out. It's about respect. Or should I say lack of. Why would I take your money and go when I could kill you and *still* have the money? Win-win to me."

Jamie opened his mouth to speak as Zack pulled the trigger, the blast of the gun echoing around the living room.

Chapter Fourteen

LEX HAD ONLY heard gunshots on TV, but she recognized them like she recognized the thudding sound of a body hitting the floor a minute later. She sat bolt upright, heart racing with her desperate urge to get free of her shackles and see what was going on upstairs.

A thousand scenarios flashed through her mind.

Someone had broken in and killed Jamie.

Jamie had a partner that he had turned on or had turned on him.

Jamie killing an innocent person.

Had he killed *himself*?

Alex screamed. With the shackle still holding her firmly in place, it was the only thing she could think of doing. Maybe the Gods above would show her some kindness and present her with someone who could save her.

The creak of the basement door cut through her panic. She gave another desperate pull on the restraint with such force that the metal sunk into her flesh, freeing a line of fresh blood. Dragging her eyes from the wound to the staircase, she sagged with relief.

It was only Jamie.

Creak, creak. He inched down the staircase with an odd gait that made her wonder where he was hurt. Blood soaked Jamie's face and arms. She was ready to launch into a stream of questions until she saw the body in his arms, and the words lodged in her throat.

Jamie's eyes were wide as he stepped off the last stair and entered the basement. Alex didn't ask if the person he was carrying was dead. She already knew he was. No one could lose that much blood and survive. Jamie moved to the corner opposite Alex's before he dropped the body with a *thump* that sounded like a sack of potatoes.

"Who the fuck is that?" she screamed, backing herself against the wall as if it could somehow save her if Jamie decided to kill her too.

Jamie took in a sharp inhale but didn't turn away from the corpse. Alex couldn't decide if not being able to see his face was better or worse. Before she could make up her mind, Jamie turned, moving toward her. Alex tried to throw herself backward, but she was already as far as the wall would let her go, and the movement did nothing but cause a ripple of pain to shoot up her back.

Jamie's eyes were glazed over in undecipherable emotions as he sat down on the edge of the blanket, his long legs stretching out so that his foot rested against her thigh. Instead of looking at her, he buried his face in his hands. Alex didn't know what to do, so she did nothing.

When Jamie looked up, blood was smeared on his cheeks and locks of his black hair were matted with the substance.

Alex stared at him, face blank for the sole fact that she wasn't sure which of her emotions was the most prominent—fear, rage, hopelessness?

"Fuck, I never wanted you to know about this side of

me," he said at last.

Alex wanted to question what that meant. If he meant his dark side, she had seen that the moment she'd woken up in his basement. The painful glint in his eyes told her that wasn't it. There was something guarded deep down in his soul, and the man he had killed was part of that.

Her eyes drifted to the body. There was so much blood on Jamie that she wouldn't think the man could have had any left. The puddle around the body made it impossible to distinguish the wound that had killed him.

"Who is he?" she asked, voice a soft whisper as her eyes moved to him. It was soothing like a mother would use on a newborn baby, because like a mother of a newborn, she was afraid of doing *anything* that would snap Jamie out of his lax state.

"He…he was my dealer," Jamie admitted, tilting his head to watch her reaction.

She blinked rapidly, trying to process the information. Drugs. Drugs certainly made some of this make sense. Kidnapping her seemed like something someone under the influence of something would decide to do.

Except Jamie looked sober.

Alex didn't know what to make of it. "You just…make a habit of throwing people into your basement?"

He cracked a smile, but it fell, and he turned away, looking at the body in the corner as if to remind himself that this was the worst time possible to show any semblance of happiness. "No. I never thought I'd see him again. It's been years. The last time we saw each other, it was ugly. I owed him money, and we had a plan that I would work for him to make up for it, but I…I got out of that life and turned things around. I waited for him to show up on my doorstep, but he didn't and so much time passed that I thought he let it go. Turns out, I was wrong."

"He came here?" Alex asked with a shiver, thinking of the creaking floorboards she had heard ten minutes earlier.

"Yes. He broke in. I tried to talk him down. I wanted him to go on his way, but he attacked first, and well, I couldn't let him go. Couldn't risk him coming back and finding you." He bent one of his legs toward himself, resting his elbow on his knee so that his bloody hand dangled in mid-air.

Alex's mouth went dry. If she'd had any food in her stomach, she was positive she would've thrown up. "You killed him for me?"

"I killed him for *us*," Jamie said, bending forward to put his hand on her knee. "I can't lose you. Not again."

Alex drew her eyebrows together. "Huh?"

Jamie pulled his hand back, eyes clearing as if he had returned from wherever he had gone. He gazed at her then looked down at the blood on his hands, the smear he had left on her knee, and jumped to his feet.

"Now I have to figure out how to get rid of a body," he said. "Fuck!"

Alex flinched, her bottom lip quivering with a question that she didn't want to ask but knew she had to. "Have you ever killed anyone before?"

Jamie cut her a sideways look, eyes smoldering with intensity, before he turned away, heading for the staircase. Hand on the railing, he glanced at her before ascending the stairs without a word.

Alex didn't want to look at the body but did anyway. "No! Please don't leave me down here with him! Jamie!" She screamed over and over, long after the click of the door announced that he was already gone.

Chapter Fifteen

JAMIE THOROUGHLY LOATHED himself. Not for what he had done, *that* had been in the name of survival. No, he hated himself for the fact that Alex had seen that side of him. The side he vowed he'd never let anyone see again.

It was inevitable.

People spent their time searching for answers. They'd get jobs to give themselves titles, a sense of purpose, but for him, his title had been assigned at birth, the one thing that defined him more than anything else.

Monster.

Somehow, the Greater Gods had determined that was who he was and all the soul searching in the world wouldn't change that. He had spent years trying to run from the truth of himself, and that had only caused him pain. The title would probably always have hold over him.

What else could he do but embrace it?

Jamie ran his fingers through his hair, cringing at the blood dried to the ends. He wanted to hop in the shower and scrub himself until his skin was raw and no trace of blood remained anywhere on him, but he couldn't do that yet. Not when he still had a body to dispose of.

Alex's screaming hadn't waned, and he closed his eyes. It was too easy to imagine how terrified she must be. She wasn't sure about Jamie, still sure that he would hurt her, and the fact he had hurt *someone* probably only escalated that thought.

Jamie wiped his mouth. Her hysteria would only grow the longer Zack stayed down there with her. If Jamie waited too long, Zack would start to rot. Jamie might have air conditioning, but it was a sweltering Texas summer, and he wanted to take no chances.

Jamie scooped up a water bottle and crushed a handful of sleeping pills to dump inside. Shaking the bottle, he dissolved the powder and then soaked a rag in chloroform. One way or another, Alex would not be conscious to see the next terrible thing Jamie would have to do.

It took several breaths to prepare himself to open the door. The second it creaked, he expected to hear Alex's screams start up again. They didn't, and he almost expected her to be asleep. Or at least, he hoped she already was. It would make this easier.

When his foot hit the concrete at the bottom, he saw her. She lay sideways across the blanket, staring at the body on the other side of the room. Her face was emotionless, but her bloodshot eyes told him she had been silently sobbing. Most likely, she had worn out her throat screaming. As soon as she heard him, she peered up. It was so red underneath her eyes he was sure it hurt.

"Go back to sleep," he said, setting the water bottle beside her.

"How could I possibly sleep?" she asked, eyes landing back on Zack's body.

Jamie crouched beside her, expecting her to flinch away, but she didn't move. "It'll be easier that way."

"What will—"

He wrapped his arms around her, pressing the rag to her face before she could finish the question. She flopped in his grasp, and he planted a kiss to her forehead before he settled her against the blanket, making sure none of her limbs were bent at an awkward angle that would cause her pain later. Satisfied, he stood to his feet, looking down at her for a moment longer before he turned toward Zack.

"Couldn't stay away," he grumbled, searching the shelves of the nearby rack for his machete.

Before this, he had only ever used it to kill snakes in his yard. It was a large blade, the length of his forearm, but Jamie had enough muscle to use it with ease. *Big step up.* When he turned back to Zack, he lost some of that confidence.

With a snake, it was easy to do what needed to be done, but this was different. At one time, this man had been his friend, his *only* friend, and now he was a chunk of rotting meat. Jamie's eyes welled with tears, and he held them back, trying to focus on Alex's sleeping frame on the other side of the basement.

This is for her, he told himself.

Yet, when he looked to Zack again, he couldn't stop the memories from playing.

Juvenile hall hadn't been a fun place, but it had been Jamie's home over the past two years. Being released out into the world didn't leave him feeling good. All he had were the clothes he'd worn when he was brought in, and he had grown so they were uncomfortably tight.

Better get used to being uncomfortable, he thought,

trying to subtly undo the wedgie his pants had bunched up into.

Jamie stood on the side of the road, waiting for his prearranged ride, and yet, all he wanted to do was go back inside the building. What did it matter if he was a prisoner or free? He had no one on this side waiting for him anyway. Life wouldn't be glorious. At least when he had been a minor, he was guaranteed a place to live. Now? That comfort was beyond him. He didn't want to imagine the possibility of homelessness, but it was there, and so was a get-back-in-jail quick plan.

When the car pulled up, he hardly looked at the man in the driver's seat. His clothes were clean and pressed, and he sat ramrod straight as Jamie climbed into the passenger seat.

The man didn't introduce himself right away. He waited a few minutes and said, "I know it's scary what you're going through."

Jamie cut his eyes at him. What he had learned in juvie was that the less he talked, the less chance there was of saying something stupid and possibly angering someone who could come back to do damage later. He did that now, keeping his mouth shut with the wonder of what else this man would say.

"Being on your own? It's terrifying. I've been there. In almost the exact same situation as you. That's why I took this job. Since I can't go back in time and tell myself everything is going to be alright, this is the closest I can come. I hope to one day be your friend, and if not, then a guide to a better life."

He smiled as if it was supposed to be a joke, but Jamie kept his face passive, not letting any emotions free. He said, "I don't think you told me your name."

"Paul," the man replied coolly as if Jamie's reservations hadn't hurt his feelings. They probably hadn't. If he dealt with prisoners like Jamie on a daily basis, he was probably used to getting the cold shoulder among other things. "My name is Paul. Now, I will tell you that things on the road ahead are going to be rough over the next year, but as long as you do what's expected of you, then things will go much smoother. If not, you could find yourself right back where you came from, and since you're not a minor anymore, you'll be going to the big leagues."

"Noted," Jamie said, turning his face to look out the window so he could roll his eyes in peace. Silence would be better than this dead-end conversation.

Jamie was glad that Paul decided to stay silent for the rest of the trip. He nearly dozed off in the comforts of it when they at last came to their resting point. Hope Haven, the halfway house. It was a large three-story building with gray siding and white window frames. It looked like an inn or perhaps a shop. Jamie didn't say any of it out loud as he climbed out of the car. Paul didn't waste time leading him inside, calling greetings to all the men they passed. Some of them were cold and mean, extensive tattoos showing off their history. When they ascended the stairs, Jamie was surprised to see men closer to his age.

Paul gestured to a room. "This is yours," he said. "I'll give you a proper tour and meet-and-greet tomorrow. Take tonight to get settled in and try not to cause trouble in the meantime."

"Right," Jamie muttered.

Paul disappeared into the hallway, calling after one of

the men who ran past.

Unsure what to do, Jamie sat down on the edge of the bed. "Guess I'm already settled."

The room was barely furnished, and the more he looked around, the more he realized it wasn't that different from his cell. The bed was comfortable, and he relaxed against it. His eyelids started to droop when a voice said, "You the new guy?"

Jamie sat up at once, eyeing the thin man in the door. He looked a year, maybe two older than Jamie. Unease settled into his stomach, but he wasn't sure why. "Yeah. Who're you?"

"Name's Zack," he said, plopping down next to Jamie without invitation. "You get used to Paul. He's got a stick up his ass, but I guess someone around here needs to keep order somehow."

Jamie smiled, some of the tension easing. At least someone could see it from his point of view.

"So what's your poison?" Zack asked, cracking the knuckles on his left hand. "You don't look the type, but uh…" He gestured to the raw wounds on Jamie's arm.

Quickly, Jamie reached up to cover them and looked away, tension coming back. He wasn't ready to talk addictions with a stranger. Especially when he had no idea of who could be trusted around here and who couldn't. The wrong words in the wrong hands could land him in more trouble than he had gotten himself into.

"I'm not a narc," Zack said, holding his hands up as if he could read Jamie's thoughts. There was an easy smile on his face that Jamie wanted to trust. "I'm holdin' most things, so if you're in the market, let me know."

Jamie ran his hand through his hair. A voice told him not to reply, but it was weak in comparison to the voice telling him he needed his fix. "You got oxy?"

"Yeah, man, I can get you some. I got a guy. Got some brown too."

"Are you asking me to go with you?" Jamie asked, thinking of Paul's explicit order not to go anywhere.

"Yeah, that a problem?" Zack asked.

"I thought we were supposed to follow orders here," Jamie said, knowing how golden boy that sounded. "Paul said so."

Zack rolled his eyes. "Don't worry about him. You only live once, right?"

Those words were enough of an argument for Jamie. After being locked up for so long, the idea of stretching his legs wasn't a bad one. Zack showed him the window he snuck out of through the attic. They scampered across the roof, easily using the divots in the siding to climb down to the ground.

Jamie's heart pounded as he followed his new friend across the lawn. He had forgotten what a rush it was to be in the throes of something he knew he shouldn't be doing. Zack glanced over his shoulder to make sure Jamie was still following, his white teeth flashing in the dark. Jamie didn't ask where they were going, and Zack didn't say.

They ended up at a bar. Jamie took a moment to wonder how far they had traveled and how they would get back inside the halfway house without going through the front door.

Zack didn't seem to think of any of it. He kept his head up and spine straight as he winked at a group of girls near the door. Jamie was too young to be in the bar, and Zack looked to be too, but his confidence didn't waiver.

"Get that table," Zack ordered, pointing to a tiny table cloaked in shadows in the corner of the building farthest from the bartender's probing eyes. "I'll get us some drinks."

He was gone before Jamie could ask how he planned to do that. As he waited, a girl in a tight black dress approached him. When their eyes met, her lips stretched into a sensual smile.

"Well, hey there, handsome. What're you doing all alone?"

"Waitin' on my friend," Jamie said, looking across the bar to try and catch a glimpse of Zack. At first, he couldn't see him and was angered that he could've abandoned him. This entire thing a trick. Then he caught a glimpse of him bent over the counter, waving down the bartender, and that mistrust vanished.

The girl looked that way for only a moment before her gaze returned to him. "I see." She jutted out her bottom lip, teasing it between her teeth. "I could be your friend."

Jamie tried to keep his face passive. He knew what she was hinting at, what she wanted, but it wasn't in his interest. Jamie ran his tongue along his teeth, trying to think of the best way to let this woman down.

"Mallory!" an enraged man bellowed. "Yo, man! You hittin' on my girl?"

Mallory was gone, replaced with a thick scowling man. His beefy arms were covered in ugly black tattoos.

"More like *she* hit on *me*," Jamie said, tilting his head. "Maybe if you did your job and satisfied her, she wouldn't be over here trying to get my dick."

The man cocked his fist back, and Jamie braced himself for the impact when Zack appeared, catching his arm before he used his free hand to hit the man directly in the stomach. A second later, the man was on the ground, and Zack stood over him, kicking over and over until splatters of blood rained across the dirty floor.

A crowd gathered, but Zack didn't stop. Jamie was frozen in place, another body in the crowd watching the scene.

"Hey!" the bartender screeched, and Zack started to laugh.

He grasped Jamie's arm, leading him through the crowd as he said, "Time to go!"

He kept laughing as they dashed across the parking lot. When Jamie came out of his shock, he laughed right alongside him.

None of those memories mattered anymore because Zack was gone. All that remained was a vessel. With one deep breath, he reared his arm back and let the blade swing down, halting as it sunk halfway into Zack's arm and stuck.

Jamie's frown deepened. This would be neither quick nor easy—emotionally or physically. He risked a glance to Alex again as he worked the blade out of Zack's muscle. It didn't matter how difficult these next few hours would be.

He would do it for her.

Chapter Sixteen

A PAIN THROBBED at the front of Alex's brain that she recognized from her initial wakeup in Jamie's house. She had been knocked out again, but *why*? When she finally managed to open her eyes, she didn't see Zack. Maybe her half-asleep vision had distorted the basement. She rubbed her eyes, trying to clear her watery vision.

The body was gone, and in its place was a puddle of blood, a tiny reminder of the horror that had been there. Alex stared at it. This should've been one of the moments where her brain kicked into overdrive, but after everything she'd experienced, she was tired. So much so that the thought that she could be reduced to one of those puddles didn't bother her.

Death was peaceful. The blackness of nothingness had to be. That was why she was addicted to sleep. The nothingness it brought was the only time she wasn't filled with pain.

Alex's bladder ached, but she ignored it, curling up tighter into the blankets. She didn't know where Jamie was but expected him to come back soon to clean up the blood. He didn't, and before she knew it, she was asleep again.

When she woke the next time, the puddle had dried into a brown smear. She sat up, bladder demanding release. With as much dignity as she could manage, she squatted over the bucket and urinated. Ashamed of herself, she cleaned up and pushed the bucket away, sitting against the wall to watch the stairs.

When Jamie appeared, he was in much better shape than the last time she'd seen him. He was cleaned of blood and his hair was carefully brushed. She searched his hands expecting to see food of some sort, but he carried nothing.

"See you in a minute," Jamie said as he strolled into the room, and Alex realized he was speaking into a phone.

Who in the world could he possibly be talking to? Did they know about Zack? Did they know about *her*?

"What?" Jamie asked, catching the look on her face as he tucked his phone away.

"Who was that?" she asked.

"My friend and boss," he said passively.

The answer didn't satisfy her. "You don't think it's weird?"

"What? That I'm friends with my boss?" he chuckled. "A little unconventional, I suppose, but weirder things have happened."

"Not that. I mean you have friends…*friends,* but you spend your free time like this. Do they know you have a captive in your basement and a dead body in your house?"

"Dead body is not *in* the house anymore so…" He trailed off and shrugged as if he had made some fantastic point by informing her of that.

"Where *is* he?"

"Don't worry about it," he said, crouching down beside her. "He's not going to be able to interfere again."

"You say that as if it's so simple," she said.

Jamie stared, eyes almost void of the cheer they'd held only a minute prior. "It *is* actually. You didn't know him. He meant nothing to you. I took care of it, and now he's gone. End of discussion."

His voice was soft, but there was a menace behind those words. *Don't ask,* it said. Alex took the hint. "Do I get anything to eat before you go out? I-I'm starving."

"Of course," he said, fingers running softly over the skin on her ankle before he undid the chain. "But first, you need a shower."

Alex looked away, trying to forget the first day when she had wet herself and had to bathe in front of him. She was starting to stink, but her nose had gotten used to it, dulling the extent of the issue. He grabbed her by the arm, easing her up to her feet. Alex wobbled on her feet, her toes writhing in the pins and needles sensation of not using them for hours at a time.

Jamie's arm slung easily around her waist as he led her up the stairs. At the top, Alex took a deep breath, glad to breathe in air that wasn't musty. Jamie led her across the hall to the bathroom. It was tiny with a sink, toilet, and shower cubicle. A pile of clothes had been put on the sink.

Jamie pointed to it. "Everything you need is there. When you're done, meet me in the kitchen."

He pulled the door closed with a click. Alex didn't move right away, unsure what to do. This was the first time he'd allowed her to move freely in his home, and she wanted to make the most of it. She scanned the walls, looking for windows, but there were none in the tiny bathroom.

Her shoulders slumped, and she crept back toward the door, wondering if she could push it open and creep down the hall without him noticing. The second her ear touched to the wood, Jamie's voice said, "I don't hear the water."

She cursed. Of course he'd expect her to try something. Defeated, she crept toward the pile of linens, running her finger over the shirt on top. It was soft and light. Most likely comfortable. She smelled her armpit and winced. Her time in the basement was taking a toll on her. Between that and the deep ache in all her muscles, a shower didn't sound like such a bad idea.

She turned on the faucet, testing the temperature. Hesitantly, she stripped off her clothes. Usually, when she was naked, she avoided looking down at herself, desperate to avoid looking at the scars, the reminders of her past. The ugly wounds she had given her left wrist two days before meeting Jamie were scabbed over, the skin around them an angry red. She ran her finger over them then looked to the rest of the faded scars across her thighs, stomach, upper arms, and everywhere else she could reach.

Some of them were years old, but she could remember the reason behind each and every incision. Jamie's face when he'd seen them flashed into her head. What had he thought? And why hadn't it been enough for him to turn her loose?

Blush on her cheeks, she jumped into the scorching stream, letting the water burn away her shame, anger, and most importantly, filth. The bucket and toilet paper left her feeling unclean as if she had gone to the bathroom in her underwear instead of the bucket. The warm water temporarily assuaged her loneliness, her desperation, and she closed her eyes, losing herself to the sensation.

When the water turned cold, she wasn't ready to get out but had no other options. She turned it off and stepped out, wrapping the fluffy towel around herself. It absorbed the water before she could do much in the way of drying off. After running it through her hair, she put the clean clothes on, grateful for the feeling of them instead of the dirty ones she'd been wearing.

Alex cracked open the door, expecting to see Jamie waiting for her, but he wasn't there. That little urge to run called out, and she gave in, creeping down the hall. When she passed the bookshelf, her eyes fell to the door. Between her and it lay the arch of the kitchen. Clattering of pots and dishes inside told her Jamie was there, but was he paying attention?

Holding her breath, she took a step, and the board beneath her foot creaked.

"In here!" Jamie called.

Alex kept her eyes on the door a minute longer but abandoned her plan. She'd been made, and the memory of the taser had her following his voice, seeking him out.

Jamie stood in front of the stove, pan posed over the burner. "How do you like your eggs?"

"Eggs?" she asked, glancing out the window. The sky was turning pink-purple with the oncoming night. "It's not morning."

"No, but after all the sleeping you've been doing, I figured you'd want something light. Something that will sit easy in your stomach."

Alex bobbed her head. He had a point. Eyeing the glass of orange juice on the table she said, "S-scrambled, please."

"Coming right up," he replied.

She pulled out the chair and sat down, eyes still on the glass. It seemed like forever since the last time she'd had something to drink, and she was aware how dry her mouth was.

"You can have that," Jamie said, pointing to it with his spatula.

Alex hardly had time to say thank you through her juice. She gulped it, not putting it down until it was empty. Jamie turned toward her, setting a plate in front of her.

"Here you go." He eyed the empty glass. "You were thirsty."

She took the fork from him. Jamie smiled at her before he picked up the cup and filled it again. When he came back to the table, it was with his own plate of food. He set the glass beside her before he sat in the empty seat next to her. Alex moved the food around the plate, lost in her thoughts. Her stomach demanded she put it in her mouth, but she couldn't bring herself to do it.

"Eat," he insisted, gesturing to her mostly untouched food.

She did. The flavor sang on her tongue, but she didn't know if that was because he was a good cook or if she was hungry. Self-control gone, she forced down bite after bite until her plate was empty.

"I have to do a better job of feeding you," he said.

Alex downed half of the glass of juice in lieu of answering. Jamie savored what was left.

"Thank you," she said, tapping her fork against the plate. "For the food."

He raised an eyebrow. "It's just eggs. I'll make you something better next time."

Alex glared down at the table, mad that she couldn't find the words to explain herself. Part of her was madder for opening this door to begin with. "No, I meant…well, thank you for cooking for me."

Jamie raised an eyebrow. "Doesn't your husband cook for you?"

Alex didn't know what to say. The truth was, if she didn't cook, her family didn't eat, but there was something in Jamie's dark eyes that kept her from saying that. "I-I'm more of a fast-food person."

"Well, that's no good. That sludge will rot your insides. You need brain food." He paused, taking another bite of his eggs. "What's your favorite meal? I mean if you could choose anything in the world. Chicken parmesan? Lasagna? I want to make it for you tomorrow."

"I'm not picky," she murmured. If *eggs* could be this good, she wondered how other dishes made by him would taste. Then she felt guilty for the tiny moment of enjoyment. She shouldn't be happy about anything he had to offer.

Jamie set his fork down, and Alex was jolted back to the present. "Tell you what, I'll make *my* favorite. Then you can see what real food's all about."

Alex didn't look at him. "Why worry about my favorite food?"

"Because I want to do nice things for you. Things that will make you smile."

Alex drew her eyebrows together. "Why?"

"Because seeing you happy would make me happy."

Alex didn't know what to do with that so she stayed silent. Jamie finished his eggs and stood from the table, cleaning up the plates.

"Thank you again for the food," she said, standing up as well. Numb, she held herself as she went toward the front room.

Her eyes were on the front door, and as if he sensed her desire to run, Jamie called, "Where are you going?"

Truth be told, she didn't know. The only place she could think of was barred from her. Exhaustion swept over her, and she thought of the blanket in the corner of the basement with longing. It didn't seem to matter how much she slept anymore; she was always tired. She supposed that in this situation, that was a blessing. The more she slept, the less time she'd have to be awake to focus on what had happened to her life.

At last, she said, "To the basement, right? That's where I belong."

Jamie set the dishes in the sink with a clatter before he stepped out of the kitchen. He placed a hand on her upper arm, and she looked up at him. If he were a little bit smaller, she would consider sending a palm to his nose and making a run for it.

"You know the basement is only temporary," he said, voice soothing as if he hoped those words would be enough to comfort her.

"Until what? You get tired of me and kill me?"

Jamie was silent, face twisted into a grimace as he led her down the hall to the basement door. As he walked her down the creaky steps, she expected the blind terror to start gnawing at the back of her mind again, but it didn't. She was oddly numb as Jamie hooked her back to the pipe and sat her on the blanket.

Jamie stared back as if he wanted to say something but couldn't find the words.

Alex let herself fall over, curling up into the blankets. The blackness of sleep started to claim her before the sound of the door announced Jamie had left. *Maybe I'm dying,* she thought and lost herself in the bliss of the idea until she fell asleep.

Chapter Seventeen

J AMIE FELT BAD leaving Alex alone again. For as bad as her terrified screams had been, it was somehow worse having her *accept* her place in the basement. Her face had been so defeated that all he wanted to do was curl up next to her to get her to feel something else. Even if that something was anger.

After what he had done with Zack, Jamie wasn't in too high of spirits himself. The idea of getting so drunk he couldn't remember who he was sounded too good to pass up. So he took Damien up on his offer, but that didn't take his mind off his troubles. When he met up with Damien at the club, the memory of dragging Zack's body through the grass, the moonlight giving him enough light to dig a hole and toss it in, haunted him.

If he wore any of that on his face, his friend/boss showed no sign of noticing. He wore an easy smile and already had a drink in his hand. Jamie wondered what else he had taken, but out of fear of wanting to join him, he wouldn't ask.

"Good to see you, man," Damien said, clapping his friend on the shoulder.

"Good to get out of the house," Jamie said with a laugh.

"I take it your vacation hasn't been all you were hoping it to be?" Damien asked.

"It's been good. Better than I thought. The uh…time away from everyone has been good. A great chance to disconnect," he said, and that was the truth. Getting away from the monotony of his day-to-day expectations in the restaurant had been a relief to some degree in spite of it being overshadowed by worries about Alex and what he had done.

"Glad to hear it. That means you should have no problem coming back, right?"

Jamie chuckled. "Yeah, maybe."

Damien looked over his shoulder to where a group of girls in skin-tight dresses were standing together, talking. Damien side-eyed Jamie and raised his eyebrows. "Nothing will make you feel better than one of those."

Jamie ran his tongue along his bottom lip, wishing he had a drink or some kind of distraction. There was no easy way to explain why they didn't interest him. He didn't know how much he could tell Damien about Alex or how much he could trust his friend.

Damien drew his face tight. "What is it?"

Damn. "I've kind of started seeing someone." He prayed that Damien wouldn't push for details.

A wide grin broke out across Damien's face. "Oh? What's she like?"

Jamie froze up, not wanting to answer the question. One of the girls Damien had been leering at called him, and Jamie went weak with relief. He'd never been happier to be alone. Figuring Damien would be busy for a minute or two, Jamie slunk off to the bathroom. Bending over the stone sink, he splashed water on his face, staring at himself in the mirror. There were bags under his eyes, but there was something else that spoke of better times.

He went into the stall, locking it behind him. He didn't

have to use the bathroom, but he wanted his privacy in case anyone else came in. He sat on the toilet and pulled up Alex's social media. His heart dropped. The more he scrolled, the worse he felt.

Where are you at? someone had written.

Are you okay?

They know. They've finally realized she's gone.

At the top of Alex's husband's page, there was a post that drew Jamie's attention: *My wife, Alex Alpine, is officially missing. If anyone has any information about her whereabouts, please, please contact the police. We are doing all we can to get her home safely. Please circulate these pictures.*

Attached to the post were two pictures of Alex. They looked outdated. Alex's hair wasn't as long, and her skin was much paler. He squinted at them, wondering when they had been taken. The bathroom door opened then the sounds of the club flooded into the silence.

"Jamie, man, are you in here?"

It was Damien.

"Uh…yeah," he said, scrambling to put his phone away. "One minute."

He left the stall, pretending to wash his hands. Damien leaned his hip against the sink, watching him. "Thought you skipped out on me."

"Nah," he said, avoiding looking at his reflection.

Damien bobbed his head, eyes looking from Jamie to the stall, and Jamie could guess what he was thinking. Somehow, the idea of his boss thinking he was doing coke was less of a concern than him figuring out the *real* evil that he had committed over the past few days.

"Come on," Damien said, leading him back to the dance floor.

Jamie obliged, but the entire time he and Damien mingled and made their way around the club, he sorted through escape plans. At one time, this would've been a perfectly enjoyable outing, but now, with the knowledge that people were looking for Alex, he was on edge. He wanted to go back to her, to hold her close.

Should I tell her? he pondered, teasing his lip between his teeth.

He cursed under his breath and raked his fingers through his hair. The more his nervousness chewed at him, the more he desired to ask Damien what he was on. A hit of ecstasy didn't seem like such a bad idea anymore.

***

WHEN JAMIE MADE it home, the effects of the drug were wearing off, and he was glad. He hated himself for giving into old urges, but it would've somehow been worse if Alex had seen him vulnerable. For her, he wanted to show nothing but strength and sureness, but he was nothing but a weak, fragile kitten inside.

Feet on autopilot, he went to the basement door and popped it open, creeping down the stairs. Midway down, he ducked to see her. Alex was curled up among the blankets, asleep. He knew he should've been concerned at how much time she spent unconscious, but right then, he was glad for it unsure if he'd be able to face her.

Exhaling, he went back up the stairs, closing the door as quietly as he could. Jamie plopped down on the couch, stripping off his shoes as he flicked the television on, going directly to the news. If there was news of her disappearance on social media, there had to be some report on TV too.

And there was.

Wincing, Jamie rushed to turn down the volume of the reporter's grating voice, convinced that Alex would hear it and start wailing. Cringing, he hit record before he passed out on the couch. He snorted awake a few hours later, and the news was still on. It looked like Alex's husband on the screen.

That couldn't be right.

He closed and opened his eyes, but the image was still there, and he realized what it was. A plea from the family for Alex's safe return. Though he'd just woken up, Jamie's heart started to race as if he had run a marathon. He turned the volume up, desperate to see if they had any suspects.

Any leads.

"Whoever you are," Peter was saying, "Please don't hurt her. I'll give you anything you want if you return her safe and sound."

Jamie laughed. "Fucking hypocrite."

The TV went black with a click of the remote.

Chapter Eighteen

ALEX WOKE TO Jamie poking her in the ribs. His hair was spiked and messy. It looked as if he had fallen asleep in the clothes he'd been wearing the night before. She didn't fight as he aided her up the stairs and pushed her toward the shower. The hot water was starting to become her favorite part of the day, the only thing she had to look forward to.

When it went cold, she wandered out to the kitchen as Jamie put two plates of pancakes on the table. Jamie had a smile plastered to his face. It was nervous and guilty—he was hiding something from her. As he ate his pancakes, he didn't look at her. Alex didn't taste the food, instead staring at the part in his hair on top of his head as she chewed each bite slowly.

At last, she'd had enough of the silence and said, "What aren't you telling me?"

Jamie licked his lips and set his fork down, looking up at her without lifting his head so she could see most of the whites of his eyes. "Why do you assume I'm keeping something from you?"

"You're different today," she said. "Weird different."

He wiped his mouth with his napkin and set it down before he focused his gaze on her. "Different how?"

"Not different in how you're acting…more of how you look. You look like you're…hiding something."

He laughed and gestured to her before taking a sip of his

juice.

Alex's face flushed with frustration. "I don't mean *me*. I mean you're hiding something *from* me."

When the glass was empty, Jamie sighed. "Is it that obvious?"

"Yeah," she said, forcing out her air in a rush to make the word sound harsher than normal.

Jamie pursed his lips. "Okay, fine. Last night, I saw something you're not going to like."

Alex widened her eyes. "What is it? My replacement?"

Jamie stared into her eyes as if he were trying to telepathically get her to reach the conclusion he wanted.

"They know I'm missing," she said, nearly breathless. She tried to calculate how much time had passed. Had it been four days or five? She didn't know. It had all been one long nightmare of a day.

Jamie stared into the arch leading to the living room and stood up, pushing away from the table. His face was hard, features showing none of the warmth he'd been full of ten minutes prior.

Alex flinched away, unsure if he would turn that hardness to her. "It's okay. It'll be okay," she said. "Let me go. Let me go back. It's not too late. I'll tell them this was all my fault. That I ran away, and you brought me home. Or I won't mention you. Your choice."

Jamie stepped around the table, softly slipping his fingers through hers as he grabbed her hand. "I appreciate the offer, I do, but I can't do that."

She tried to pull away, but he tightened his grip. Panic rushed through her, and she found herself wondering where Zack was again and if she was about to find out. There was no hint of what was happening in Jamie's head as he eased her from the chair and into the living room. She waited to be walked back to the basement when he perched her on the edge of the couch instead. Some of the tension eased as he picked up the remote and sat beside her.

"This aired last night," he said, carefully studying her every feature. "I recorded it, in case you wanted to see it."

She didn't know what *this* was, but the tone of his voice didn't sit right with her. It was like he was getting her fully prepared to be delivered news she wouldn't want to hear.

Why?

She *wanted* people to notice she was missing, wanted them to come looking for her and find her. The only person this was bad news for was him.

She said none of that as she sat, waiting for the recording to start. Jamie pressed play, and she was staring at a crowd. A search party. She ran her eyes over every person she could make out. Most of them were strangers except for Peter and Katrina. Alex had to bite her lip to keep herself from yelling out. She was mad at Jamie for keeping her here, mad at Peter for allowing Katrina to be exposed to the truth that she was gone, and mad that her life had come to this.

Alex missed her daughter so much, and the image of her made it worse. There was sadness in the little girl's eyes, and she hurt more knowing it was her fault her daughter looked like that.

"That's your husband, right?" Jamie asked, pointing to the profile of Peter's face.

"Yeah."

"And…uh…who's that?" he asked, pointing to the woman beside Peter.

Alex picked out her details, so like Peter's. "That's his sister, Katherine."

Jamie looked at her patiently, but there was a hint of annoyance as he said, "No, not her." He got up and pointed to a space between Katherine and Peter. Someone was running their hand down his arm, and it wasn't his sister.

Alex tilted her head, tracing the arm up to the woman standing behind them. She studied her, but nothing came to mind. "I've never seen her before."

On screen, the woman reached out to squeeze Peter's hand, and Jamie turned to look at her. "Looks to me as if *he* knows who she is pretty well."

Alex felt a lump in her throat, and her fingers dropped to the fresh cuts on her left wrist. The whispered phone call and stupid fight that had led to this outcome. She was right all along. Warm tears rolled down her face, and the prodding to her wounded flesh turned to frantic digging. The need to hurt was there, followed by a desire to get home, to hug her daughter and confront Peter.

"Is this why he waited to say anything?" Jamie asked.

Alex successfully tore into one of the scabs, watching one red droplet run down her arm. Jamie turned off the television and reached out to pull her into his arms.

She didn't resist.

Chapter Nineteen

ALEX THOUGHT JAMIE was going to pull her in for a hug, but he didn't. He grabbed both of her wrists, so tightly she could feel the bones grinding together. His thumb barely missed the bleeding wounds.

"What the hell are you doing?" he demanded, shaking her.

Alex looked at the cut she'd managed to open, the first drop of blood leaking free. There was no way to explain her need to destroy herself, so she opted for silence. Jamie's face morphed from rage to sorrow as he turned her arm toward him, studying the stream of blood.

"You're mutilating yourself," he said.

Alex set her jaw.

"This has gotta be cleaned up before you get an infection," Jamie said, letting her uninjured arm go before he dragged her down the hall, in the direction of the bathroom.

Alex's heart pounded at the idea of him forcing her into the tub again, but she had no choice but to comply as he sat her on the toilet seat. He gave her a warning glare before he pulled out a first-aid kit from beneath the sink. Rummaging through the supplies, he said, "I don't know what you used to do with your husband or how much he knew about you. But this is gonna stop."

Before Alex could say anything, he sprayed antiseptic onto the wound, and she cringed at the stinging pain.

"I said I was going to help you, and this is how I'm going to start. You're not gonna hurt yourself anymore."

Alex frowned, glaring at him as he carefully mopped away the blood and gazed at her wound.

"Okay?"

She stayed silent, and he peered at her as he began to wind an ace bandage around her wrist.

"You're not going to like what happens if I see you do this again."

"I don't like *any* of this," she hissed.

"Then you'll *really* hate what'll happen if I see you spill any more of your own blood." He tapped the edge of the bandage into place with a clip and stared through dark eyes.

For some reason, she believed him. She wasn't sure how he would make things worse, but she didn't doubt for an instant there were ways of making it come true.

"Now that the ugliness is out of the way, what do you want to do?" he asked and grabbed her hand, pulling her to her feet. "We could play a game or watch some television?"

"I want to go to sleep," she said, frowning down at the bandage.

"You've been sleeping a lot. That's a sign of depression, you know."

"Can't imagine why I'd be depressed," she said and hugged her free arm around herself.

"Come on," Jamie said, dragging her down the hall.

Reluctantly, she followed him. He tried to lead her past the basement and to the living room, but spending a *normal* evening with the man who had ripped her away from her family seemed crueler than drowning in her memories in the basement. She set her hand to the wood, digging her heels in until Jamie stopped walking.

"Please, Jamie, I'm tired," she said, not looking at him.

Defeated, he said, "Alright."

They didn't speak again as he walked her down the stairs. She laid down on the blankets, hardly noticing Jamie's gentle work as he snapped the chain into place. He crouched beside her, watching her closely, but she didn't return the look. Hardly looked up at him as she settled among the blankets, the makeshift bed that was starting to feel like the only constant in her life.

"I know you don't want to be around me, but I don't think you should be alone right now," he said and crawled onto the blanket behind her.

He wrapped his arms around her, and Alex stiffened, heart thudding as her exhaustion gave way to her fear. She pulled herself as far from his body as she could in the embrace, but he was strong. Jamie murmured soothing things in her ear, and she felt betrayed to find that it was working. Her discomfort started to ease, and before she knew it, she was asleep.

***

WHEN SHE WOKE up, Jamie was gone. The loss of his warmth made her colder, and she hugged herself. The movement jarred the wedding ring on her third finger, and when she looked at it, she remembered everything that had happened. The woman at the search party with Peter. How unbothered he'd looked. He didn't miss her. He was *happy* she was gone. She closed her eyes, letting tears gather as memories coursed through her.

From the time of her Mom's last breath, Alex cried until she didn't think she'd ever be able to cry again. Her eyes hurt all the time, and she hardly ate. She'd lost weight but only noticed when it came time to put on clothes that hung off her frame. Staying locked in her grief made it easy to lose track of the time. Days, weeks, and months went by with her in that state, but to her, it felt like one long never-ending nightmare of a day. Her father was an enabler to that effect. Like her, he was so wrapped in his grief that he didn't make her go to school. It could've been days later, or it could've been weeks, she didn't know. And really, she didn't care.

Occasionally, the phone would ring, the only bit of reality that seeped into her mind, but as soon as it stopped, she would slip away again. Nothing existed. Nothing mattered. One night, there was a tapping at her window. It was so faint that she didn't notice it at first. Not until the squeak told her someone had opened it. By the time she rolled over, a figure stood in the middle of the room. She opened her mouth to scream when a familiar voice cut her off.

"You didn't answer the phone. I was worried."

Peter.

The tension eased from Alex's shoulders, and she flopped back into her bedding. "Sorry," she murmured, but she wasn't. That would've required feeling something besides the soul-crushing sadness that had hijacked her body.

"You don't have to be sorry," he said, sitting on the edge of the bed.

"Oh," she said, mood nowhere near a place where she was conversation ready. If he hadn't come for an apology, what did he want?

"How've you been holding up?" Peter asked, crouching beside the bed.

Alex squinted, trying to make out his features, but everything was lost to the shadows. "Not…good," she said at last.

"I can imagine," he said, reaching out to tuck a strand of hair behind her ear. The soft brush of his fingers soothed her, and when he tried to pull his hand away, she reached out to hold it, marveling at the feeling of something after so long of not feeling anything at all.

"Things have been unreal…detached," she said for lack of a better explanation. "Like I'm dead, and I'm watching my life from someone else's perspective."

"That sounds unpleasant."

She bobbed her head, wishing he could understand how unpleasant it really was.

"You don't seem like you're in the mood to talk. If you want me to leave, say the word and I'll go," Peter said, at last pulling his fingers from her tight grip.

She couldn't see him through the shadows, but she hoped he could see her, could see the spark of something akin to life in her eyes that his visit had inspired. She held her arms out.

A gentle smile crossed Peter's face, and he stood to his feet. "It's okay if you're not ready to talk yet. When you are, I'm here. I'll always be here for you."

Something about the tone of his voice, and his word choice, was exactly what Alex needed to hear. Peter crawled into her bed, and she wrapped her arms around him, glad to feel the warmth of love after the bitter cold of her own despair.

Their relationship hadn't felt like that in years.

How far they'd come. How far they'd *fallen*.

Tears misted her vision, and she slipped the ring off, throwing it across the room. She couldn't see where it landed, but the tiny *ting* as it connected with the concrete floor gave her an idea.

It would never be far enough away.

Chapter Twenty

JAMIE STAYED WITH Alex until soft snores erupted from her. He squeezed her tight, glad she was at peace, and untangled himself from her. Doing his best to not disturb her, he stood to his feet and stared down at the bandage on her wrist. He couldn't decide exactly how it made him feel. The entire scene with her tearing herself open like a wild animal was so unexpected that all he could do was shake his head.

His stomach growled, reminding him that he was yet to eat for the day. After what had happened, food was the last thing on his mind. He ambled up the stairs. When he'd first seen her scars, he'd fixated on them, wondering how she'd gotten them, and now he knew the ugly truth. She was a danger to herself. Prone to detonate at any moment.

Gathering everything sharp in the house, Jamie bundled the items together in a towel and put it on top of his closet where he was positive Alex wouldn't look. If she did, she wouldn't be able to reach that high on her own.

Jamie paced the hallway, feeling helpless. He wanted to make Alex feel better, to cheer her up so she'd forget all about the scumbag who had hurt her like this. Jamie couldn't understand Alex's husband. If he was the one married to her, he would've done nothing but treat her like royalty. Bitterly, he sat down on the couch and pulled up Peter's social media. The plea about Alex was still there, and Jamie had to refrain from typing something snide. Instead, he went to Peter's friends, searching for the girl from the broadcast. It wasn't hard to find her.

She tagged Peter in a lot of posts, and he wasn't shy about responding. The more that Jamie saw, the more his heart broke for Alex. Could she have already known about this? Was this the reason she'd had those fresh wounds on her wrist to begin with?

"Ugh," he said out loud, forcing his phone off.

He was torturing himself with things he could do nothing about. Desperate to take the edge off, he grabbed his keys and went out to his car. He didn't like the idea of leaving Alex alone after what kind of day she'd had, but he would make it up to her.

First, he needed a drink. That was all he could think as he pulled into the closest bar which also happened to be a restaurant. Inside the dimly lit building, he tried to sit as far from everyone and anyone he could. It was hard to be completely solitary because he knew almost everyone in town.

After gauging his mood, they left him alone. Jamie was glad for that. He tipped back one shot, then two. Flashes of Alex tearing into her wrist came back to him again, and he realized alcohol wouldn't be enough to get him to stop worrying about her.

You might've made your own image of me in your head when you were stalking me, but I promise you, I'm not her, Alex had said.

Until that day, Jamie hadn't realized how right Alex was. When he had come up with this plan, he hadn't imagined her purposefully trying to hurt herself. In her pictures she looked so confident, so battle ready, that he never guessed how broken she was. Jamie downed the third shot. If he had known how hard it would be to take care of her, would he have changed his mind?

Of course not.

She was still Alex.

Still the girl who had poured her heart out into those books that had moved him. If anything, the show of her humanity only made her more precious. What happened had been a sign that she was very much in need of help of some kind.

Do something nice for her, that little inner voice urged.

Wiping his mouth, he grabbed a nearby menu and opened it, scanning the selections. He'd promised her a fancy meal, and he would deliver on it. It wouldn't be much, but at the very least, he hoped she would see he was trying.

Chapter Twenty-One

ALEX HAD NO idea how long she laid in a sorrow-induced haze, or where Jamie had gone, but she knew the moment he came home. The sound of a slamming door and footsteps caused her to wince. He was so loud she almost thought he had brought a friend home with him. Less than ten seconds later, he was clambering down the stairs. Alex peeked over her arm, watching the smile on his face as he approached. When he got closer, she could smell the alcohol, and all her questions were answered.

"Smells like you had a good day," she said, not rising off the pillow.

"Not particularly," he said, crouching beside her. "It's been a rough week for both of us."

"Yeah," she said and turned over. She didn't want him to see her face, to see how much rage and hatred she was capable of holding onto. Sometimes, she scared herself with it. One day it would all come out of her, and she didn't know when that day would be.

Jamie was silent as he laid a hand on her arm, gently turning her toward him. "Want to talk about it?"

"No. Why would I?"

"It might help you process what you saw."

Alex wasn't convinced.

"I got you something. Maybe it'll help cheer you up," he said, grasping her elbow to ease her to her feet.

Alex was wary, but she had no fight left in her. She watched as he undid the chain and laced his fingers through hers. Her instinct was to pull away, but she didn't. Since he was so much taller than her, he had to bend his neck at an angle to look at her. She pretended not to see as he led her to the kitchen, sitting her down in the nearest seat. A plate of food sat on the table in front of it, a glass of wine to the side. The smell was intoxicating, the presentation rivaling any cooking show she'd ever seen. Alex stared at it, but she had no desire to eat.

"I told you I'd get you some real food," Jamie said, pulling up a chair to sit beside her. "And here it is. It's prime rib. The most expensive I could get."

"Th-thank you," she said, fidgeting under his stare.

Somehow, the look he gave her was more intense than the first moment she laid eyes on him. He didn't turn that penetrating gaze away. To break some of the tension, she started to eat. Her plan was to get down a few bites and say she was full, but once the flavor hit her, it triggered her hunger. She started to devour the food as if she had never eaten before.

Jamie looked pleased as she put the last bite of food into her mouth. "Good?" he asked.

She nodded, and he reached out, running his thumb over her cheek before he stood up and gathered her plate. Flushing from the contact, she picked up the glass of wine, downing a few swigs. Her face twisted at the taste, and she was glad Jamie's back was turned so he wouldn't see.

After what happened at the bar, she despised alcohol, but Jamie hadn't offered her anything else to drink. Jamie dropped her plate into the sink with a clang. She expected him to wash it as he usually did after a meal, but he turned back to her, leaning his hip on the sink as if he contemplated the next words he wanted to say.

"Now that you're nice and full, I think it's time to talk about what you saw," he said.

"No."

The bit of satisfaction garnered from her meal vanished. She and Peter had had their problems for a long time. So long that she had almost become numb to it. The fact that he hadn't left her led her to believe that deep down, he still cared for her somewhat, but now, she didn't have that to hold onto. She didn't want to admit that to anyone. Least of all her kidnapper.

Jamie held his hands up. "That's fine for now, I suppose, but in the future, I expect you to open up to me."

Alex continued to stare at the table, pretending she hadn't heard him. If she responded now, it'd be out of anger. After the work he had gone through to cook for her, she didn't want to do that. Then she was mad at herself for the manners that had been bestowed on her. She didn't want to be *polite,* she wanted to be angry, a venomous swirling cloud of rage and hatred.

Instead, she was a statue.

Jamie approached her. "Look, I'm getting a headache, so let's call it a night." He grabbed her elbow, pulling her to her feet with a strength that could've frightened her but didn't. "C'mon."

She let herself be hoisted out of the chair, but when her feet finally hit the ground, she dug her heels in. The basement hadn't bothered her earlier, but it did now. Maybe it was the alcohol, but she didn't want to be alone.

"Please," she whispered, too afraid to meet his eyes and see what emotion was there. "Don't make me go back down there."

Jamie pursed his lips and breathed out through his nose. "I…might have a solution."

"Anything," she said, grasping onto his arm.

The expression on his face didn't make her feel better as he led her out of the kitchen and into the living room, fidgeting with the drawer beneath the bookshelf. There was a thin silver band inside, open at one section.

He scooped it up, opening it and closing it before her eyes. "Now this is a little unorthodox, but…"

"A shock collar?" she asked with a sarcastic laugh. He couldn't be serious. Goosebumps spread over her skin when she remembered the pain of the taser. A shock collar would border on cruel.

"Not my favorite," he said, "but it's either this or the basement. I don't trust you enough for anything else, and I certainly don't have the heart to hobble you."

Alex eyed the collar but couldn't manage the nerve to tell him that the electricity could damage her in far worse ways than a shattered kneecap could. "Fine."

"Sorry," Jamie said, swiping a lock of hair from her eyes before he looped the band around her neck, snapping it shut.

Alex reached up, prying at the edge of the collar to get an idea of the lock before the fabric hid it from view. She wondered how effective it would be, but she didn't have the time to ask before Jamie was leading her down the hallway.

Jamie popped open the door at the very end. The room inside was small with only a bed, desk, and dresser. A closet sat in the opposite corner from the bed and the desk was in the space between them. As Alex picked out more details, she noticed that his bed didn't have a frame. The mattress rested directly on the floor, a black and red comforter spread out across the top. It looked like such a normal room for any guy his age, except he wasn't a normal guy.

Alex shivered, not knowing what to think. Her mind worked at top speed. Zack's death. Peter's infidelity. Jamie's kindness. It was all a lot to take in, but at least Jamie's bed was comfortable. More comfortable than the blankets in the basement at least. Her spine was rigid, but she forced herself to relax. When she collapsed onto the mattress, her joints thanked her for the softness.

She glanced at Jamie, waiting to see what would come next. His fingers were working their way down his shirt, easily undoing the line of buttons. On instinct, she looked away, heat lining her cheeks.

"You're embarrassed," Jamie said, sitting on the edge of the bed after he tossed his shirt to the floor.

"Of course I'm embarrassed. Y-you're a stranger, and you're stripping in front of me. You've seen me naked. I'm in your bed, and I…I have a husband, a *child,* for crying out loud."

"It's an adjustment," he admitted with a soft bob of his head. "I'll give you that, but I don't know how many times you're going to make me say this. You don't feel like a stranger. To me, it's as if we've known each other our entire lives. If you give me the proper chance, I am positive you'll feel the same way about me. Besides, your *husband* isn't much of a husband if you ask my opinion. Who waits to look for someone as precious as you?"

Alex dropped her eyes to the blanket. No one had ever called her precious before. She didn't like the tingle, the *warmth,* that it gave her.

"No, you're better off forgetting about him. About everything your old life had to offer."

"Why?" she asked, sitting up with a huff. The collar pinched her skin, and she winced, adjusting herself. "Who says I *want* to?"

Jamie's eyes ran up and down her frame, landing at last on the bandage still wrapped tight on her wrist. He crawled onto the mattress next to her and reached out, gently tapping his fingers to the fresh wounds. "I think these do."

Alex *hmphed* and laid back against the bed. She didn't have a good argument that could counter that. For the last few months at least, she'd felt trapped, a secondary character in her own life. Part of her had wanted to escape, to take Katrina and start a new life, but she had been too afraid to do it. Too afraid of how life would treat her on her own. At least with Peter, she could hide in his shadow. Being on her own would mean she'd have to step into the light.

Be seen.

"No one who's happy does this to themselves." He paused to glance down at his abdomen, at the toned stomach and muscular arms. "My life has been far from perfect, but even in my world, I never mutilated myself."

Alex's eyes fell to the crook of his arm. There were a few faded scars there. Track marks she knew. She wanted to call him on the hypocrisy but decided it wasn't worth the battle. Neither was pointing out the fact that he had mutilated *someone else* too.

"Talk to me," he said. "I want to be your friend, your confidant, your *everything*, but I can't help you if I don't know what's wrong."

Alex looked into Jamie's eyes as he finished his sentence. He looked cold and warm at the same time, like he could hurt her at any indiscretion but would comfort her immediately afterward, and that trill of danger ran through her again. This was an unbalanced man. One she shouldn't play with.

"If I can take a guess, I'm gonna say it's related to why your *husband* waited to report your disappearance."

Alex ran her finger along the scars that Jamie had pointed out. Some of them were purple, some white, and a few which were still pink. She stopped on the bandage. They were all reminders that the life she was hoping to return to was the one she had loathed and wished to desperately escape.

Alex scooted away from him, annoyed though she didn't know if it was more with him or herself. She had allowed her life to get to that place, hadn't she? She had wallowed in her misery instead of trying to fix it, and it had landed her here with this man who was calling her out on all of it.

"Why does it matter? It's in the past, right?" she snapped, barely fighting the urge to dig her wounds open all over again.

"It matters because you did this to yourself," he said. "It's not as if it's someone else's fault, and by taking you away, you're safe. You're still in danger, but you're better than this. You are beautiful inside and out," he said, tapping the side of her forearm. "Even with those scars. Now, I don't know if you're religious or not, but you have to believe that God didn't put you on this Earth for you to throw it all away."

Alex closed her eyes. "I don't believe that God has a plan or that this life really means anything. I think if God exists, he sees us the way we see a spider in the drain. We turn the water on and watch to see if it will live or die, not really caring about the outcome either way. I think that's what he does with us. Whether we live or not is a reminder of our own luck and tenaciousness. Nothing else."

"It feels like that sometimes," Jamie agreed. "In the system, they pushed Catholicism. I had the whole nine yards learning it, but it never sat right with me. If we're God's beloved creation, why would he keep us in this place, watching while we inflict senseless violence on one another, day after day? It makes no sense."

Alex rested her head on the pillow, eyes on the wall as she said, "Those thoughts plague me all the time. It was…why

I started writing to begin with. It was my way of making sense of things."

"And then you gave up on yourself, which is ridiculous because you have everything you need to succeed except confidence."

Alex squeezed her hands into fists. She wanted to be angry for the sole fact that she didn't want to be sad anymore. Her eyes started to tear up and she tried to will them away, not wanting to see how deep his words cut, how much she had needed kindness like that. They were words that at one time she wished Peter would've told her, long before she felt as if he had stopped caring about her.

Jamie grasped her shoulder, pulling her away from the wall, and pushed her onto her back before he cupped her chin, bringing her face toward him. He kissed her. It was a soft brush of his lips to hers. She didn't react at first, trying to decide what her best course of action would be.

Maybe this was the opportunity she'd been waiting for. Get his guard down, incapacitate him, get the collar off, and get the hell out of there. She relaxed, letting him run his fingers down her body. She deepened the kiss, their mouths moving together surprisingly well. Alex was very aware of every spot his fingers grazed on their descent from her shoulders down to her hips. When his hands trailed over her thigh, she gasped and pulled away, her fingernails digging into him.

"Woah, hey. Relax," he said, pulling his hand away to show her his empty palm as if he were afraid she would claw deeper if he didn't.

"I-I'm sorry," she said, eyes wide, and pulled her nails out of his skin, not liking the tiny crescent moons left behind.

"It's okay," he said, features crafted in concern.

Alex was so wrapped in her panic that she didn't hear him. "It's not you," she continued. "It's…I…I don't like to be touched."

Jamie held his hands out, the gentle curve of a smile on his lips. "You don't have to explain a thing to me," he said, voice soft. The opposite of what she had expected.

Whenever she rejected Peter, his instant go-to was anger. It didn't matter to him what she felt as long as his needs were gratified. Part of her had grown so used to that reaction, she believed it was a normal response. That all men were wired the same way. She narrowed her eyes, suspicious, but Jamie either didn't notice or didn't care.

"You're hurting," he said in way of an explanation. "That much is obvious. I'm not heartless. I'm not going to make you feel things you don't need to. The only thing I ask is that you reach out to me when you feel comfortable. Remember that whatever pain you feel, you don't have to do it alone. I'm here."

Alex shivered but didn't fight as he slid his arms around her, holding her close. He kept his hands away from her thighs, and she found herself burying her face in his chest.

Jamie watched with eyebrows raised. When she pressed her forehead against him, he leaned down and planted a kiss on the top of her head. "You can keep your secrets for now, but I'll be here when you're ready to let them out."

Chapter Twenty-Two

JAMIE KEPT HIS arms around Alex, convinced she would try to take off the first chance she got. He was surprised when no more than ten minutes later, she fell asleep. Her soft snores filled his ears, and he sat up, pulling his arms loose. Alex groaned in her throat but didn't wake, and Jamie froze, waiting for her eyes to open. When they didn't, he swiped a lock of hair off her cheek, studying her every feature.

It hurt to see someone so beautiful be so sad.

Peter was poison. Not the kind that acts instantly upon digestion, but the kind that seeps into every organ, slowly causing damage. The damage builds up over time until it's so severe, it shuts the entire body down. Like arsenic. That was what he had done to Alex. He had destroyed everything that made a person vibrant—their confidence, their self-esteem, and their sense of self-worth. All of it was gone from Alex because of the careless way that Peter had treated her. Jamie wished the worst for him. Wished he could have every sense of his own humanity stripped away until he was a husk wishing for death.

It was clear something else had happened in Alex's past too, and he debated with himself over whether he truly wanted to know what it was or not. He could guess, and that was more than enough to anger him because she reminded him of another girl. One who had been close to his heart. One who was now dead.

At one time, she had been the only light in his life, until that light had been extinguished for good, of course.

Jamie's eyelids had fluttered with the onset of his nightmares. When his eyes opened at last, he realized the muffled screaming had followed him from the darkness in his head.

Lana.

Heart pounding, he jumped up, running to her room. Lana started to cry and as Jamie reached the door, the sound of fists landing could be heard. Lana's door wouldn't open at first, and Jamie yowled, barreling his shoulder into it. With all the strength his tween body could muster, he managed to bust inside. Lana screamed again, and Jamie's brain was overwhelmed with panic as he tumbled into the room.

Their foster father, Greg, was hitting her over and over. In the darkness, Jamie couldn't tell if he was using something to do it or was barehanded. The sounds told him that either way it didn't matter. Lana was hurt. Bad. With no regard to his own safety, Jamie charged forward, grabbing one of Greg's massive arms.

"Get off her!" he screamed, landing punches that his foster father couldn't feel.

"This isn't your business!" he roared and struck out, hitting Jamie across the face with a blow that sent him stumbling backward into the wall as Lana's wails started again.

Jamie was dazed, the spot where his head hit the wall pounding, but he shook it off, knowing what he had to do. Dizzy, he got up, stumbling out of the room.

"Get back here, you prick!" Greg demanded.

Jamie didn't stop. To do so would be foolish. When his

vision started to blacken around the edges, he forced himself to keep going. He rushed into his foster parents' bedroom and flicked on the light.

The motion had his foster mother awake instantly.

The blanket was pulled up to her chest as she peered at him through wide eyes. "Jamie! What's happening?"

He said nothing as he pulled the gun out of its hiding place in the back of the closet.

"Jamie, no! What are you doing with that?" she yowled.

He was out the door before she could stop him, but the sound of her footsteps told him she was following. Greg wasn't in the hall anymore, but Jamie kept the gun up, finger poised over the trigger, ready to squeeze it. Jamie hurried back inside Lana's room, but she wasn't screaming anymore.

The moonlight streaming in through the window highlighted Greg's massive form hovering over Lana's battered body. Greg turned to him, light glinting off his eyes, and Jamie pulled the trigger.

Chapter Twenty-Three

WHEN ALEX WOKE up, the soft blankets beneath her came as a surprise until she remembered the night before. Jamie's bed. She peered over her shoulder, seeking out Jamie. He was gone. She sat up so fast, she had vertigo. Had he left her *alone?* As she struggled to regain herself, a soft voice from the hall caught her attention.

Intrigued, Alex got up out of the bed, creeping toward the door. As she moved into the hall, her steps hardly made a sound. Soft singing came from the bathroom. The door was open a crack, spilling the light from inside. Alex grabbed the frame as she peered inside the bathroom. Jamie stood in front of the mirror, working on rolling up the sleeves of the white button-up shirt he was wearing.

"…back to the night we met."

Alex was transfixed. The door creaked as she pushed on it, and Jamie turned to look at her. She expected a verbal lashing for catching him in such a vulnerable moment, but there was a warm expression on his face.

"That was beautiful. What was that?"

Jamie smiled and rolled the sleeve in place a bit before his elbow. "A song I heard a few years ago. It…makes me think a bit."

"About what?"

The smile fell from Jamie's face, replaced with a crestfallen edge as if he had been delivered bad news. "It's not important."

Alex's face mirrored his. Anything that could make someone's emotions do a complete one-eighty was far from *nothing*.

Jamie didn't give her the chance to speak as he said, "C'mon. I've got breakfast in the kitchen."

Alex's stomach growled at the mention of food, and she was disappointed in the fact that her body would have such a normal reaction. Mentally chastising herself, she didn't speak again as she followed him to the kitchen. Jamie was quick to serve her food before he sat down with his own plate. She stared at him, studying the way his shaggy hair was neatly combed and his face carefully groomed.

"You look dressed up," she said.

Jamie twitched his nose. "Yeah, I have to go back to work today."

"What do you do?" she asked.

"I'm a waiter. Damien was kind enough to give me some time off, but my vacation is over now."

Alex stared at him without really hearing. He would leave again. For an entire shift at a job? That would give her ample time to figure out some kind of escape plan. The pinch of the collar around her neck reminded her it was there, but she wasn't worried about it. If no one was around to trigger it, it wouldn't go off anyway, right?

Jamie set his fork down and looked at her through narrowed eyes. "I don't want to have to put you back in the basement."

Alex took a sip of her juice, trying to hide her expression with the fear that whatever she showed in the moment would be misinterpreted.

"I'm not sure I can leave you up here alone," he said. "I want to trust you, but if you betray me…it'll ruin my life."

The bite of pancake that she had taken stuck in her throat. "N-no! I won't do that." She forced the food down. "Please don't put me back down there." The band around her neck seemed somehow smaller, and she poked it. "I have this after all so it's not like I'll be free."

He studied it for a long time, unreadable emotion on his face before he pushed away from the table and stood up. "I'm still worried," he admitted, dumping his mostly untouched breakfast into the trash.

Alex stared at the back of his head, but he didn't turn to look at her. He turned the tap on, washing his plate. Alex watched him, considering what else she could say. If she were him, what would she *want* to hear? "You know, I can't get you to trust me if you don't give me the chance."

It was a lie, and she was hardly getting it through her teeth. Of course he couldn't trust her. He had taken her against her will, and he'd be a fool to think she would so readily accept this fate. She was sure he could tell she was lying, but she would plead her case until he left. Seeing what lay beyond Jamie's front door was powerful motivation.

Jamie turned off the faucet and turned back toward her, drying his hands with a red dish rag. "That's a fair point," he said, approaching the table to clean up the rest of the dishes.

Before he picked up any of them, he approached her, setting his fingers under her chin. She looked up at him, into his eyes that were both foreign and familiar. Softly, he pressed his lips to hers before he whispered, "I'll give you this chance." He pulled away, light eyes hardening to flint. "Don't make me regret it."

Alex withered under the look, but he didn't seem to notice. He picked up Alex's plate and empty glass and dumped them in the sink. On the way to the living room, he gave her a meaningful look and plucked his jacket off the hook beside the door. He pulled it on, glanced at her one more time, and left. Alex let out the breath she'd been holding, not realizing until that moment how afraid she really was of Jamie. Sure, he had been mostly kind, but there was something about the look he had given her that chilled her.

Alex's first instinct was to bolt out the door and immediately make a break for it, but she was sure Jamie expected that. It would be her luck that she'd break free only to run right *into* him. She would wait. Wait until she was sure he was gone, and she was truly alone. She bided her time by cleaning up the pile of dishes he had left in the sink, listening to the fading sounds of a car outside that she pegged to be Jamie's.

The second she stopped hearing it, the urge to dart out the door was strong again. To keep herself rational, she dug her nails into her palm, telling herself that if she waited this long, she could wait a few more minutes. She peered through the thin yellow curtain over the kitchen window. Jamie had taped some sort of plastic over the screen so she couldn't see anything beyond other than some blurs of green and brown.

Now or never.

She hurried to the door but paused before opening it. The shock collar was still in place, and she frowned, once again wondering if it was remote activated or if other factors would come into play. Would it feel like the taser had or would it be worse?

"Doesn't matter," she whispered and hurried out the door. This was too perfect of an opportunity to let pass her by because she was afraid.

She made it a few steps outside the door and stopped. From the inside of Jamie's house, it had been all too easy to imagine that they were in a city somewhere with help only a few feet away. Beyond Jamie's door, it looked nothing like the picture she'd created in her head. A stretch of grass littered with leaves and branches led down to a lake. Around the rest of the space were throngs of trees.

Alex did a three-sixty, searching for *some* sign of other humans. From what she could tell, there were no other houses nearby. She studied a flattened part of the grass that was almost worn away to pebbles and dirt. Tire tracks. The path that Jamie must use to come and go from his house.

Alex glanced back once over her shoulder. What if there was no one to help her? For once, she would do what she never did and help herself. She ran. Five steps gave her a sense of freedom until a bolt of pain ripped it away. It felt as if someone had lit her face on fire, and her body refused to cooperate, dropping her onto her knees. She screamed out and pulled herself backward.

Then she understood why Jamie had been so comfortable leaving her alone. The collar was rigged to an electric fence. His actions had all been a game because he knew she wouldn't be able to leave. He'd been testing her…or trying to get her hopes up.

She wasn't sure which.

A laugh-sob fell from her lips, and she laid back against the ground with a thump, staring up at the cloudy sky above. A slight billowy breeze cooled the water streaming down her cheeks.

It was a nice day.

Chapter Twenty-Four

THERE WAS ONE table left. One table standing between Jamie and home. Between him and Alex. The couple at it were so drunk they barely knew where they were, and Jamie doubted they cared about his schedule, but if only they knew. Alex being home so alone so long made his skin crawl. He missed her and wondered how she'd done on her own all day. No police had come to arrest him, and he took that as a good sign.

"Can I get you anything else?" Jamie asked for what had to be the fifteenth time. After the incident with the man and the drink, Jamie was on thin ice with his job and didn't want to do anything to risk it. Damien had warned him that if things went down like that again, he'd have to let him go. So Jamie was restraining himself, trying to get rid of the couple with hostile hospitality.

"No…w-we're good," the man slurred.

"Okay, so you can be good at home," Jamie said, sneering tone but a smile on his face that might pass for friendly for someone as drunk as this man.

The man cut his eyes at him, but Jamie started to gather their dishes, pretending not to notice. Neither of them said any actual protest, so he took the armful to the kitchen, and when he came back for the rest, the couple was gone.

"Thank God," he said loudly to the ceiling.

Damien laughed from his place nearby where he'd been

cleaning the tables. "Got a hot date?"

"Something like that," Jamie murmured, quick to clean the rest of his table.

He was proud of Alex, but there was something about Damien knowing too much that made his skin crawl. If his friend knew exactly what he had done, he wouldn't approve. Probably wouldn't be his friend anymore either.

That thought hit him hard, and he tried to hide it as he finished the last of his tasks and bid his goodbyes. He was so eager to get home that his hand shook when he turned the key in the engine of his car. Uniform discarded into the passenger seat, he pushed his car into action.

Driving up the narrow dirt road leading to his house, he let out a relieved breath. Everything looked normal. No cops, no mysterious vehicles. No sign that anyone besides him and Alex had ever been there. There were lights on in the front room and kitchen. He turned off the car, eager to see what she was up to. When he stepped into the living room, he looked around slowly. The TV and his bookshelf looked undisturbed.

"Alex?" he called, louder than necessary since the house was dead silent.

"In here!" she said from the kitchen.

That was when he picked up the smell of food and his stomach growled. He wandered into the kitchen, eyebrows raised. Alex had four pots going on the stove, and the table was set. There was a bottle of wine between the glasses, and the more he took in, the more surprised he was.

All day he'd been positive she would've tried to escape,

to go for help, but he hadn't considered the possibility that she might not. She might already be acclimated to his house, to *him*. He remembered their first day together, how little it had taken to convince her to strip and get in the tub. If he hadn't been sure before, he was positive now that life had broken her spirits long before he'd met her.

"What's this about?" he asked.

"You've been cooking for me so…I thought I'd return the favor," she said and turned to smile at him.

That would've warmed his heart if he didn't notice the red marks on her cheeks. They were worse than they'd been before he went to work.

She'd been crying again.

Maybe she's not so obedient after all. He had the sudden realization that she *had* tried to escape and couldn't. This was a woman trying to make the best of her situation. Or maybe there was something more insidious behind her actions.

Would she drug his food? He made a note to check it before eating anything she presented.

"Thank you," he said, taking off his coat before he sat down, uncorking the wine. "What's on the menu?"

"Meatloaf," she said and looked away as if she were embarrassed. "It's the fanciest thing I know how to make."

"Meatloaf is perfect," he said, filling the glasses halfway with merlot. He set the bottle down and said, "You know, I have a candle in my closet. I'm gonna go get it."

She simpered before she turned away, stirring the contents of the largest pot.

Jamie didn't know what she was thinking, but if there was ever a time to wish he could read someone's mind, it was right then. He waited until her attention was off him before he padded down the hall, stopping at the closet. A glance over his shoulder to see if anything changed. Nothing did. He slipped into the bathroom, closing the door with a quiet click before hurrying over to the medicine cabinet.

Prescription drugs had been a vice at one point, and he blamed the doctors who were supposed to look out for his best interest. The same drugs that had ailed him had been the ones he'd been prescribed. Keeping a supply in the house was always a dangerous move because at any second, any slight inconvenience, he could relapse and throw away everything. Knowing he had a supply nearby if he *did* want it comforted him.

In some weird way, he was sure that was partially the reason he'd been able to cope as well as he had. He picked up each bottle, shaking them. They didn't look as if they had been disturbed. He uncapped one, but the level of pills hadn't changed. Alex hadn't touched them. Content with his findings, Jamie closed the mirror and left the bathroom, plucking the candle out of the closet on his way back to the kitchen.

When he stepped into the room, Alex was pulling the meatloaf out of the oven, and Jamie had a surge of pride. This was a moment of domestic bliss, one he'd never thought he'd have.

"This should give us a more appropriate atmosphere," he said, setting up the candle in the golden holder in the middle of the table.

He lit it, watching the first bead of wax run down the side. Alex said nothing as she turned to get their plates ready. Alex hadn't touched his medicine, but Jamie still watched her to make sure she didn't slip anything else into the mix. She didn't. When she approached the table, she gave him a plate piled with more food than he could hope to eat. In comparison, her own plate was nearly empty.

"You'll need to eat more than that," he said as she sat down across from him.

"I don't really eat much," she assured him and put a bite into her mouth.

"Mmm, that's why you're all skin and bones," he said, taking a bite. "This is amazing! And you said you couldn't cook."

"This is the fanciest meal I can make," she reminded him.

"Well, you did wonderful."

She drew her eyebrows together. "What is it?"

"Are you going to tell me the real reason behind this?"

She licked her lips and looked away.

"You can be honest with me. I'm not going to be mad. I understand if you tried to leave while I wasn't here," he said, reaching across the table to clutch her hand. "I understand there's going to be an adjustment period

Her eyes were wide. "I di—"

He held his hand up. "Like I said, I understand."

She deflated then. "Fine, I tried. I couldn't get far."

"Don't be sorry," he said. "Learn from what it's taught you."

"It taught me we live in the middle of nowhere," she said. "Where *are* we anyway?"

"I like it out here," he said. "No neighbors to get in your business. Plenty of land to live and breathe. This, uh, was my dad's house. He wasn't a fan of cities, but he liked to know that if he needed to get to town in a hurry, he could. When he died, he left this place to me."

"Where's the rest of your family? Your mom?" she asked.

"I don't know," he admitted, but his mind was a series of memories. Days of listening to his mother's screams and nights of his father's beatings. Foster parents, orphanages, asylums, and pills. Police. Handcuffs. Alex's bottom lip jutted out, and he paused, confused for the reaction. "Does that upset you somehow?"

"It's not fair," she said, dropping her fork with a clang.

Jamie flinched, uncertain of the reaction. "*What's* not fair?"

"It's been what…a *week* since you took me from my home, and yet the only thing you've let me know about you is your name. And honestly, I'm wondering if that's real. You don't look like a Jamie."

He took another bite. "Oh, yeah? What *do* I look like?"

"I'm serious."

Jamie didn't want to tell her the truth about his past. Not yet. Not because they barely knew one another, but because remembering it was like reliving it in a way. And he didn't want her to see how it affected him. It was bad enough that Alex had reminded him of Lana on more than one occasion, but to admit that would be to let all the negative spirits in to fester.

"You know every intimate detail down to my bra size apparently," she said, snagging the strap of the camisole bra he'd bought during his supply run. "And I know nothing about you."

"Not true," he said, downing the last of the merlot in his glass. "You know something about me that *no one* else does."

"What's that?" Alex asked, voice quivering.

He bent forward, resting his elbows on the table. "You know I killed a man."

Chapter Twenty-Five

LEX WAS ON edge for the rest of the night. Jamie's unpredictable moods made her wary. When he was ready to go to bed, she wanted to go to the basement to be away from him. She thought of the night before, being wrapped in his embrace. The kisses they'd shared, and she shivered with the feeling that tonight might bring more than that if she let it. She shouldn't, but she felt guilty. As if she were betraying Peter. As if he hadn't betrayed her first.

Alex tried to voice her request, but Jamie didn't give her the chance. He herded her easily to his room, stripping down as he had the night before. She lay on the mattress with him beside her. He was propped up on one elbow, studying her over like an artist studying their competition's work in a museum. It was an appropriate comparison because she very much felt as if she were on display.

Then he said the words she had dreaded. "Take off your clothes."

She hugged herself tighter, looking at him like a wounded animal.

He held his hands out. "Let me try again. You look stressed. I can see it in your muscles, in the way you carry yourself. I'd love to give you a massage. To help you deal with some of that stress. I know that right now you don't have many outlets for doing so, and I want to make this easier."

She didn't change her pose or expression. He was lying. He had to be. Alex searched his face for the glint of danger she had seen at the dining table, but it was mysteriously absent, wrapped back inside the warmth and joy that usually radiated from him.

Where does it go? she wondered, leaving his eyes for last.

They weren't soulless like she'd expected of a murderer. They were light and haunted. They spoke of pain and anguish. Guilt and hope. They were everything an artist could ever hope to capture in a piece of artwork.

She dropped her arm from its protective position across her chest but didn't obey him. Instead, she stared at him until he reached out, brushing away the hair from her face. "I gave you a chance to earn my trust, now you've got to do the same for me."

She wanted to argue but couldn't find the words. Giving in, she pulled off her shirt and pajama pants. He had already seen every inch of her. What difference did it make anymore? The collar around her neck caught on the blankets as she lay on her stomach, and it took a little bit of awkward maneuvering to fix it.

Jamie sat up on his knees, and Alex turned her face against the bedding, trying to see him from the corner of her eye. His clothes were still on, loose pajamas hanging from his hips, showing the beginning of the V lines on a guy that drove women crazy.

His fingers pressed into the muscle and tissue in the middle of her back, and she melted. Like magic, he erased away all her tension. He worked from the tops of her arms down to her hands, leaving her body feeling weightless. Next, he moved to her thighs, calves, and took extra time on her feet. Alex was nearly a puddle, drool leaking from the corner of her mouth as she threatened to doze off. She had never been so relaxed.

At last, his fingers pulled away, and she would've let herself drift right off to sleep if he hadn't touched back down on the clasp of her bra. Her eyes were open, tension instantly back as she tried to prop herself up and glare at him.

He held his hand up so she could see it, but not nearly as far away from her as she'd like. "Trust. You're trusting me, right?"

She wanted to raise a lip to snarl at him, to tell him he could choke on that trust if it meant taking advantage of her, but he was right. She'd given him her word, and without it, she was nobody. Instead of saying any of that, she buried her face in the pillow, readying herself for whatever would come next.

A second later, his fingers grazed her back, massaging softly before they slid under her bra, unhooking it. The band fell to either side of her, and Jamie's fingers brushed softly over her skin as he did his best to move it without disturbing her.

She let him get the straps off her arms but continued to lay on her stomach, pinning the most important piece in place. Jamie didn't argue. He left it there as his fingers played with the waistband of her underwear. Tears misted her vision, and she bit down into the pillow, contemplating a hundred different methods of escape. At last, she decided on a palm to the face and sat up, trying to jab the heel of her hand into Jamie's unsuspecting nose. He caught her easily, almost as if he had been prepared for her to strike out.

Jamie's grip was firm but delicate. He held her, staring into her eyes, and only after he was certain she wouldn't continue the assault did he let her arm go. It dropped to the mattress with a thud, and that was when she realized her bra was still in its place on the bed.

Jamie kept his eyes on her face and reached out to touch her under the chin. "It's okay," he said softly. "Thanks for trusting me this much."

Alex was frozen, unsure how to respond. What was the logical response to any of this? *Fight like hell and run,* she thought, but those hadn't been lucrative ideas in the past.

Jamie didn't wait for her to speak before he reached for his own pants and pulled them down, revealing his boxers, and the outline of his manhood through them. Alex didn't want to blush, but she could feel the warming in her cheeks.

Jamie didn't say anything to it. He laid on his side, holding his arms out. Alex looked from him to the door and back to him again. For a reason she couldn't understand, she longed to lie down, wrapped in his embrace like she'd done the night before. It felt as if it had been ages since Peter had held her, like she was frail and delicate and something he would protect with his life. Her lip trembled, and she found herself diving into Jamie's outstretched arms. The feeling of her bare chest to his sent shivers through her. The same kind she had gotten the first time she'd been intimate with Peter, and she wondered what it meant to feel that way now, in the throes of such a dangerous situation.

Jamie said nothing. Head rested on the pillow and eyes closed, he took his own enjoyment from the moment, leaving her to sort out her feelings for herself. She envied his peace, wondering what it truly meant to be okay with who you were.

Alex had always been self-conscious, always worried about what people thought of her. Walking down the street she feared that strangers would see her and think she was ugly, know that she was an outsider of some kind.

Jamie didn't show any of that. He had the smallest hint of a smile on his face as if he had been given a Christmas gift he'd wanted all year round. He looked carefree and happy. So much so that she wondered if the story he'd told her about his addiction and past had been nothing but lies.

Alex relaxed against him, trying to turn her brain off, but it wasn't easy for her to go to sleep. Soft snores told her Jamie was sleeping, but she had the irrational fear he would wake up and tear the underwear off her, demanding she give him the last shred of dignity she had left.

The fear from her first day had never gone away, but it had dulled considerably. Now, it was back. Jamie's madness could be dangerous, she knew that now. What she *didn't* know was how capable he was of hurting her. She poked the collar around her neck. The only other thing she wore besides her underwear. She fidgeted with the clasp, but for all her trying, she couldn't get it off.

Somehow, during her own self-torture, she managed to fall asleep. When she woke in the morning, it was to Jamie softly rubbing his fingers up and down her arm. When she first became aware of the sensation, she kept her eyes closed, feigning sleep. How long had he been awake, watching her?

He called her bluff almost instantly. "Come on," he said, warm breath fanning her face before he pressed a soft kiss to her lips.

When she opened her eyes, she realized he was already dressed in a white T-shirt and jeans. Clutching his comforter to her chest, she sat up. Jamie turned to grab a stack of clothes off his dresser and handed them to her. She took them, expected him to take the collar off so she could shower.

"Put those on. I want to show you something," he said.

Alex was both intrigued and fearful. She did as he instructed, glad to hide her body beneath a layer of fabrics. Once she was dressed, he grasped her hand, leading her out to the hallway. There was a door across from his room, and they stopped in front of it. Jamie let go of her as he pulled a bundle of keys from his pocket and sorted through them. Alex watched, fidgeting from foot to foot. The suspense was killing her. And so was her full bladder.

"What are we doing?" she asked, more curious to find out than she was desperate to relieve herself.

He turned a key in the lock, pushing the door open. Inside was a desk and a computer. There was a padded office chair in front of the monitor and a stool not far from that.

"This is my office," Jamie said. "Or I guess I should say it was my dad's office since I don't really use it. I think it'll be handy for you with your work."

"Wait…what?"

"I told you I'm going to help the world see how brilliant you are. Or have you forgotten?"

"No, I remember. Just like I remember telling you I'm not interested," she said, trying to pull away.

Jamie easily caught her arm. "And I told *you* it's not really your decision. You want to go home, right? Well, do this for me first."

Alex narrowed her eyes, staring at him. After all this would he really let her go? He avoided her gaze, and she was almost certain he was lying. She knew too much, had seen too much. He'd never make the choice to free her. It was something she would have to do on her own.

Jamie set his hand on her lower back, leading her to the computer to sit her down in the padded chair. He picked up the stool and set it down beside her, face unreadable as he studied her over.

"What do you want from me?" she asked. "You keep staring at me as if you expect me to miraculously crawl out of my skin or something."

"I want to get inside your head. To know what it's like to be you," he said, propping his elbows on his knees as he leaned forward. "Walk me through what you used to do online. How you published your books and all that."

She didn't want to. She wanted to shower and eat. To forget about everything that had happened so far and put her brain back into coming up with some kind of escape plan. She glanced at Jamie from the corner of her eye. His face hadn't changed in expression, and she gave up. An argument could happen, but she was positive she wouldn't win.

She tapped the mouse.

Jamie's computer hummed to life, and she was looking at a picture of herself. It was professional, the one she'd had taken for the back of her books. Jamie had put a decorative border around it of hearts and roses. It turned her stomach. Somehow, it was better to be a nobody than somebody's focus of worship.

"Like it?" Jamie asked, the slightest hint of a smile on his lips.

"No," she replied flatly, honestly.

"Pull up the browser."

Alex didn't argue. The sooner she didn't have to look at her own face, the better. She navigated to the website she had published all her work through and looked to Jamie. "This is it."

He bobbed his head. "Log in."

Her fingers hovered over the keyboard. "Aren't you worried about the IP address being tracked?"

"Not particularly. I have two VPNs working to disguise it. Please sign in."

"Okay," Alex said, not sure what a VPN was. Unshaking, she typed in her familiar username and password.

"You're in? Good. Now delete the account."

Alex glanced up at him, eyes wide and questioning. While she had been so certain that she wanted to call it quits, this felt like a solid step in that direction, one that couldn't be undone if she had a change of heart.

"What are you worried about?" he asked, eyes on her frozen fingers. "You don't need a website like this that won't help you. You will write another book, and that book will get an agent."

Alex drew her eyebrows together, wanting to argue again, but she didn't waste the breath. She clicked the *Are you sure* button before she minimized the browser and turned to Jamie. "If you have all this knowledge of the publishing world, why don't you write something yourself?"

"Because I don't have the talent. You do, but you need guidance to make it flourish," he said, pausing to cup his chin with his hand. "You…understand me in ways that no one ever has, and that's why I want you to write my biography."

"Your biography? My, that seems a bit narcissistic, don't you think?"

"No," he said. "I haven't…told you a fraction of the things I've been through, but my life has been far from easy."

"I don't think you've really thought this plan through," Alex said. "Say I write the book and it does become big. People will be able to find me."

"Pen names, my dear," he said. "And if there's any actual contact info, I'll use my own. They'll never know."

Alex's shoulders drooped. "So there will be no actual way for anyone to know it's me?"

"Nope, but *we'll* know. It'll be our little secret."

"You really just…expect me to sit down and write like everything is normal after all that you've done?" she asked. "You want me to write your life story in a way that favors you?

I don't see that happening."

"You have no faith," he said, gazing at the scars on her arm. "But I think in time, you'll warm to the idea."

"Alright. All of that aside, even if I agreed, I can't work on the computer," she said. "My head isn't wired like that. I need pens and paper. Not to mention I need to know everything about you."

Jamie smiled but it was pinched, pained. "You're full of surprises, aren't you?"

"Yeah, but not the good kind."

"Nonsense," he said. "Tell you what. Try to make a chart of everything you've learned about me so far, and I'll go get you supplies."

He stood up, and Alex followed, glad to get out of there. The sooner she got away from the computer and the creepy blown-up image of her face, the better. Jamie locked the office door behind them, and Alex wilted as she watched him. It didn't seem as if there was a landline anywhere in the house, the only phone being Jamie's cell. The computer was most likely her only way to reaching out to the outside world, and for the time being, she didn't have access to it.

So many doubts and fears flooded her mind that she was surprised Jamie couldn't hear them leaking out of her ears. Somehow, she plastered a fake smile to her face and maintained it as Jamie went out the front door. She stood at the entrance to the hall, waiting for the sound of Jamie's vehicle to disappear into the distance. When she was sure she was alone, she rushed back to the office door, ramming her shoulder into it. The wood was solid and firm, unyielding to her wants, and she gave up, staring down at her scarred arms, the bandage still in place.

Jamie thought she had stories in her, and he wasn't wrong. Except it wasn't *stories,* it was *a* story. One specific tale that screamed in her head over and over.

A girl who wanted to die.

Long before the monster had stolen her innocence and brought along the pain of adulthood, she had wished for death. Every day in this place only made her realize how much she craved it. It would put an end to all of this—the pain caused by Peter, missing her daughter, fearing for her safety. She could end all of it so easily.

Chapter Twenty-Six

J AMIE DIDN'T MAKE it far down the road before he realized he had forgotten his wallet. As he drove, he did his best to tap the pocket, certain he had grabbed it, but it was still empty. Groaning, he did a U-turn, maneuvering back up the long, winding dirt road to his house.

When Jamie went inside, it was quiet. *Too* quiet, but that wasn't unusual. Alex didn't make a lot of noise. She was as mousy as her appearance had suggested.

"Alex?"

On instinct, Jamie wandered to the kitchen, searching for her, but she wasn't there. There was no sign she had been there since their dinner the night before.

"Alex! I forgot my wallet."

Nothing.

Panic scratched at his insides as the silence closed in on him. It wasn't normal silence; it was the quiet from the aftermath of something terrible. Jamie tore through the living room, eyes wide with possible horrors. What if Zack didn't work alone? What if he had sent someone else and they had hurt Alex in revenge for Zack's disappearance?

"No," he said out loud. "No, no, no."

Seeing was believing, and since he saw nothing, he couldn't confirm what had happened one way or the other. Frantically, he hurried down the hall and checked the basement. He didn't expect her to be there, but he was at a loss when he didn't see her there either. At last, he made it to the bathroom.

"Oh, God," he breathed.

Time slowed down.

Alex was lying on the bathroom floor, a pool of blood under her from the wounds on her wrists. She was usually pale, but now, she looked as white as a ghost.

Or a corpse.

"Oh, no," he moaned.

While his first instinct was to rush to her side and cradle her, it would spend time he didn't have. He backed away, snagging his first-aid kit from its spot beneath the sink and rushing to her. He threw himself to his knees so hard that they audibly cracked against the hard floor. Jamie hardly noticed the resulting pain as he fidgeted with the case, opening it to scoop out the bandages.

With gentle pressure, he wrapped the long white strands into place on both wrists, hoping it wasn't already too late to save her. She was breathing, the slow rhythm of her breaths stirring the strands of hair that had fallen over her face. The puddle of blood beneath her was massive, the cracks in the tiles spreading it farther than it should've traveled on its own. She didn't stir, and he pulled her up, holding her close against his chest. Her skin was still warm, and when he squeezed her tighter, he could feel the slight puff of air from her lips.

He wasn't too late.

"Stay with me," he whispered and carried her into his room, hardly conscious of the blood that was smearing onto his shirt and through to his skin.

He tried without success not to think of Zack's body in his arms, how similar it had felt. Biting back his sorrow, Jamie laid Alex down, gently pulling back his blankets, and then laid next to her. He buried his face in her hair, breathing in her scent and trying to ignore the copper tang that came from her blood. Her scent was a smell that was oddly familiar to him after their short time together. In a month, how much more familiar would it be?

If she lives, the darkness in his head mused.

"Alex, please hold on," he said, holding her close.

He disconnected from himself then. From the girl dying in his arms. He wasn't twenty-six anymore. He was twelve. In his arms was a different girl with brown hair and blood across her body. Lana. He was holding her in his arms, sobbing as her battered eight-year-old body stopped moving, as the heart in her chest ceased its final beat. Her blood had been warm too, but there had been so much more of it, enough to drown in, and he wished he would've.

"Why are you crying?" Alex's soft voice rasped.

Jamie was immediately pulled from his memories, slamming back into his body with a force that left him momentarily disoriented.

Alex didn't look at him. One of her bandaged arms was held up, and he could tell that was where her attention was focused. A blot of red soaked through the white on her left wrist, but other than that, there were no signs of the carnage beneath.

"Why did you do this?" he asked softly before she could say anything else. He wanted the question to be gentle, but it came out accusatory, harsh, and he hated it. He was torn between chastising her for the reckless move and coddling her after how close he'd been to losing her for good. "I told you to never hurt yourself again."

"You fixed me," she countered. "*Why?*"

"You're no good to anyone dead," Jamie said, sitting up to better see her face. "Why would you do this? Haven't I been good to you?"

Alex's eyes welled with tears, and he wondered how it could be possible to be filled with so much sadness that a brush with death wasn't enough to make it go away. "Because I'm better off dead."

"That's ridiculous."

Alex looked down at the bandages again. "Says a random internet creep who's known me all of a week."

Jamie straightened his spine, staring at her with a mix of hurt and anger. The way she so blatantly disregarded his feelings, disregarded *him* after everything, cut him in a way he never imagined words could do. He imagined things to have gotten better between them, but the look on her face made him doubt everything. It had been wishful thinking on his part. Of course she'd never accept him. Never accept what he had done.

He had been a fool for thinking otherwise.

"I know what I am," Jamie said.

"And I do too," Alex whispered, wrapping her arms around herself. The venom was gone, and the lack of emotion in her voice so much worse as she stared straight ahead at the wall. Jamie wondered if she was actually looking at what was before her or if she was lost in the depths of her memories. "I'm the disposable friend, the black sheep, the outsider. As much as I've always wanted to belong, to be loved, to matter, I never will. Seeing the news? The whole thing with Peter? That was nothing new. I've known he hasn't cared about me in some time, but it's been easier to pretend. Pretend that everything was fine. That I was loved."

"Peter is a scumbag," Jamie said slowly, carefully. "You can't possibly derive your value from him. If anyone deserves to have their wrists slashed, it's him. I wouldn't mind doing it myself to see the look on his face."

Alex held up her hand, eyes closed as she said, "Don't. You don't think I know what he is? But…sometimes it's easier to see the distant monster than the one beside you. I've known Peter since middle school. We were young and impulsive, and we married right out of high school. We thought it was love, but it wasn't. It was an escape. One that both of us needed."

"An escape from what?" he dared himself to ask, but he doubted he would get a straightforward answer.

"My…family was never much of a haven," she admitted. "My mom was sick with cancer from the time I learned to walk, and it finally claimed her not long after I met Peter. Dad…he didn't know how to cope with Mom's death. Never really did, I guess. He found his solace in a bottle, and I became nothing more than a nuisance. Peter was all I had left, and I guess I fooled myself into thinking that if I cared about *him,* then that meant he had to do the same for me."

Alex flopped back against the pillows, covering her eyes

with the backs of her hands. "As pathetic as it sounds, I used to have the theory that if I up and vanished one day, no one would notice. I'd argue back with myself, saying that *someone* would notice. Someone had to. In my twenty-three years on Earth, I can't have *not* made an impact on anyone, right?"

"Right. You have a daughter," Jamie spoke up. "I bet she misses you like crazy."

Alex let her hands drop to her sides. "She's been a daddy's girl from the start. Plus…*look* at me." She poked one of her faded scars so hard that the skin around it turned red. "I'm a monster. She deserves a better mother, and I know it. I always have."

"All of that is your depression *lying* to you," Jamie said softly. "I fell in love with you from your words alone and being with you for this week has strengthened that, not weakened it. Everyone has their scars. Some people don't wear them on the outside, but you can bet they're still there. Everyone you see on the streets has their own mask of strength on. I think that's what adulthood is. Pretending that you've got it all together when really, you're confused inside. Yearning for someone to take the responsibility off your shoulders. At least, that's how it's been for me. That's why I can say with confidence that you're not a lost cause. And you're certainly *not* better off dead."

Alex closed her eyes, the wetness of her tears causing her eyelashes to stick together.

"Why do you…do that to yourself?" he asked, finger tracing the nearest scar.

Alex stared at it, lip jutting out into a pout.

"It's…cleansing, like the feeling that comes after a good cry. Like a huge weight has been lifted off your shoulders."

Jamie wasn't ashamed to admit that he cried quite often. It was the only way he could be sure his own pain would escape him. It was either that or pills, and he was done with those.

"It's like that. Getting the blood out…it feels like I'm letting out the sadness, the anger, the hatred, and I'm keeping all the good things inside of me." Her eyes fell to her bandages, to the tiny blot of red that was steadily seeping into the white. "In the old days, they used to believe that the blood held onto toxins and evil. That was why they used to bleed those who were sick. They believed ridding them of some of the evil would cure them. I don't know how well that worked from a medical standpoint, but I understand the theory."

Jamie pressed his lips together to consider her words before he said, "That might be true, but how do you know you're not letting it all out? The good with the bad. How do you know you're not dying a little more with every cut?"

"I guess I don't. Not really. I was a different person when I first turned to this. Maybe I've been siphoning myself away with it, but everything good has a cost, right?"

"If it was good, you wouldn't have to sacrifice yourself to keep doing it." Jamie winced almost as soon as the words were out of his mouth. It reminded him of a conversation he'd had with Zack at the halfway house not long before his father passed, and Jamie's life changed. Jamie had been on the verge of getting over his addiction, and Zack had wanted nothing more than to drag him back into his old ways.

Alex opened her mouth, and Jamie prayed she wouldn't call him on the tiny slip of emotion, but she didn't. She broke down into tears again, and Jamie was relieved. Then he felt guilty. He'd never been the type of person who was happy for the bad things that happened to other people.

Jamie squeezed his eyes shut, trying to hold in his own tears as he rubbed soothing circles into Alex's back. She fell asleep, and Jamie let a few tears leak free, confident that no one would be any the wiser. Jamie stayed with Alex for hours, the only indicator of the time was the moonlight shining through the cracks in the blinds.

When his arm started to fall asleep, he looked down into her peaceful face and pulled himself free. She murmured something and turned over, still deep in her slumber. Confident that she wouldn't notice his absence, he got out of bed. He peered at Alex again before he crept out of the room and went down the hall, putting his shoes on. As quietly as he could, he opened the door and crept out to the yard. The moonlight overhead spilt silver light across the grass, and he walked through it, imagining himself to be part of the darkness. Before he reached the edge of his yard, he sat down and sighed, loud and long.

"This probably isn't appropriate etiquette since I killed you and all," Jamie said, peering down at the mound of dirt before him. It was still strange to think Zack was down there somewhere, feeding the worms. That Jamie was the reason he was dead and not the assortment of demons that had ruled Zack's life. "But I wanted to sit with you for a while. I don't know what it's like on the other side, but if some part of you is aware of what's happened, it must be lonely. I know I would be."

Some crickets chirped, and Jamie tilted his head back to look up at the sky, counting the stars in the constellations above his head.

"Alex has got me thinking about you. About everything really."

An owl hooted from somewhere in the distance, and he imagined it to be Zack responding to him.

Jamie looked down at his fingers through the shadows. "We were kids in that place," he said. "We had our entire lives ahead of us. I don't know why you didn't want to come with me. Why did you want the drugs more?"

A stirring sensation filled his gut, and he was uneasy. He knew the answer to his own question because Jamie still wanted the drugs too. It took a great deal of restraint and an ironclad will to remind himself he was better off without them.

Not everyone had the same resolve.

"I hate that this is the way things ended with us. You were my best friend. Probably the only person in the world who knew it all and still accepted me. Wherever you end up, I hope you find the peace you never could on Earth."

A shuffling sound came from the foliage nearby, and he jumped up, hand on his pocket where his knife was tucked away. Heart pounding, he waited to see what would emerge. Two emerald eyes peered back at him.

Chapter Twenty-Seven

WHEN ALEX WOKE in the morning, she expected Jamie to still be there, comforting her, but he wasn't. She sat up, gaze dropping to her wrists. Angrily, she thought about everything she'd let slip when she had been drunk on her depression and hated herself for the vulnerability. People were likely to exploit your weakness, the cracks in your armor, and she had given him an entire arsenal.

She couldn't blame Jamie for not wanting to be by her after that. If she could run away from herself, she would've a long time ago.

Desperate to cause herself more pain, she unwound the bandages that Jamie had carefully secured into place. They dropped to the bed, revealing the carnage underneath. The red marks were almost purple, dried blood crusted to the skin around them. The ugliness against her pale skin brought her some pleasure but not as much as she'd hoped for.

She could've been dead. *Would've* been without Jamie. There was no way he'd run away. If he had been desperate for escape, he would've let her die, not gone through what he had to save her life.

"Jamie?" Alex called, uneasy with the silence, and stood from the bed.

Sunlight streamed through the odd plastic covering of the window beside the television, and she wondered if Jamie had gotten up and gone to work without telling her. A strange mix of relief and unease whooshed through her like that. It wasn't like him to vanish. What if something had happened? The strange feeling in her gut turned to despair when she remembered Zack. Did Jamie's disappearance have something to do with him?

Her only way of finding out would be to ask Jamie, but she doubted she'd get a straight answer. Alex got out of bed and relieved her bladder before she went to the kitchen, pouring herself a cup of juice. After the amount of blood she'd lost the night before, she was weak. She needed nutrients, but she wasn't sure she could eat. Her nerves were still a frazzled mess. As she finished the last sip of juice, she considered going out into the yard when the front door popped open. Jamie came in, silver pet container in his right hand.

"Good morning," Jamie said, voice bright with enthusiasm. The look he gave her told her he hadn't expected to find her out of bed.

Alex wanted to ask him where he had gone, but her eyes went to the container. "What's that?"

Jamie glanced down at it before looking back up at her. "See for yourself."

Alex narrowed her eyes, taking a small step closer to peer through the little silver grating on the front. Two big green eyes stared back at her from the shadows.

"A cat?" she asked, glancing up at him uncertainly.

"More than that," Jamie said, placing the container on the counter. He opened the door and pulled out a black kitten. Softly, he patted its head before he held it up, smiling at her. "I got you a friend."

Alex felt her steely expression melt away as the kitten mewled. She could feel its fear as clearly as she could feel her own. She took the ball of fluff, cradling it against her chest. "She's adorable," she said, scratching the cat under the chin. Then she looked up at Jamie with narrowed eyes. "What's this for?"

He put his hands in his pockets. "Last night, after you went to sleep, I went outside to do some thinking, and I found this little thing in the yard. I figured you'd appreciate the company. After all, life can be lonely, with or without other people. The connection we can form with animals heals us in ways no other relationship can."

Stunned and unsure what to say, Alex managed to get out, "Thank you."

The kitten squirmed in her grasp, but Alex felt an instant connection to it. Like her, it was a prisoner, brought into a strange place that it didn't understand or care to be in. This kitten was to her what Alex was to Jamie.

"You'll take good care of her, right?" he asked, tipping his head in a way that gave him a boyish flair.

"Of course," she said, running her hand down its back. She gauged it for injuries or other potential issues. It was underweight, and in her head, she ran through a list of things she could cook that would be soft enough for it to eat with its tiny teeth.

"Good," Jamie said and bent forward to kiss her on the forehead. "What are you going to name her?"

Alex stared into the cat's face before she tucked its tiny body back against the safety of her chest. Curled up beside her heart, it relaxed the tiniest bit. "I think I'll call her Chloe."

"Cute name," Jamie said. "But why that?"

"My mom had a cat when I was a baby. It was named Chloe too. It was a big fat thing that liked to sleep directly on top of people."

Jamie laughed then his gaze went down to her wrists as if he just noticed she no longer wore her bandages. "You're going to be okay, aren't you?"

Alex swirled her tongue along the inside of her teeth. She was fine for the moment, but that wasn't something she could expect other people to understand because she barely understood it. The whirlwind of emotions that could overtake her out of nowhere and disappear again.

"I'm fine," she said, looking down at Chloe instead of him.

"I have to go to work today," he said, gaze not moving off her wrists. "But I don't know if I should leave you alone again. I thought I did such a good job of hiding all the sharp stuff in the house that I blame myself entirely for what happened. How could I forget razor blades of all things?"

Alex's lip twitched with veiled annoyance. She didn't want to be fussed over. Didn't want to be babysat. Not when she hadn't sorted out her feelings about living through the attempt. "Well, don't. It wasn't your choice, it was mine."

"It's not a choice you should have," Jamie said, some of the warmth visibly leaving him. "Look, if you're still thinking about it, I can tell Damien to switch my shift and—"

Alex set her hand on Jamie's arm. "I'll be *fine*. I'm not going to do anything stupid." She looked down at Chloe, and her voice went up an octave. "Not with this little girl to take care of."

Jamie smiled, a look of absolute relief. She realized then what his emotion had been when he'd first seen her. It was fear. Fear that she was still on the verge of destroying herself. Fear that he'd lose her for good. Fear that she would never truly be at home with him. For some reason, it warmed Alex to know that. To know that someone was *afraid* of losing her and didn't consider her to be a burden that they would gladly dispose of like yesterday's trash. Maybe it was foolish for Jamie to believe that she wouldn't attempt to hurt herself again, but she was glad that he did.

Glad he had the fear *and* the faith.

"I'll see you later," he said, eyes both soft and warning before he kissed her on the lips.

Chloe let out a little *mew* from her place between them, and Alex pulled away, kissing the top of the cat's head instead.

Chapter Twenty-Eight

JAMIE DIDN'T LEAVE without doing a full search of the bathroom for anything sharp that he had overlooked during his initial search. He took the towel from the top of his closet and put them into a string backpack that he threw under the passenger seat of his car. He didn't want anything dangerous in Alex's vicinity.

As he drove to work, his heart felt lighter than it had in a while. He was terrified about what Alex would try to do to herself next, but she had opened up to him in a way that she had previously refused to do. Whatever walls she'd had up to keep him and everyone else out were starting to come down.

Partly, Jamie wondered if that was one of the reasons behind her attempt. It couldn't all be about what Peter had done. If she was as numb to his tricks as she claimed to be, then there had to be other influences. Whatever the case, he hoped the kitten would be enough for her to change her mind. To know that something else depended on her for survival might be enough.

He hated that he had to leave her alone. There was a chance he was completely wrong. That she was waiting for any opportunity to finish the job, and he had handed it to her. He wished he had a landline at home, some way of checking up on her every hour on the hour. Until he clocked out of work, all he had to comfort him was his anxiety.

It was *not* kind.

Jamie tried to keep a smile on his face as he went into the restaurant. Damien stood at the hostess' station, leaning on his elbows on the podium. "Glad to see you doing so well," he said. Then reconsidered. "Wait, I've seen that smile before. You *are* doing better today, right?"

That was a loaded question. One Jamie wasn't quite sure how to answer. He forced himself to say, "Yeah. Things are starting to look up."

"You have no idea how glad I am to hear that," he said. Jamie could imagine. It probably wasn't easy to be his friend. To have to manage everyone on the staff without seeming as if he had his favorites. Jamie was lucky to have him as a friend. "That girlfriend of yours is doing wonders for you."

"That she is," Jamie agreed and felt the sentiment.

Jamie had steered away from women and relationships. He'd spent so much time doing that that he hadn't realized what it was that he was missing out on. Loneliness was something he'd gotten used to. So much so that he hadn't realized how lackluster his life really was. He did now. Alex had taught him that. The thought she could've died yesterday made him cold inside, because if she'd been successful, Jamie had no idea what he would've done. Going back to a life filled with such loneliness hurt him worse than anything else.

It was amazing what the right person could do.

As Jamie went through the rest of his shift, his mind buoyed between hopeful optimism and pessimistic fear. He was glad for his life but worried that something, specifically something with Alex, would go horribly wrong.

Chapter Twenty-Nine

WHEN JAMIE WAS at work, the house seemed too quiet. He kept the door to his office locked, but Alex wasn't surprised. Their relationship was slowly improving, but it was nowhere near the point where he'd allow her communication with the outside world unsupervised. After what had happened, Alex doubted they would ever get to that point.

With the cat in the house, Alex was more than occupied. Chloe followed her everywhere she went.

"Are you hungry?" she asked it.

Chloe stared up at her through wide eyes.

Alex checked for supplies, but Jamie hadn't bought anything for a cat. No bowls or toys. No litter box and no food. It was so small she hoped it was weaned from its mother's milk. Alex went into the refrigerator and pulled out the container of lunch meat. Carefully, she shredded it to bite-sized pieces and stacked it on the floor. Chloe scarfed it down as if it had been a few days since she'd last eaten anything.

"Poor kitty," Alex cooed, sitting down beside the tiny creature.

Chloe hardly noticed her as she ate. When she was at last full, Alex pulled out the smallest bowl from the cupboard and filled it with water. Satisfied that she had done all she could, she looked around the house, staring at the clock.

It would be a few hours before Jamie would come back.

Frowning, she glanced down at her tiny shadow then the marks on her arms. Out of ideas, she started to pace and ended up in their room.

Our room, Alex echoed inside her head as she entered the bedroom. It was a strange thought, maybe stranger for the fact that it wasn't unwelcome when it should've been. When had it changed from *his* to *theirs,* and how had she not noticed the change in herself?

On the dresser, in front of the television, Jamie had stacked plenty of paper and supplies. He had bought her a fancy notebook, but she hadn't taken the time to look through everything he'd gathered for her. Alex's heart soared a little bit as she rummaged through the supplies. The pens and paper were much fancier brands than Peter had ever allowed her to buy. As she stared at the neat piles, trying to decide where to begin, she picked out a book among them.

East of Eden, the spine read.

She scooped it up, smiling to herself before it fell away. It seemed like such a time had passed between her life now and what used to be her normal, that seeing a tiny detail of her old life like this was almost jarring. She opened the cover, staring at the fancy script on the title page. Alex had finished the book maybe days before she met Jamie, and in everything that had followed, she had nearly forgotten all about it. Holding it now reminded her of a few passages she had particularly related to.

Surely, she wasn't the same naïve woman who read this book and memorized quotes for strength on a rainy day. She felt stronger, a better version of herself than she had been back then.

That was a story, wasn't it?

Jamie had said he wanted her to write his biography, but this moment they were living in together would be a huge part of it. Or at the very least, it would be a beginning to work from. Hesitantly, she picked up a handful of papers and one of the fancy pens. She moved out to the living room and spread the supplies around her. Chloe watched her with intrigue from her spot underneath the couch.

When Alex turned away, Chloe batted playfully at one of Alex's spare pens. She offered the tiny kitty a smile before turning her attention to the blank pieces of paper. Something stirred in her, something she hadn't felt in a while—the desire to create.

Writing had always been therapeutic to her. She could've created a hundred different worlds, lost herself in the crevices of a fantastic place far away. Yet, when she picked up the pen, there was only one subject she could think about.

Jamie.

She *wanted* to tell his story if only to find out what it was that had happened to him. He was mysterious but kind. Loyal but detached. Again she was left with the knowledge that she didn't really *know* him, didn't know what had happened to make him who he was today. As she prepared herself to write, she decided she would try to figure it out.

When she closed her eyes, she could still hear the sweet song he had sung in the bathroom. He had a beautiful voice, the hint of sadness telling her more than his words. That song meant something to him. There was something in his past that was hurting him. Something that haunted him.

She thought of everything she'd learned so far, focusing particularly on the incident with Zack and the moment he declared "he wouldn't lose her again."

He had lost *someone*.

The question was, *who*?

Chapter Thirty

URING THE DRIVE home from work, Jamie thought about his home and Alex. He didn't know what would be waiting for him tonight, but the suicide attempt hadn't been forgotten. He was on the edge of his seat with anxiety, hating that he had left the house at all. Of course Alex had seemed fine this morning, but it could've been a lie, a front, to get him to leave her alone again, and he had fallen for it hook, line, and sinker. He hated that he had to work, hated that he had to leave her when she was so vulnerable.

When he hit the winding dirt curve that led up to his house, he pressed a bit harder on the gas and parked. Grabbing the bag out of the passenger seat, he hopped out, hurrying to the door. His fingers shook so much it was harder than it should've been to get the right key. At last the door opened, revealing the living room. A handful of papers were laid out across the floor. In the center of them, Alex was on her hands and knees, marking on one of the pages. Jamie raised a questioning eyebrow, closing the door behind him. One of the papers skittered toward her, and she looked up, startled.

"I didn't hear you come in," she said, sitting back on her haunches.

"What's all this?" he asked, crouching down to her level.

"Brainstorming," she replied, holding one of the papers to her chest as if she didn't want him to read whatever she'd written on it.

"Ah, don't let me stop you," he said, pleased. He set his bag beside her. "Got some supplies for the kitty."

"Good, good," she said and opened it, peering inside. "Food's on the stove." She set the bag down and went back to scribbling on one of the pages, a tendril of mousy brown hair escaping the bun she'd tied it into.

Jamie didn't move at first. He was transfixed by this image, this very picture he'd had in his head. He kept that goofy smile trained on her, but she was so focused on her work that she didn't notice.

At last, the trance was broken by his churning stomach. He couldn't remember the last thing he'd eaten or if he'd eaten that day at all. He'd been so consumed in his worries of Alex that nothing else had mattered. He fixed himself a plate anyway.

From his place at the kitchen table, he could still see her work. Occasionally, Chloe would skitter out from under the couch and attack one of Alex's pens, to which she'd respond by tickling the cat's stomach until it scampered away, and the cycle started again. As he chewed, he decided that maybe he was worrying over nothing. He had assumed he'd have to keep a closer eye on her, but it was as if her demons had left with the blood.

Just as she said they had a habit of doing.

Alex hadn't said anything about it, and he decided he wouldn't either. If it had helped her feel better, helped her adjust, then he would live with what had happened, only mentioning it when it came time to clean up the wounds. He eyed her wrists, wondering if she'd bothered to put any medicine on the wounds to keep them from getting infected.

The next few weeks passed in a similar routine, summer leaving way for fall then winter.

Jamie would go to work, and Alex would make sure he was fed when he came home. She spent her afternoons writing and caring for Chloe. Overall, she seemed to be in a better mood, and Jamie started to ease from his careful vigil. He wasn't worried about her trying to run away anymore or hurting herself, but he had yet to return the sharp things to the house.

Things went into a fragile sense of normalcy.

Then tragedy struck.

A vicious fever claimed Jamie, and he buried himself in bed, convinced it was the stomach bug going around at his job. He wanted to spend time with Alex, but he did his best to sequester himself away from her, worried she'd catch his bug with her vulnerable immune system.

Alex had noticed his lack of enthusiasm at meals. Not too long after he got home from work and promptly skipped dinner, he heard her footsteps as she wandered down the hall toward him. She peered into the room warily. He was wrapped up with the pillow over his head.

"A-are you okay?"

"I'm fine," he said and peered out from under his shield, squinting at the light.

Alex extended a glass of water to him, and he gratefully accepted it. "You're sure?"

"Yeah," he said and handed her back the cup. "Just a

bug is all."

Alex squinted at him. "Okay," she said, crossing the room to pause in the doorframe. "I'll go back to work. Holler if you need anything."

Jamie watched her go. Her moods went hot to cold, day to day, and he couldn't tell if she hated him or not anymore. He licked his dry lips and had the fear that maybe she had poisoned his drink. It looked clear enough—no traces of powder or residue.

If she hadn't done it before, she won't now, he tried to convince himself.

It was impossible to believe that fact when his fever turned to chills. His sickness had come so suddenly that he wasn't about to rule anything out. Before the evening was done, he started to throw up, and then the pain came. A burst of fire in his abdomen. He screamed out, desperate to do anything to keep himself from focusing on it.

Alex appeared in the doorway, eyes wide and mouth open in a perfect *O*. "What is it?"

"I-I think it's my appendix," he said, hand pushing to the spot in his stomach that hurt the most in his desperate attempt to block out the pain.

Alex stared, hand clutching tight onto the edge of the dresser beside her. "You need to go to the hospital!"

"No," he said at once, mind reeling for a solution. "If I call 911, they'll take you."

"If I do nothing, you'll die," she retorted, rushing to the side of the bed. "Take the collar off, and I can drive you to the hospital myself."

Jamie stared at her, stared hard. If this sickness had been her fault, she would run off as soon as the collar came off. But she was right. Whatever this was, he couldn't fight it on his own. The room around him started to swirl, and before he could stop himself, his fingers worked the lock. The band slipped to the floor, and he looked up into Alex's wide eyes, pleading for help, before he slipped to blackness.

Chapter Thirty-One

A S SOON AS the band dropped off Alex, a thousand emotions ran through her. Hope, relief…and one she didn't understand—fear. Not for herself, but for Jamie. He was dying. She knew that. If he didn't get to a hospital soon, he *would* die. Alex licked her lips, and then she wasn't inside her body but watching herself from a place far away.

Jamie had passed out, face contorted in pain in his state of nothingness. Alex scrambled into action, patting his pockets in search of his keys. Next came the most difficult part— moving Jamie to the passenger seat of his car.

Heat blazed off his skin. He had to have a fever close to 104. *Don't panic, don't panic,* she told herself over and over as she put her hands under his armpits. Unconscious, he weighed a lot, and she doubted herself as she dragged him down the hallway. She tried to focus on her mission and not her exhaustion as she maneuvered him over the stoop and out the front door. Chloe watched with wide eyes from her hiding place under the couch.

"No…hospital…" he murmured as she situated him in the car, but he didn't open his eyes.

Alex paused, waiting to see if he would look at her, if he would voice the request twice, but he had passed out again. She got into the driver's seat, fumbling with the key. Jamie was going through fever dreams. That was bad.

As soon as the car started, she floored it. She had no idea

where she was going and didn't know if they were going closer to town or farther away. The dirt road looped through endless trees on either side. Nervously, she drove a little faster, telling herself that a road, *any* type of road, would always lead to more. With roads came towns and with towns came people.

Jamie vomited all over himself.

"I'm sorry," she said repeatedly, for every bump and turn, for every minute she wasn't able to help him.

She doubted he was awake to hear her, but she repeated it like a mantra, unsure what to do with herself if she stopped. Between the smell of his vomit and her sloppy driving, Alex was ready to throw up herself. It didn't take long to find the town and less the hospital. Alex pulled to a screeching halt in front of the emergency room doors and ran inside.

She cared little about her appearance: her ratty hair, disheveled bed clothes, and scabbed wounds across her wrists as she ran through the lobby. "Please! He needs help!"

Everyone turned to look at her, but no one approached. Their eyes were wide, watching her as if she were a raccoon that had wandered in off the street. After a moment of silence, she started to sob, twin tears trailing down her cheeks. Every moment they hesitated was a moment closer that Jamie got to death. "Please."

A nurse and security guard ran up to her, and it didn't escape Alex's notice that the security guard was one step ahead the entire time. "Ma'am, what's happened? Who's hurt?"

Alex couldn't speak, so instead, she pointed toward the car she had parked haphazardly outside. Jamie, leaning heavily against the window, was visible from inside the lobby. She watched as they went to pull him out and loaded him onto a gurney. As they whirled past, Alex tried to keep at their side, but the nurse who had been behind the counter stopped her. She set a hand to Alex's elbow, guiding her to sit down.

"What's your name, sweetheart?" she asked after they were seated.

"Al—" she started and stopped. She couldn't give her *real* name, right? For as worried about Jamie as she was, she couldn't let anyone know the truth about her. About him. "Alice Drayden."

"Okay, honey. It's going to be okay. Your boyfriend is in good hands." The nurse reached out, taking one of Alex's hands in her own, but Alex hardly felt the contact.

She stared toward the hall that Jamie had disappeared down, eyes misty with tears. If he died, what would that mean for her?

"Can I get you some water or something to eat?" the nurse asked softly. "It might be a while."

Alex shook her head. She couldn't remember the last thing she'd eaten, but with the smell of Jamie's vomit in the back of her nose, and the worry in her heart, she didn't think she'd ever be hungry again. The nurse stopped asking questions, but she didn't leave. She kept Alex's hand protectively wrapped in hers, her thumb soothingly working circles into her skin while Alex fought back silent tears. Alex didn't know how long they sat like that, but she was sure the nurse had surveyed her from head to toe. Several times she caught her eyes on the ugly scars across Alex's wrists, but neither of them commented on them.

The nurse released her and stood up, pointing toward the counter. "I've got to get back to work, honey. If you need anything, I'll be right over there, okay?"

Alex watched her take her seat. Usually, Alex liked to be alone, but she wished the nurse would've stayed. Her company had been the difference between holding herself together and breaking down entirely. The security officer approached her then, and she tensed, eyes wide with the assumption he would call her out on everything.

"Ma'am, if you can, I need you to move your car so our ambulance can pull up."

Alex fumbled with her keys as she stood. She didn't look back as she went outside, climbing into the car. Her eyes were so dewy with tears that she didn't trust herself to move Jamie's car, but she didn't have a choice. The officer watched her from the window, almost as if he expected her to crash. When she turned the engine on, she tried to regain herself by taking a couple slow breaths. When she thought she had it together, she recognized the song on the radio.

It was the same one Jamie had sung in the bathroom.

She wanted to sit and concentrate on it, but the security guard had taken a step outside, and the last thing she wanted was for him to check up on her again. With a shaky breath, she started to drive, pulling into the nearest spot before she parked and sat with the engine running, listening to the rest of the song.

It made her think of death which in turn led to her

thinking of Jamie again. She didn't believe in the afterlife or a God, but right then and there, she found herself bowing her head in prayer.

"Please let him be okay," she whispered for any omnipotent being to hear and potentially grant. For as wrong as it was, she felt that prayer in every inch of her body.

Jamie had gotten under her skin in the time she'd been in his care. She didn't know how it had happened, but it had. With stiff determination, she turned off the engine and went back to the waiting room. As she slid into her chair, the nurse at the reception desk offered her a tiny smile.

Alex couldn't work up the energy to return the smile.

What was she *doing*? Sitting here and worrying about a man who had kidnapped her? She could go for help; she could tell these people who she was. Her eyes looked to the nurse behind the reception desk. She had been kind. Alex knew she'd believe her.

So why am I not doing it? she wailed inside her head.

Alex's need to save herself was loud, but she couldn't get her legs to cooperate. In her head, she imagined telling that woman she had been kidnapped, that she was Alex Alpine. That she needed help. The woman would call the police, and then it would be over. She would be able to go home. To see her daughter again.

Her heart lifted for only a second before it plunged again. She didn't *want* to go home. She wasn't sure when that feeling had first hit her, but it had been inside her for a while. She didn't want to go back to Peter and the dysfunction of her every day. For all she knew, Peter had let his new girlfriend move into their place.

For all she knew, there *was* no place for her back home.

And if she was gone, who would take care of Chloe?

Who am I? she wondered, full of despair for the fact that she couldn't answer the question.

Her eyes were so bleary with tears that she hardly saw the doctor approaching her. "Miss Drayden?"

Alex didn't respond at first, so the doctor repeated her soft question. It took Alex a minute to remember her fake name. She stood up so quickly that she nearly fell over the leg of the chair. "Yes, that's me. How's Jamie? Is he okay?"

"Mr. Knox was on the verge of sepsis when he went into surgery, but we were able to successfully flush his system and remove his appendix."

Alex wrung her hands together in front of her chest. "So…he's going to be okay?"

The doctor nodded. Then her eyes moved to the wounds on Alex's wrists, and her eyebrows drew together in concern. "Before we go back there, you let me know if you need to see someone, okay?"

Alex had no patience to pretend she cared about herself. Part of her assumed this woman was lying about Jamie. That he had actually died, and she was trying to distract Alex from finding out the truth.

"C-can I see him?" Alex asked.

"He's resting right now, but I don't see why not."

"Thank you," Alex said, following the doctor.

Her mind buzzed, and her palms were sweaty as she followed the doctor up elevators, around corners, and through a set of doors that required a key card to get through. Alex risked a glance at the woman from the corner of her eye, and though it wasn't welcome, the thought was there again. How easy it would be to reach out for help, but she shot it down as they came to a halt in front of a room. Jamie's name was on the whiteboard by the door.

She stared at it, her resolve melting.

"He's in here," the doctor said.

"Thank you," Alex whispered and turned to go inside.

The lights had been dimmed, the glowing monitor showcasing Jamie's pulse the only light she could see. Alex stopped a step inside the door. Jamie's bed was in the middle of the room. In the darkness, she could see how pale he was with purple bags under his eyes and a dozen white sheets on top of him. His bed was surrounded with the melodic beeping of the machines monitoring him.

Alex couldn't decide how she felt. This scene should've brought her joy. He was her kidnapper. This was karma in real time, but the longer she looked at him, the more relieved she felt. Relieved the surgery had been a success. Relieved that she had gotten him here in time.

Relieved that they had met.

She made her way to the side of his bed. Jamie's breaths were rugged with the oxygen tube taped under his nose. She wrapped her fingers around the side railing, afraid to touch him directly for fear she'd accidentally knock some essential wire out of place.

"I'm glad you're okay," she whispered, voice haunted with the ghosts of a thousand emotions all at once.

Jamie's eyes fluttered open, focusing on her before his gravelly voice said, "Alex?"

She bent closer to him. "I'm here, Jamie."

"Why?" he asked, eyes focusing on her with such an intensity that she flinched. "Why did you save me? Y-you could've been free. You could've let me die."

"You saved *me*," she reminded him.

"You could've run away," he whispered.

"Yeah, I could've," she said, seeking out his massive hand. She wrapped both of her hands around it, pressing her lips to his knuckles before she said, "But I didn't want to."

Chapter Thirty-Two

WHEN JAMIE WAS officially released from the hospital, Alex wasn't sure what to expect. Not only for herself, but for their entire situation. There was no denying the fact their dynamic had changed in the two days Jamie spent at the hospital. Alex drove him home and Jamie said very little. She helped him inside. Of all the things she could've felt, relief wasn't expected, but standing with him in the front room of the house, it was all she could feel.

This felt like home.

Jamie had not only saved her life, he'd breathed the will to live back into her as well, and that was something she could never thank him enough for.

"Are you thirsty?" she asked him.

He sat down at the kitchen table. Chloe padded out from her place in the shadows, sniffing cautiously at Jamie's foot as Alex went to the fridge, preparing a glass of orange juice. Chloe scampered over to Alex as she handed Jamie his drink.

As Jamie downed the liquid, Alex bent down to pet the kitty between the ears, "We should get you in bed. You're going to need plenty of rest."

He handed her back the glass. "You're right."

Alex put the cup in the sink and led him to their room. She eased him onto the bed, visible pain flashing across his face as he shuffled to get situated in the red and black bedding.

He rested his head on the pillow. "I forgot how comfortable my own bed is."

"Compared to a hospital bed, *anything* is more comfortable," Alex pointed out, sitting down beside his legs.

"That's true, I suppose," Jamie said and then his eyes moved to something on the floor.

Alex followed his gaze to the shock collar. The moment he had taken it off her, it felt as if the entire world had changed. What if he decided he wanted her to wear it again? Would she let him put it back on her? In his current state, he couldn't fight her.

"Are you going to make me wear it again?" she asked, not looking at him as she said it.

His gaze went to her, and his face softened as he said, "No. Why would I?"

Dumbfounded, she said, "Really?"

"If I can't trust you after all you did to save my life, then I never will. But I...I have one question, and I need you to be honest with me."

Alex blinked expectantly.

"Did you really mean what you said? That you don't want to leave?"

She looked down at her hands, guilty. "I know how it sounds," she said, without looking up. "I tried to make sense of it myself, but feelings and logic aren't one in the same. You know what I was thinking about when I was in the hospital lobby, waiting to see if you would survive the surgery?"

"What?"

"I didn't think about me or what you've done. All I could think was that I didn't want you to die. When you passed out, I was scared…for you. And I contemplated how fucked up that was, that I *should* wish bad things to happen to you, but I didn't, and I don't. You treat me better than anyone has for a long time. In the hospital, I tried to imagine telling someone who I was, that I was the missing girl from the news. It would've been so easy but…the thought of going home made me cringe."

Jamie reached out to clutch her hand the same way she had his in the hospital. "That's because this is your home now."

Alex had known full-well the consequences of her decisions but those words from Jamie's mouth had her questioning herself all over again.

Jamie noticed the change in expression. "Okay, let's watch TV or something."

Before she could stop him, he got up with a groan and made his way down the hall, Alex following close behind in case he tripped. She couldn't see his bandages and stitches through his shirt, but it was hard to forget they were there.

When he sat on the couch, she handed him the remote before she sat down beside him. Jamie slung an arm over her shoulders as he turned on the TV. Since the news was the last thing they had watched, it was still on that station, playing the day's broadcast.

A picture of her was in the corner of the screen. She could hardly breathe. At the hospital, she'd been so wrapped up in her own decision that she hadn't stopped to consider that other people outside the scope of her focus might've recognized her. Might've reported her to the police.

They would've said something, she assured herself.

Then she remembered the doctor's concerned looks and words. She'd been there for hours. How many people had seen her in that time? How many people recognized her?

"…calling off the search," the reporter's voice said.

Alex couldn't move.

"In other news, police in Tangipahoa Parish are giving up the search for a missing twenty-three-year-old woman—"

The TV went black, and she turned to Jamie as he tossed the remote to the side. "That's enough of that for now."

"They called off the search?" she asked softly.

"I guess so," Jamie said, pulling his arm off her shoulders to scratch the back of his neck.

"W…why would they do that?" Alex asked, balling her hand into a fist around the blanket. Pain shot through her, and she felt herself falling from the precipice of happiness, of warmth, that she'd been balancing on. Peter had found ways to hurt her all over again.

"I don't know, but this is a good thing, right? It means we don't have to worry about the hospital trip. We don't have to worry about you being seen."

Alex's eyes went misty. "Yeah, but…don't they want me home?"

"They must've realized it isn't going to happen," he said. "It's been months, and they're no closer to finding you than they were that first day. It's for the best they put it in the past. This is *good* news."

"But…" she said again, unable to process the

information. Familiar stinging in the corners of her eyes warned her that she was about to start crying again. "There are families who search for decades for their missing loved ones, and my family is ready to give up on me after only a few weeks?"

Jamie stared into her eyes, pain glinting in the depths. He wanted to say something that would make her feel better, that much was clear, but there was nothing he could say. Both of them knew as much. Chloe jumped up onto the couch, staring up at Alex with an expression mirroring Jamie's.

"Come on. I think after yesterday, we're both sleep deprived. Let's get some rest, and I'm sure we'll feel better in the morning."

"No!" Alex said, standing. "I need to go back. I…I need to remind them why I was important. Why I mattered."

Jamie narrowed his eyes. If it was out of pain or annoyance, Alex couldn't tell. In that moment, it was all the same. "You've got to be kidding me. You just sat here and told me you didn't want to go home."

Alex's bottom lip trembled. "I don't but…I miss my child, Jamie. She deserves to be with her mother. It's nothing against you, but…I don't belong here."

He stood up to take his place beside her. Injured and hunched over, he was still much taller than she was. "And what about everything you told me about this feeling like home?"

"I meant it, but that doesn't stop me from missing *her*. It isn't fair of Peter to make her forget about me. I birthed her. I was her world, and she was mine for four years."

"I understand," he said. "But you can't go back. Not

now. Not ever."

Alex wanted to snarl at him but couldn't think of a thing to say.

"If a baby would get rid of the wanderlust, we can make one."

Alex stared at him, taking a small step backward. His expression didn't change, and Alex's eyes dewed up with tears. It was clear he had no idea how insensitive his words were. How could he? He'd never had a child of his own. He didn't know about the instant, overwhelming love that a mother shared with her child.

"Just say the word," he said, wrapping her in his arms. He planted a kiss to her neck, his forehead brushing her chin as he brought himself closer to her.

Alex was tempted to push him away, but she didn't because part of her worried she would somehow mess up his stitches. Fresh tears leaked from her eyes, and Jamie broke away to grasp her hand. He tried to tug her down the hall, but she didn't budge.

"How can you say something like that to me?" Alex asked. "After everything…how can you talk about something so…normal? We can't have a family. I *have* a family."

Jamie flared his nostrils. "Had. Okay? You *had* a family. Now you have a new one. Or you could if you'd stop fighting. It's all up to you."

Alex tried to pull herself free. "I'm crazy. I am absolutely insane. That's why I didn't go for help."

Jamie whirled on her. "Stop it with that. You're not

crazy to miss your family. You're not crazy for wanting me to live. You're…*you*. Don't you get that? You're allowed to feel multiple things at once, and then nothing at all, if it suits you. However, I'm not going to stand by and allow you to threaten leaving me again. I will put you back in the basement, and we'll start all over if that's what it takes."

Alex was stunned. Jamie's face was flushed with red by the time his speech finished, and he looked as if he wanted to do nothing more than lock her away again for a few moments of peace.

"Don't you dare."

Jamie frowned. "What can I do to make this easier?"

"I want the truth."

Jamie knitted his eyebrows together. "The truth about what?"

"You."

"You know as much about me as you need to know."

"That right there is bullshit," Alex said and pulled her hand free. "How can I commit to this when you aren't?"

Jamie laughed. "You're joking, right? I'm risking jail time for this. I *killed* a man for this. I don't know how much more you want from me to prove I'm dedicated."

"I want to know why you chose me. There are other authors out there, better authors. If this is all for a book, why did you choose me?"

Jamie plopped down on his bed, exhausted in every way that mattered. "Will it really make you feel better if I answer your questions?"

"Yes, it would," Alex said, sitting down beside him. "All I know are the things you've shown me…and they're not good. Drugs? Murder? Is that really all you want me to know?"

"I've shown you other things too. Kindness. Love."

"And the prerequisite to all of that was fear."

Jamie dug the heels of his hands into his eyes. "Alright, alright." He breathed out and stared into the corner of the room before he looked back at her. "Where should I begin?"

"Wherever it is that put you on this path," she said. She wouldn't admit that she wanted to know *everything* about him and would take anything he offered at this point.

"You…remind me of someone I used to know," he said so softly that she barely heard him "When I told you Zack was the only one I ever killed, that was a lie." He paused to give Alex a chance to say something. When she remained quiet, he added, "I've killed one other person."

Alex wasn't sure how to react so she didn't react at all. Somehow, she knew that he was watching her every fidgety movement, desperate to get inside her head. "Who was it?" she asked at last.

"My foster father," Jamie said.

Alex pulled a face.

"Don't look at me like that. Everyone looked at me like that after what I did, but I'm not the problem. I had…so many people tell me that killing someone was wrong. And maybe it is, but he wasn't a person." He paused. "I killed a child rapist, and *I* was the monster."

A cold rock sat in Alex's stomach. Maybe they were

more alike than she imagined. "Did he…touch you?"

"No," Jamie said, running his finger along the seam of his pajama pants. "My foster sister, Lana." He reached over to grab his wallet from its place on the nightstand, opening it to stare at the single picture he had of her. He showed it to Alex as he said, "She was eight years old."

Alex didn't take her eyes off it. She could've been looking at a photo of herself as a child. Keeping her unease away, she asked, "What happened to her?"

"He killed her. I was twelve."

Alex's eyes moved to him. "I-I'm so sorry."

Jamie turned the picture back toward himself. "Me too. I spent a long time mourning her. Probably still do. I never got to go to her funeral. Never got to say my proper goodbyes. God knows how badly I wanted to."

"So why didn't you?"

"It wasn't up to me. The people responsible for me said, for legal reasons, it was best for me to step away from the entire situation. And it wasn't as if I could run away and go myself. I had no idea where I was. They bounced me around homes and clinics after that. I took this picture so I could try to remember her by. I wish this was the image that came to my brain, but more often than not, her body moments after she was murdered is what I remember." The haunted look she had seen in his eyes on that first day was there again, and she wanted to reach out, to hug him, but was afraid of how he would respond. Jamie brought the picture a bit closer to his face, running his thumb gently over the corner before he tucked it safely back into his wallet. "You remind me of her."

Alex watched him, face neutral. "So that first day… you were talking about her."

"Yeah," he whispered, the word louder for his forced exhale. "When I first saw pictures of you online, I saw someone who was hurting, someone who deserved a second chance. I couldn't save Lana, but I can save you."

Alex looked at the wallet, at the edge of the photo still sticking out. It couldn't be easy to lose anyone to such tragedy, let alone someone so young.

"What happened to you after…after you killed him?"

"I went through a series of foster parents and therapists. Even spent some time in an asylum, and they all wanted the same thing. They wanted me to express remorse for what I had done. I couldn't do that. I had none, and I refused to fake it." He ran his tongue along his teeth. "I had a reputation after that. No one in their right mind would adopt me. It was as if it didn't matter anymore that I was a child. Everyone was afraid of me like I would go off and kill them too."

"You didn't have any friends?"

"The only person I met who didn't treat me like I had the plague wasn't exactly a friend. He was a foster brother living in the same temporary house. But he handled his pain differently from mine. He was a bully."

Alex knitted her eyebrows together. Jamie had such a large stature and confidence, it was hard to think anyone had ever bullied him.

"He was the reason I first went to juvie. I stabbed him

in the leg with a pair of scissors."

Alex flinched, imagining the sensation of cold metal plunging into her thigh.

"I know what you're thinking, probably the same thing that *everyone* thought, but he deserved it. He made a joke about Lana, and I…lost it. It was too much, too soon." He tapped the top of his wallet as if he wanted to bring his lost foster sister's picture out again but didn't. "I came out at eighteen then moved into a halfway house. I spent a year there, and that was where I met Zack. Then Dad died, and you can put together the rest of it."

"So you…are you clean now?"

Jamie bobbed his head, swiping his thumb across his lip. "Besides the occasional drink, I am. It wasn't easy, but it needed to be done. The pills—they got me through some rough years, but when it was a few months before my release from the halfway house, I started to really look at my life. I wanted to be a different person. That was how the rift between me and Zack started."

"You did the right thing," Alex said, finally reaching out to touch her fingers softly to his arm. "With Zack and with your foster father. Never be ashamed of that."

Jamie stared into her eyes again with that concentrated look that made her sure he could see her soul. "It happened to you too, didn't it? What happened to Lana."

Alex looked away instantly.

Jamie reached up, almost cupping her face, before he dropped it again. "It's okay. You don't have to tell me."

Alex buried her face in her hands. Flashes of a cold basement and rugged breathing filled her memory again, and she squeezed her eyelids tighter. "You told me about you." She paused and looked up. Jamie's face was neutral as hers had been. "I told you about my mom, and the fact my dad wanted nothing to do with me, but that wasn't all of it. He'd lock me in the basement. Sometimes, days at a time. He wouldn't feed me or give me water. I spent a lot of days thinking that I would die down there, and I was almost relieved for it because it meant that I would be back with my mom again."

"So was it…" Jamie trailed off, staring at her as if he hoped she'd understand the question without him saying it out loud.

"My dad? No," she said, eyes blurry with tears. "His friend. He'd sneak down in the dead of night. I don't…I don't know if Dad knew or not."

"I'd kill him too, if I could," Jamie said.

Alex didn't want to smile, but for some reason, those words caused her lips to betray her and make a face anyway. She'd never had anyone to protect her. Never a sibling or friend looking out for her well-being. And she'd always longed to have that. The expression flitted away as she continued, "Peter knew about all of it, and that was why we married so young. So he could take me out of there, set me on solid ground."

Jamie breathed out audibly through his nose. "I don't want to give him any compliments after the way he's treated you, but that was admirable of him. I'm grateful he did that for you, but as far as I'm concerned, he fulfilled his role in your life."

Alex curled up next to Jamie, narrowing her eyes to try and clear the tears that had welled in the corners.

"Just so you know, I'm never going to force you to do anything you don't want to do. We could be together the rest of our lives, and I'd be fine with us never having sex."

Alex gazed at him in wonderment. It seemed as if every man she'd ever met was only programmed to think about one thing. "Really?"

"Really," Jamie assured her, twirling the black ring on his right hand for added effect.

Alex's eyes were drawn to it.

"I'm ACE," he said, showing it to her. "I don't *prefer* to have sex, but I'm not against it or anything. I think you're beautiful, and I want to be close to you, but intimacy for me is you falling asleep on my chest. I'm sorry if that's weird for you."

"Not weird," she said quickly. Her heart swelled in her chest. A long time ago, she'd imagined the perfect man and believed he didn't exist, but here he was before her, offering her everything that Peter had failed to deliver.

"I'm not saying it's never *going* to happen or never will. I mean, if it was what you wanted occasionally, I wouldn't be opposed…" He trailed off, peering up at her sheepishly.

She looked back at him, twin tears running down her cheeks.

Jamie wiped them away with his thumb, and Alex rested her cheek on his chest, right above his heart.

"Good to know."

Chapter Thirty-Three

A WEEK PASSED, and Jamie's wound slowly began to heal. Alex hadn't mentioned the broadcast again or the conversation afterward. A small blessing? Jamie wasn't sure.

Things fell back into the routine they'd had before his hospital trip. Alex's attention went into Chloe, writing, and food. She cooked him three meals a day, and as far as he could tell, she didn't try to run away. On the days where she woke up before him, she did what she could around the house, greeting him as soon as he woke up. She didn't talk back anymore, opting to barely talk at all.

She wrote more than she spoke. She had two different projects—scribbles in the fancy notebook he'd picked out for her, and thoughts and feelings, a diary of sorts, jotted on loose leaf paper held together with a black binder clip.

Their relationship seemed to be everything that Jamie had hoped for, but there was still a hint of sadness in Alex's eyes. She was compliant, but he was positive she still thought of her daughter, and that wasn't something he would expect her to forget anytime soon.

There's gotta be a way to make that go away.

Partly, he wondered if it had always been there, and she had somehow masked it. Maybe this was her way of bringing up the broadcast without saying a word.

He'd broken down and dug out Alex's wallet from the belongings she'd had the day he'd brought her home. He gave the picture of the little girl to Alex, but things didn't get better. If anything, Alex grew more reserved.

Jamie stood up off the couch, the sudden silence in the living room deafening as he padded into the kitchen. Alex stood at the sink, the clatter of dishes ringing around the room as she washed them from their meal earlier. True to her position as Alex's shadow, Chloe watched from her place under the kitchen table.

Jamie stayed like that for a moment, leaning against the doorframe and watching her. He could imagine the kind of mother she must've been. Dedicated. Fierce. The kind to do anything to make her daughter happy. The kind of mother he had never known.

"I want to take you out tonight," he said at last.

The water switched off, and Alex turned to look at him, uncertainty drawing her eyebrows together. "What?"

He took a step into the room. "Everything that's happened hasn't been easy. I know that, but you've been amazing through it all. I want to thank you. I want you to know how much I appreciate it."

"You don't have to do that," she said, turning back to the sink to shield whatever emotions might've popped up from the offer.

"I know I don't, but I want to," he said. "Most couples, they go out on dates. For us, we can't really do that, but maybe just once, you know? It could be fun."

Alex said nothing, but the tiny twitch of her shoulders told Jamie that she had gone back to washing the dishes. She was deliberately shutting him out.

Jamie tried to keep himself from taking offense. "Meals aren't your favorite thing, I get that, but I think it'd be nice to have a romantic meal with candlelight and wine. One not prepared by me or you."

Alex didn't answer, didn't turn around, and he wondered if she had heard him.

Anger started to slip through then. He was trying everything he could think of, and she couldn't look at him? "Look, it's not up for debate. Get dressed, and we'll go."

The water turned off again then Alex said softly, "Okay." She tossed her wet dishrag to the counter with a *plop* and disappeared from the room.

Jamie watched her go but didn't follow. He would give her space, let her sort through whatever emotions were controlling her.

She cares about you, he reminded himself.

When he closed his eyes, it was easy enough to conjure the image of her wide eyes peering at him through the shadows, the feeling of her squeezing his hand as she hovered over his hospital bed.

The only real question was which did she feel more—love or hate?

When Jamie finally got himself to move down the hall, he saw the bedroom door was closed and figured Alex was inside, changing. Again, he found himself wishing he could read her mind as he went into the bathroom, cleaning himself up the best he could. Staring at his reflection in the mirror showed him a version of himself he wasn't entirely proud of. He was still gaunt and pale from his surgery, but the color was starting to come back to his cheeks, and the darkness around his eyes was fading. He almost looked back to himself. Self-consciously, he reached up a finger to poke at his protruding cheekbone.

"How's this?" Alex asked, pushing her way into the bathroom.

Jamie's eyes widened at the interruption, and he turned to look at her, a smile on his face as he studied her over. She wore a soft blue V-neck shirt and black jeans which on her came across as firm and professional. Sweet in a way.

"Perfect," he said, reaching out to cup her face, gently pressing a kiss to her soft lips.

She smiled back at him, but her gaze dropped to the floor. At first, he thought she was hiding her face from him until she said, "Is that what you're going to wear?" and he realized she was giving him a once over the same way he had done to her.

He looked down at the stained sweatpants and T-shirt. "Of course not," he said. "I wanted to give you your privacy. Hold on one minute."

He left her in the bathroom and dashed across the hall to the bedroom. In a flash, he tugged on some jeans and a button-down collared shirt, careful of the angry stitches in his side. When he emerged, Alex was leaning against the wall with her arms folded, waiting for him.

"Well?"

"You look great," she replied.

Smiling, he walked up to her and slung an arm over her shoulders, leading her to the car. Before they got in, he risked a glance to Alex's face, expecting to see the tiny frown she wore when she thought he wasn't paying attention. It wasn't there.

Jamie stopped walking, and Alex looked at him through wide, concerned eyes. "Is something wrong?"

He shook his head. "I got to thinkin' that we don't have any pictures together. I want one."

"I don't like pictures."

Jamie tipped his head to the side. "Please? Just one? For me."

Alex stared at him for such a long time he was sure the answer would be no. At last, she said, "Okay."

"Thank you," he said as he brought her close and pulled out his cell phone.

He maneuvered to the camera and held it up. Jamie pressed his face close to Alex's so he couldn't tell what face she made. She was smiling in the reflective image of his phone screen. He wasn't sure what it meant, but he wanted to believe she was happy about him, about *them*.

With that hope in mind, he snapped the picture. "We look good together," he said, showing it to Alex.

Her eyes were big as she peered over the top of the phone at him. "We do."

That tiny comment was enough to put him on Cloud Nine as he helped Alex get into the passenger seat. It was their first real date, and another surge of pride coursed through him.

They had fought through everything strange about their relationship, and now, they could do the normal things that other couples enjoyed.

As they drove down the winding dirt road, Jamie dared a look at Alex from the corner of his eye. She looked so content, so peaceful, and it didn't take much for him to remember the first time he'd seen her face on this road. When the only time she'd been peaceful around him had been when she'd been unconscious.

Stop it, he chastised himself.

He forced himself to think nothing but happy thoughts as they drove into the next town over. For a moment, Jamie considered taking Alex to the restaurant that he worked at, but he changed his mind. Alex wouldn't appreciate being shown off. He was sure of that. He pulled into the parking lot of the fanciest restaurant he could find, watching her face light up as the car came to a halt.

"Are you sure about this? It looks expensive," she said, eyes wide.

"I'm positive," he replied, climbing out of his seat. "Come on."

Alex bobbed her head and traveled beside him, lacing her fingers through his. The low lights inside the place reminded him of that day they'd met in the bar. And like that day, her eyes were huge and full of wonder as she looked around. Unlike that day, however, he wasn't a stranger. He was someone she legitimately cared about.

They sat at a table near the center of the dining room.

The red tablecloth between them was highlighted by the candle in the middle of the table. The waiter set their drinks down and took their orders. When he walked away, Jamie reached across the table to hold Alex's hands.

"Didn't think I'd ever go out to eat again," she admitted. "This place is beautiful."

Jamie gave her a reassuring squeeze. "We've come a long way," he agreed. As he glanced at the tables around him, he didn't catch anyone's eye. They weren't watching him. Weren't watching her.

They were a normal couple.

As if she could read his mind, Alex asked, "Do you regret it?"

"Not a single second," he replied. "Not now, not ever. This feels right. I can't…remember what my life was like before you." Embarrassment flushed through him as soon as he finished the sentence, and he hoped it was dark enough to conceal that fact. He didn't mean his life before he'd taken her from the bar. He meant his entire existence before he'd ever stumbled across her work. Everything that had mattered then was forgotten now.

When the waiter set their plates of food on the table, Jamie reluctantly let go of Alex's hands, glad for the interruption that brought him back to reality. Jamie picked up his glass, taking a swig of the white wine, and Alex picked at her spaghetti. Jamie's happiness reached its peak. She'd been working to starve herself as a form of punishment, he was sure of that now. Seeing her eat felt like progress.

Jamie tipped his glass, getting the last sip of his drink. Through the clear bottom, he saw the distorted image of a waitress with brown hair and a foxlike face two tables over. The glass slipped from his fingers, crashing to the floor below. It was a ghost from his past—his biological sister, Angelica.

Alex stopped mid-motion on the bite she had taken. "Jamie?"

Jamie tried his best to compose himself. He could hear Alex calling to him, but her voice sounded far away. His gaze had dialed in on the waitress, and before he could stop himself, he hopped up out of his chair.

"Angelica?" he called, pulling the gazes of everyone nearby. "Angelica! It's me!"

The woman stopped to stare at him, clutching her tiny notepad over her chest as if she were afraid Jamie would attack her. Jamie was hurt. Of all people, she shouldn't look at *him* like that.

"Jamie!" Alex said, concerned as she got up, trying to grab him.

Jamie didn't notice. "It's me!" he said as he approached the waitress, stepping through the shining shards of broken glass. "It's Jamie!"

Alex stepped between them, putting her hands on his shoulders to block his path. "Jamie!" she called, snapping her fingers in his face. "Jamie!" He stared over the top of her head, eyeing the woman. Fearfully, she gave one glance to Alex before she turned on her heels and rushed for the safety of the kitchen.

"Wait!" he called, catching one last glimpse of her as she slipped away.

Alex's cold fingers reached up to grasp his jaw, angling his face in her direction. "Listen to me carefully, Jamie. It's okay. We're okay. Come back to me."

"Alex?" he whispered, the trance breaking as suddenly as it had taken him.

She bobbed her head slowly, eyes wide as if she were afraid he would break into another fit as soon as she let go. Jamie took a step backward, studying the scene around them. Everyone in the restaurant had gone silent to watch him. Glass crunched under his feet as he took another step backward, embarrassed.

He'd been so concerned about keeping a low profile that he couldn't believe *he* was the one to draw such attention to them. *Stupid, stupid, stupid,* he chastised himself.

The restaurant was so quiet Jamie could hear the blood thundering in his ears. He had to escape. With shaky fingers, he passed his wallet to Alex and ran out the door, trying to get a hold of himself.

What have I done?

Chapter Thirty-Four

ALEX USHERED A thousand apologizes to the waitress and the manager after Jamie stormed out. She kept her head down as she paid, pretending she didn't notice the fact that everyone was still staring at her. The manager led Alex to the door. His face and voice were friendly, but he told her they probably shouldn't come back to the establishment.

Alex readily agreed.

Sweating profusely, she turned away from her humiliation and went out into the night. Of all the things that could go wrong, Jamie having a *breakdown* wasn't one of them. Outside, he sat on the curb near his car, head in his hands. With his shoulders hunched, he looked somehow smaller, more fragile.

"Are they going to call the cops?" he asked, without looking up.

"No," Alex said softly, sitting down beside him.

Jamie looked up with tears on his face. He attempted a smile, but it didn't last long as he wiped his face with the back of his hand. "That's good at least."

"What happened in there?" she asked, uncertain if she should ask or let it go. The panic on his face had been so real, so heartbreaking that Alex wondered if it had something to do with Lana and his time under the same foster home as her.

Could it be something else?

Jamie stared at the cracked cement in the parking lot, his eyes glassy in the moonlight, pools he drowned his emotions in.

By that expression, Alex knew he wouldn't answer the question.

She was right.

He got up and slid into the car. Resolved, she followed him. After all that attention, she was ready to go home and hide, never to be seen again. As she climbed into the passenger seat, it was hard to believe that less than a half hour prior, she had been filled with such hope and wonder. Things had seemed *better* between her and Jamie. Life had been a glowing thing. She had no idea he had all the trauma lurking beneath the surface. As they drove home in silence, she wondered what else he'd kept from her. Jamie was layer upon layer of secrets. Would she ever get to the bottom?

When they made it back up the winding dirt road, Jamie was the first out of the car. Alex spent an additional minute sitting in the darkness, thinking about her entire life before she worked up the courage to follow him inside.

In the safety of the living room, Jamie tossed his keys onto the table next to the couch and went straight down the hall, tossing himself onto his mattress, face buried in the pillows. Alex followed, making it into the room in time to see him strip down to his boxers and climb under the blankets. She couldn't see his face as she pulled her uncomfortable jeans off and laid down beside him, curling up as close as she could.

"You don't have to say anything. I know I'm an utter moron," he said, voice muffled by the fabrics.

Alex stared at the back of his head, surprised for the self-loathing. "That wasn't what I was going to say at all."

Jamie moved the pillow enough to peer at her, searching her face for some sign of a lie.

"What happened, Jamie?" she tried asking again. She didn't like how guarded his eyes were. It reminded her of the first time she'd seen him in the bar.

The pillow moved back into place as he said, "I...I thought she was my sister."

"Lana?" Alex asked.

Jamie shook his head. "My biological sister. I don't have many memories of my family before the foster homes, but the few I have of Angie were the best ones."

Alex considered his words. It must've been hard to lose family member after family member. She might've gone insane too if she had lived his life. "Where is she now?"

"I-I don't know," Jamie said and sat up watch her closely. "Dad died and Mom went to prison. No one talked about what happened to Angie during all that. Maybe she was adopted, maybe she went through the same as me, maybe she ended up on the streets. There's...no way for me to know."

Alex recognized the sheen over his eyes as if he were barely managing to hold back tears. The gears in her head started to turn. "I listened to that song I caught you singing," Alex said, unsure what else to say. "It came on when you were in surgery, and it got me thinking a lot about you. I-I had the feeling you were missing someone, and when you told me about Lana, I assumed she was the one, but there's a lot more to your past that you haven't told me, isn't there?" She paused then reconsidered her words. Now wasn't the time for a confrontation. Not when Jamie was already clearly upset. Before he could form a response, she added, "You should try to find her."

Jamie tossed the pillow to the floor with a muted thump. His eyes were red and swollen when the light touched his face. "I don't know how I'd go about it."

"Maybe not, but you could try. With computers, nothing is impossible. Plus, if it works, and you find her, it'll probably help you feel better." She didn't want to say her next sentence but knew it was necessary anyway. "You said your Mom's in prison, right?"

"Yeah. I'd rather not go into details on the why."

Alex waved a hand. She was sure her father was also sitting in prison at this point if he was still alive. "Don't need 'em. Bottom line is that she would know where your sister was, right?"

Jamie bit his lip. "Not necessarily. I mean, it wasn't as if they gave us up and asked to be kept updated. Me and Angie were taken away by child protective services. I don't know how much Mom and Dad were told about us. Maybe they knew everything. Maybe they knew nothing."

"That's a lot of maybes."

"Bottom line, after I left home, I never spoke to either of them again. Besides, you don't know what my mother's like. She put me through *hell,* and I don't think I have the strength to face her again."

Not being able to trust her own father had always made Alex feel like such an outsider. As if there was something wrong with *her,* and that was why her father hated her so immensely. Her friends' parents didn't hate them.

Jamie was the only person she'd met who understood that pain.

Alex wrapped her arms around him, holding him like an extra-large teddy bear. "If you think of any way that I can help, let me know."

Chapter Thirty-Five

J AMIE WAS VEHEMENTLY against Alex's idea when she said it. Nothing in the world would get him to visit his mother. Or so he'd thought. Somehow, Alex's idea worked into his mind, convincing him this was the best thing he could do, and the worst part? He started to think maybe she was right.

Driving down the curving dirt road, he couldn't decide what he hated more: going to meet one of the people responsible for ruining his life or going into a prison knowing the crimes he'd committed. Thinking of his mother only kicked his brain into a chaotic mess of paranoia. He started to wonder about Alex's motives for this plan. Did she *want* him to get caught so he'd be arrested, and she could go home?

That's bullshit and you know it, he chastised himself, thinking of the way she had willingly looped her fingers through his the night before. The way she had held him while he cried. During his breakdown, she had been *concerned* for him, doing what she could to bring him out of the beartrap that was his mind. She wasn't thinking of a way to get rid of him.

Those days were long behind them.

As he parked in a distant lot at the edge of the prison's property, sweat formed on his forehead and trickled down his temples. He told himself it was ridiculous to be so nervous, but as he approached the secure building, his heart did wild flips in his chest. To calm himself, he thought of Alex. Focusing on her was a solid way to distract himself from his self-created fear.

His childhood was scarred with years of abuse at his mother's hands. He didn't look forward to seeing the woman again. The last time he had laid eyes on her, he'd been a kid. News of her arrest had come to him during his time in the halfway house. Her picture had been all over the news, and he was sure that was partly why his father had changed his will, giving everything to Jamie at the last minute rather than his mother. It was thanks to that news story alone that Jamie knew where she was.

As he approached the metal detector, his skin prickled under the gazes of the guards milling around. He told himself they weren't staring because they suspected something, but rather because it was their jobs to study everyone who came in.

It didn't make him feel better.

He had already stripped off everything metal in the car, even his ACE ring. The less chances there were to draw attention to himself, the better. At last, he passed through the metal detector and approached the desk.

"Who are you here to see?" the woman on the other side of the plexiglass asked.

"My Mom. Mary-Anne Campbell," Jamie said.

"Got your ID?"

He set it on the counter, pushing it into the tiny hole beneath the divider and held his breath as the woman picked it up, studying it closely. She started to type something into the computer then glanced at him from the corner of her eye. Tension crept into his spine, and he was certain the woman was onto him. In the back of his mind, he started to map out a possible escape plan.

"You said she's your mother?"

Jamie nodded.

"Alright, come this way," she said, handing him back his license.

Jamie said nothing as he was led past a secure door and down a dingy gray hallway. He didn't walk past any cells, but it was still too easy to imagine himself here. To think of the hard bunks and uncomfortable silver toilets.

This is your future, a cruel little voice whispered in the back of his head.

Shut up, he hissed to it. *Alex wouldn't do that to me.*

The woman offered him an encouraging smile when he started to lag behind. Jamie forced himself to go faster as he was led into the cafeteria and seated at the table farthest from the place they entered through.

"She'll be out in a minute," the woman said as he sat down.

"Thanks," he replied, but she was already walking away.

Jamie's heart started to pound. He worried he would have another breakdown like he'd done in the restaurant. Anxiously, he tapped his fingers on the table, drawing the attention of a scowling woman at the next table over. It didn't matter. It didn't change his fear or his loathing. He could've gone his entire life without talking to his mother again, and it still would've been too soon.

Jamie bowed his head, avoiding looking at any of the

other inmates and their visitors. The doors opened. When he looked up, an officer guided a woman toward his table. Her face was clear of emotion, her upturned nose her most prominent feature. Her tangled dishwater hair hung in clumps around her head and face. Through the gaps, he could see her baby blue eyes.

The officer sat her down across from him. "The hell are you doing here?" she asked, wicked laughter pouring through her lips as she looked him up and down.

Jamie took a deep breath through his nose, trying to center himself. He thought he'd been prepared for this moment but looking into the eyes of the woman who had given him life, he realized how wrong he'd been. There was nothing that could prepare him to see her again. Nothing that could prepare him for the cascade of memories that came with her presence. "I have some questions…some things about our family that I need to know."

"You mean with all that fancy stuff you got from your daddy you still can't figure it out? Guess you were blessed with looks not brains."

"Mom, please don't make this harder than it has to be. I'm not exactly thrilled to see you either, but I'm trying to be a better person," Jamie said slowly, carefully. "And that means not letting you get under my skin anymore."

This time, she tilted her head back, her laughter growing loud enough to draw the attention of everyone at the nearby tables. A year ago, Jamie would've wilted under their stares, but now he sat up straighter, shoulders tense and ready for battle.

"No one told me you were coming with jokes, but I guess I should expect nothing more from a clown," Mary-Anne said once she'd finished laughing.

Jamie forced his lip stiff against the urge to pull it back into a snarl. There had been a time when he was vulnerable, young. A time when he had clung to his mother's words and believed her every insult. He had done so simply because he thought that as his mother, she was incapable of being wrong.

He knew better than that now. Growing up the way he had had given him clarity. Her words didn't hurt him anymore. So what if she hated him? He hated her too, and by the time their meeting was through, he'd make sure she knew as much.

"Ha, ha. Sad you have all the time in the world to come up with new material, yet you use the same tired insults you used when I was in diapers. Guess that's why Dad got tired of you and left all that stuff to me. I can't say it's *all* your fault. I mean those with less intelligence aren't privy to the creative ways of people better suited for conversation. After all, without exposure to things they can copy, they're forced to use their own brains for once, and let's face it. Yours has been lacking for some time. The drugs didn't help. With your looks *or* brain."

"Look, you little bastard," she hissed, leaning toward him. "The only reason I agreed to see you was to get out of my cell. You think I actually *want* to see your face? Hell no. From the very first moment I saw you, covered in the blood caused by *my* pain, I hated you. I knew you would be another bastard like your father. And lo and behold, you sit before me looking just like him. It's uncanny."

Jamie breathed out through his nose. "As much fun as it's been catching up, I need one question answered so I never have to see your sorry ass again."

She rolled her eyes and sat back in the chair, arms hanging at her sides as if her anger had exhausted her so much she could barely move. "Alright, what's the question?"

"Where is Angelica?" he asked, trying not to let his pain bleed through his words. If his mother sensed *any* vulnerability, she would use it against him, a twisting of the knife in his emotional wounds. "What happened to her?"

Mary-Anne stretched her eyes wide, the tiniest hint of a smile crossing her face. She looked almost…*gleeful*. Jamie tried not to jump to immediate panic, but he recognized that look. The only time his mother felt joy was when others were in pain.

"You don't know?"

"If I knew, I wouldn't be here," Jamie stated, voice flat, tired.

She chuckled, sitting forward so her elbows rested on the metal table. "She's *dead*. Gone. Expired."

Jamie wanted to show nothing of his emotions, but he felt the color drain from his face. "What?"

Mary-Anne's eyebrows shot up, the cruel laughter louder. "You should see your face!" she shouted and wiped the tears out from under her eyes. "Yeah, she's dead. Suicide or some shit a few years back. I don't know. It wasn't long before your daddy kicked the bucket."

"You're lying," Jamie snarled, not taking his eyes off

hers.

She quirked her lips to the side. "No, I don't think I am."

"You're lying!" he repeated, standing to his feet. "You've always been such a manipulative bitch doing what you can to keep everyone around you down. I should've known better than to come talk to you. You wouldn't know honesty if it bit you in the ass." He turned and started to storm across the cafeteria, not caring if he had to wait for an officer to escort him out or not.

"Getting mad at me won't bring her back to life!" she called after him.

Jamie didn't look back. He never wanted to see her again.

His heart beat with such conviction that his head buzzed, and he wondered how high his blood pressure was. How close was he to total meltdown? Jamie was hardly aware of passing back through the building and going out to his car. He slid into the driver's seat and put his ring back on, fidgeting with it as he drove home. As he drove, the anger drained away and left him with the one thing he hadn't let himself feel in the prison—sorrow.

It's not true, he told himself. *She's trying to get in your head like she's always done.*

There was a wriggle of something in his gut that he didn't like. Indecision, uncertainty. It stayed with him for the rest of the drive. The curving dirt road to his house didn't bring him the joy it usually did. Robotically, he climbed out of the car and went to the door.

Alex was there to greet him the second he walked inside. "How'd it go?"

Jamie ran his fingers through his hair, staring at the wall rather than looking at her. "About as well as expected," he said and moved toward his office door. He didn't want to look at her. To do so now in his state would burden her with emotions that she didn't need to bear. His mother could do what she wanted to *him,* but he wouldn't let her get inside Alex's head too.

"What'd she say?"

Jamie sat down in the office chair in front of his computer before he looked up at her and said, "She told me my sister is dead…that she killed herself not long before my dad died."

"I'm so sorry to hear that," Alex said, setting her hand on his shoulder.

"Don't be. I'm ninety-nine percent sure she's lying," Jamie said, logging in to his computer.

Alex's hand slid from his shoulder. "Why would she do that?"

"Why not?" Jamie retorted. "That's exactly what kind of a person she is. Wild, selfish. She doesn't care who she hurts as long as she's happy. And most of the time, hurting other people *is* what makes her happy."

"T-that's terrible," Alex said, a tremor in her voice.

She was hurting, but if it was for him or her all-too-similar childhood, he didn't know. Jamie said nothing as he typed his sister's name into the search bar. Partly, he wondered why he hadn't done this to begin with. It would've saved him a migraine, that was for sure. A hundred results came up, most of them social media pages for women with similar names to his sister.

At the bottom of the first page came a result that left a rock in his stomach.

Angelica Campbell Obituary.

"Oh no," Alex said softly as he clicked on it.

As horrible a thought as it was, he hoped it was a *different* Angelica Campbell. One who had never, and would never, mean anything to him. As soon as the page loaded, his hopes were dashed. There was no denying the picture. Then he read his name. *She is survived by her mother, Mary-Anne Campbell, and her brother, Jamie Knox.*

"She wasn't lying," Jamie said at last, not moving his eyes from the screen.

"I'm sorry," Alex whispered.

Jamie couldn't quell the emotions in him. "No," he said, frantically closing out the obituary page. He started to check every other result on the search page, a handful of tabs opening all at once.

Alex pulled back to watch him. From the corner of his eye, he could see the way she teased her lip between her teeth as if she contemplated something. At last, she said, "Jamie," and set her hand softly on the top of his arm.

Tears bubbled in his eyes, but he tried to ignore her, continuing his search. "This isn't right."

Alex moved her hand to his, stopping him from fidgeting with the mouse. He wanted to push her away and go back to scrolling. He would prove his mother was wrong. He would prove this wasn't real. Then Alex's arms slid around him, and his fight faded away. An echoing sob ran up from the pit of his stomach, and he dissolved into tears.

Chapter Thirty-Six

THE NEXT DAY, Jamie's face was still scoured with red marks from his tears. Alex had never seen someone filled with such anguish. When she'd been drowning in sadness and felt her only escape was to cut herself open and let it out, she'd never been where Jamie was. She hardly slept that night, worried about dozing off and not being there for him if he needed her. It was obvious how much he needed love. It seemed that in his entire life, Jamie had never known what real love was.

Alex had.

Those few fleeting years of her healthy mother combined with the unconditional love of her daughter gave her some sense of what it was like.

Desperate to cheer Jamie up, she got up long before he began to stir. To distract her worried mind, she played with Chloe and made sure the cat was satisfied with wet food and milk. Then she went to work arranging necessary supplies for the breakfast she and Jamie would share. The food didn't take long to cook, and she hoped the smell would rouse him, but it didn't.

By the time Jamie finally rolled out of bed, it was cold.

Alex was nursing a cup of orange juice when he appeared in the doorframe. The first thing he usually did in the morning, *every* morning, was to greet her. To let her know he was glad she was there. Today, he said nothing. He sat down at the table, staring at his food with such an intensity that Alex started to wonder if he had fallen asleep with his eyes open.

Before she could ask, he reached into his pocket and pulled out his phone. She didn't ask who he was calling as he held the device up to his ear, but the question was there anyway.

"Damien? Yeah, hey, man. Sorry to leave you hung out to dry like this, but I don't think I can come in. I got a uh…throat thing going on. I should be fine tomorrow, but I don't wanna get anyone sick, you know. Cough once and there goes an hour's worth of tips."

A beat of silence as Damien said something on the other end.

"Yeah, I'm healing fine. I really appreciate it."

Another moment of silence.

"Right. I will. Thanks again," Jamie said and clicked the end button before he tossed the phone onto the table with a thump. He reached up to run the heels of his hands over his cheekbones, and the wince he made a second later told Alex the skin was still raw.

"Morning," she said to him tentatively. As illogical as it was, she was afraid that if she didn't alert him to the fact that she was still there, he might've forgotten she existed.

He tapped his fingers to the wooden surface as if his mind was deep in thought. After the previous day, she would've had a harder time thinking it wasn't. Alex didn't have siblings of her own, but it was never easy to lose someone you cared about.

"How'd you sleep?" she asked, looking at his plate.

The food was solid with grease and looked

unappetizing. She wouldn't have been offended if he decided not to eat it. His face didn't change as he stared at it with that same concentration from a moment prior. Alex shivered. He had already proven that his emotions could make him unstable. She didn't want to think he could ever revert to being dangerous, that he could hurt her again after all they had been through, but as long as she was here, that was always a possibility, wasn't it?

No, she told herself. *He's grieving. If he's going to hurt anyone, it's going to be himself.*

"Decent, I guess," he replied at last. When he looked up at her, the brims of his eyes were as red as the marks on his cheeks, and she understood that was the true reason he had called in to work. He didn't want to let anyone beside her know how deep his pain was.

"That's good," she said, trying to sound soothing and reassuring rather than dismissive as she turned away to make her own plate.

He reached out, his cold fingers grasping the crook of her arm. "You can have mine."

Alex drew her eyebrows together as she slid into the seat beside him. "Not hungry?"

Slowly, Jamie shook his head. When he looked up at her, his eyes were touched with such sadness she was caught off guard.

"No—I'm…" He paused and looked up. "Was I—was I *wrong* for bringing you here?"

Alex fidgeted in her seat and shoved a bite of the chewy

bacon in her mouth to stall for time. She wasn't sure how to answer that. Of course it had been wrong what he did. At the very least, it was for the pain he'd caused to poor Katrina who was too little to really understand any of it. She might've been glad for what he had done now that she knew him, but it didn't change the fact that it never should've happened in the first place.

"Why are you asking me this?" she asked once the bite was gone.

"That's a yes, huh? You still don't want to be here?" He bobbed his head twice, as if he were confirming a deep-rooted suspicion, and rose from his seat.

"I didn't say that," she said, eyes wide when she imagined the shock collar being put back on her.

"You've said it in the past," he said and approached her.

"What are you doing?" she asked as he hooked his arm through hers.

"I'm fixing this situation," he said, hoisting her up out of the seat.

Desperately, she tried to grip onto the edge of the table, the doorway, *anything* that would keep Jamie from dragging her along.

"Where are we going?" she asked, fear stabbing into her. Flashes of Zack's bleeding corpse played in her mind, and raw terror stabbed into her.

"I'm letting you go," Jamie said, and that was when she realized he was leading her to the door. He thrust it open, letting the early morning sunshine spill inside.

Alex clung to him, heart thrumming as she stared at the foliage outside the door. "I don't want to go."

"I've made up my mind," he said, pulling his arm away from her before he put his hand to her back, pushing her forward. "You're free to go. Do with that freedom what you will whether it be to send me to jail or go start a new life."

"No, please," she said and turned, hurling herself over the doorframe to wrap her arms around him.

Alex had always been a homebody so being turned over to miles and miles of endless woods made her sick. There was *too* much air, *too* much freedom, and all she wanted to do was crawl back inside her prison so she wouldn't have to think of all the responsibility her freedom would require.

Jamie dropped his arm to the side, the door clattering shut. "If you're sure."

Alex held him tight a moment longer, making sure he wouldn't push her back outside before she hesitantly pulled back and pecked him on the lips. "I am. I am." A pause. "If this is about me pushing you to find your sister, I'm sorry. I just wanted you to find some peace, honest."

He pulled himself away, moving across the room to sit on the couch. "It's not your fault. It's more of the fact that everyone around me is fated for destruction."

Alex threaded her fingers together, unsure of how to approach this new mood. "That's not true."

Jamie stared. "How can you say that? There's a dead body in the backyard. If anyone ever finds out about that, about *you*, they're not going to understand. They're going to call me a monster. They're going to say I'm like my foster father. And maybe they're right. There's no redemption for someone like me. I can't lift anyone up; I drag them down into the darkness. I don't want that to happen to you."

"The whole reason I'm here is because you said you wanted to help me, and you have. You…made me realize that there's more to life than survival. Life can be a wonderful thing when it's filled with light and love. I've spent so much time living in darkness that no one ever bothered to show me the light. You have. You realized that I didn't like the darkness, didn't want it, and you found a way to free me."

He looked up at her, running his thumb over her cheek. "You mean that?"

"*Timshel.*"

"Huh?" he asked, mouth drawing down into an expression crossed between sadness and confusion.

"*East of Eden*…it's on your nightstand. I'm assuming you read it when I did."

"I have."

"Then you know what I'm talking about," Alex said softly. "What's done is done. You can either rise above it or let it consume you."

"You're right," he said. "You're absolutely right."

Jamie's phone started to ring, and he looked at it like he wanted to wing it across the room before his eyes moved back to her. He stared as if he were patiently waiting for her to speak.

Her lips pushed into a straight line, and she looked down at his phone before looking back up at him. "You should answer it."

Jamie looked down, and when he saw it was Damien's name on the caller ID, his fingers started to shake. He picked it up, clicking the speakerphone button so Alex could hear too. "Hello?"

"Dude, so you gonna tell me what's really going on?" Damien's voice bounced around the room.

"I uh…well, to be honest, it's been a rough day. I found out some bad news."

"I figured it was something like that. Want to meet up for a drink and talk about it? I'm about to take my break."

"No—" Jamie started to say, and Alex clamped her hand over the mouthpiece. He glanced up at her with an eyebrow raised. "What is it?"

"You should go," she whispered.

Jamie drew his face tight as if the idea appalled him. "You think so?"

"I think a drink will help you relax."

"You won't mind?"

"I won't mind."

"Sounds good," Jamie said to Damien. "I'll be there in a minute." He stood up on shaky legs and pecked Alex on the lips. "What would I do without you?"

Jamie picked up his keys from where he'd left them on the table by the door. With another glance over his shoulder, he disappeared outside.

As soon as the door closed, Alex looked down at Chloe perched on the edge of the couch. "I guess it's just you and me now."

Without Jamie in the house, it was too quiet. She went to their room and laid down in bed, thinking about everything that had happened over the past few days. Between the incident at the restaurant and the visit at the prison, Jamie seemed emotionally shot. She wanted to help him but didn't know how. Every attempt she'd made so far had only resulted in him being hurt in brand new ways.

Alex curled into the pillows, breathing in the whispering traces of his scent. She angled her face toward the tiny television perched on top of the dresser amidst her piles of writing supplies. On the screen, she watched the looping screensaver images of various landscapes. The longer she observed them, the easier it was to imagine that she was in any of those places.

The woods were her favorite. When she tried hard enough, she could nearly smell the crisp pine trees that used to grow around her childhood home. Her eyes opened, and she stared at the ceiling, not quite knowing how she felt.

Then her eyes turned to the piles of writing supplies around the TV. The papers she had written her thoughts on were hidden somewhere in the middle, somewhere where Jamie wouldn't easily be able to find them. She was sure he did anyway. The notebook he'd given her was filled with only half truths of her feelings, and she grabbed it along with her papers. He wanted to feel as if he'd had a positive impact on her life. If she finished the biography he'd been hoping for, it would be the best type of proof.

She carried it all to the living room and plopped down on the couch, spreading out her notes around her. Chloe watched her curiously as she opened the notebook, flipping to a new page, and started to write.

Chapter Thirty-Seven

JAMIE WENT OUT to the car and sat in it for the longest time, staring through the windshield. Alex had insisted he go, but Jamie didn't want to. He didn't want to be around *anyone* if he was being honest. The quiet of his car was serene, but it was also *cold.* He wouldn't be able to stay there for long without turning the engine on or he'd freeze. He slipped the key in the ignition and eased the car out of the driveway. As he made his way down the familiar curving roads, he started to come back to himself.

He remembered what he had done. Or rather, *almost* done. Had he really tried to throw Alex out? There was no way she could've survived in this wilderness alone. He knew that, but in the moment, he'd wanted her far from him.

I don't want to go, she'd said.

They were the perfect words, exactly what he needed to hear, but he wondered how much she meant them. Jamie had the strangest urge in his gut. He wanted to tell Damien the truth. To lay it all out on the table and see what an outside party would think. He was too close to Alex, too consumed with his own wants and needs to decide what was right anymore.

You can't do that. You'll go to jail, the tiny rational part of Jamie's brain tried to tell him.

He quieted it as he turned the engine off. His mind was made up, and whether it was a good idea or not, would remain to be seen. Inside, Damien was seated at the bar, bottle of water in front of him.

Jamie raised an eyebrow as he slid into the seat beside him. "Why invite me to a bar if you're going to drink water?"

"I have to go back to work in less than an hour. You do not," Damien said. As if on cue, the bartender placed a beverage in front of Jamie.

"What's this for?" Jamie asked, eyeing it uncertainly.

"I know you've been having a hard time lately, and I don't think it's only your illnesses. Tell me what's wrong."

Jamie stared into the glass. He was glad for Damien's foresight and picked up the cup, swirling the brown liquid. He downed it in one go, grimacing as he set it back down. "I did something bad."

Damien raised his eyebrows. "You? Never?" He grinned but Jamie couldn't mimic him.

"I mean it," he said.

"I doubt you could've gotten yourself into that much trouble."

"You're an optimist. I appreciate that."

The humor fell from Damien as he stared at Jamie. "Okay, man, you're scaring me. What is it? What did you do?"

Jamie licked his lips as he pulled out his phone. He held his breath as he went to Alex's social media and pulled up the post about her disappearance. He stared at it for a long time before finally turning the screen toward Damien. Damien didn't look at it at first, instead, choosing to study the expression on Jamie's face.

"Read it," Jamie urged.

Damien looked down, reading it over before he looked back up at Jamie. Carefully, he sat back in his seat before at last he said, "You?"

Jamie stared at his empty glass, wishing he could refill it with his mind as he replied, "Me."

"My God. I'm gonna need a drink after all." Damien waved down the bartender, getting them another round of drinks before he turned back to Jamie. "I knew there was *something* up with you lately, but this? Why?"

Jamie looked at the floor as he tucked the phone away. "It's…hard to explain."

"I'm going to need something more than that. This is...not good."

"I know."

"Then why?" Damien demanded after he downed his drink. "And is she...you know? Still *alive*?" He dropped the last word to a whisper.

"Of course, man. What do you take me for?"

"Excuse me if that was offensive. Before today, I didn't know you were capable of *this* at all."

"Well, now you know."

"Why? Why do I know?" Damien asked, sitting rigid in his seat. "What do you want me to do with this information?"

"I need advice," Jamie said. "I...I'm scared for her."

"Have you hurt her?"

"Nothing like that, but life is...so fleeting. I'm scared that I'm running out of time. That something's going to happen, and she's going to be left all alone."

"Then let her go," Damien said. "Deep down, I think you know it was wrong of you to take her in the first place."

"Of course I know that, but..." Jamie paused, thinking through the last week of his life. "But she doesn't want to go."

"What do you mean?"

"I tried to let her go today. She told me she didn't want to." Jamie stared into Damien's eyes, not caring that his friend could see him crying. Not caring that everyone around could see it too. "She could've gone to the police when my appendix burst, but she didn't."

"I don't understand," Damien said. "Shouldn't you be...happy?"

Jamie stared down at the bar. "I am, but I can't help but think that the truth is going to come out. When it does, I'll go to jail. It doesn't matter what Alex says about me; I did what I did, and I can't take it back."

Damien reached over to set his hand on Jamie's arm. "Are you thinking of going to the police? Of coming clean?"

"No," Jamie said, looking up at him. "But then I wonder if that makes me a horrible person."

"I wish I could help you, but I am very far past any idea of what I should say."

"Don't say anything," Jamie said. "I need your help with something."

"Nothing illegal, right?"

Jamie rolled his eyes. "Of course."

Damien gestured for him to continue.

Jamie pulled a piece of paper out of his jacket and slid it over to Damien. "I need you to agree to this."

Damien picked it up, scanning it over before he looked at Jamie, wide-eyed. "Your burial arrangements? Why am I looking at this?"

"Because if this comes out, I'm not going to go to jail," Jamie said. "I'm not going to follow in my mother's footsteps. I would much rather die with dignity, and when I do, I want you to be the person who takes care of me. You've always been like a brother to me, and it would mean everything to have you take care of this."

Damien carefully folded the paper over, staring at the top crease for a long time. "You're not going to kill yourself, are you?"

Jamie shook his head. "No. Never. If I did that, Alex would be alone. No. I want to have a backup plan…just in case."

Damien put one finger on the paper, pinning it to the counter. "If this will make you feel better, then of course I'll do it."

Jamie smiled from relief and sadness. He was sure that he'd be cashing in the favor much sooner than either of them anticipated.

Chapter Thirty-Eight

WHEN JAMIE CAME home, he was in better spirits. He reeked of alcohol and normally, Alex would've been concerned, but this time, she was relieved. At least he was in a better place mentally. When he walked through the door, he had a hand behind his back, and she tipped her head to the side, trying to see what he had hidden.

"I got something for you," he said then extended the arm he'd had hidden.

There was a small, flat present in his hand, and Alex reached out to take it, eyebrow raised. "What's this?"

"Open it and find out."

So she did, and a smile ghosted over her face as she realized it was the picture Jamie had taken of them together. It had been put in a beautiful silver frame. The picture of them was so happy, so normal, that they looked like any other couple.

"So…?" Jamie prompted.

She looked up at him with tears dewing in her eyes. Clutching it to her chest, she said, "I love it."

He bent toward her, planting a soft kiss to her forehead. "I'm glad."

He didn't wait for her to say anything else before he ambled down the hall. Alex admired it for another moment before she followed him. Jamie crawled into bed with everything but his shoes on. Alex carefully propped up the picture on the dresser and got into bed with him.

He fell asleep almost instantly, Alex rubbing circles into

his back. As soon as he started to snore, a look of peace crossed his face, and she had the feeling that things were going to be okay after all. He'd always have a soft spot for his sister of course, and like Lana, the pain of her loss would stay with him. With time, he'd be able to cope, as he had with everything else.

Somehow, Alex fell asleep beside him, but she was woken up by the sound of Jamie's sobs. She sat up, horrified that something was wrong. He didn't move, and she realized he was still asleep. She laid her hand on his arm, gently shaking him awake.

"Alex, is everything okay?" he asked, wiping his face with the back of his hand as if he hadn't been the one crying only a moment prior.

"Yeah, are you? I think you were having a bad dream."

Jamie licked his lips and breathed out. Slowly, he sat up, gathering himself as he said, "Yeah, I did."

"What about?"

"My sister. It was one of those dreams where I'm chasing her, but she doesn't stop moving away from me, doesn't hear me. Like I don't exist. And no matter how fast I try to go, it's never fast enough. Like running through mud." He wiped the back of his hand across the sweat on his forehead. "I know why I had it. I know why this whole thing is bothering me. I never got the chance to say goodbye. All this time I've been living, and I didn't know my sister wasn't doing the same."

"Sounds like you need to do that. To say your goodbyes," Alex said. There was a pain in her chest, empathy for the pain Jamie no doubt felt. "Otherwise, part of you is always going to look for her, to prove that what's real *isn't* real."

"Finding out what happened to her was supposed to help me with that. I saw her obituary," Jamie said, exasperated. "Any time I need the proof, I can literally pull it up with the click of a button."

"Our hearts don't trifle with logic the way our brains do," Alex reminded him.

Jamie ran his fingers through his hair, tousling the black locks. "So what should I do?"

"Maybe you need to see where she's buried," Alex said. "Put flowers on her grave and give her a real goodbye."

Jamie looked up at her through wide shining eyes. There was a hint of something, a childhood innocence that had been lost long ago trying to return. "You think that would help?"

"It can't hurt."

"You'll come with me, right?"

"Of course."

"Go get ready then, and I'll find out where she's buried."

Alex readily agreed and went to the bathroom. She looked at her blotchy face in the mirror, wondering why he'd want her to accompany him. She pushed the thought away and pulled her hair into a ponytail before tugging on a purple sweater and black jeans.

Jamie was in his office. She asked, "Find it?"

"Yeah," he said, staring down at his feet. "She's buried

in the same cemetery as my father."

"Sounds like a two-birds-one-stone situation then."

Jamie didn't look at her as he led out her out of the office. "Maybe."

"How'd you feel about your father?" she asked, realizing there was a hint of something unknown clinging to his face.

"I didn't hate him," Jamie said, eyes sparkling. "And I guess that's something. Out of all my family, he got the short end of the stick. My mom…wasn't easy for any of us to deal with. She was neurotic, quick to anger, and I used to think that me and Angie got it the worst, but now that I really think about it, Dad never stood a chance. After foster care took me and Angie away, he was still with her, for a little while at least. I'm positive the abuse didn't stop. My mother didn't kill him, but she might as well have. My dad died from liver failure. From the excessive alcohol he'd drink to cope with her antics and…" He trailed off, glancing up into her eyes uncertainly. "I'm rambling, aren't I?"

"Yes, but I think it's important to get it all out."

So that was what Jamie did.

The entire drive to the cemetery, he filled with stories of his sparse memories of his home life. Only when they stared down at Angelica's plaque did he go quiet.

Angelica Campbell. April 1990 - August 2014.

Always in our hearts.

Compared to the markers on the nearest grave, it was small, but it sat in the shadow of an oak tree which made that part of the cemetery feel disconnected from the rest.

Jamie crouched over her grave, running his fingers over the smooth surface. "Hard to believe she's really here."

"Need a moment alone?" Alex asked, holding her hands over her chest.

"No…no. Please," he said, reaching up to grab her hand. "It's better with you here."

Alex gave him her best reassuring smile, setting her free hand on his shoulder. She waited, expecting to see some of the tears he had shed during his sleep, but his face was dry.

He looked up at her, his blue eyes reflecting the sunlight. They looked clearer, more vibrant. "I think this was exactly what I needed. It hurts, seeing her like this, but it's a finale, enough for me to know that she's here. That she's really gone."

Alex nodded, relieved.

"Let's go home."

THE DRIVE HOME was silent, and Alex wondered if Jamie really felt better. She kept studying his face, but there were no definitive expressions. As soon as they walked through the door, she waited to see what he would do. Jamie wandered to the kitchen. There was a tiny bounce back in his step, the pep he'd had prior to the day he'd had the meltdown in the restaurant, but Alex doubted he felt better so easily.

Maybe now was the time to show him what she had been working on. It would do *something* to help, that much she was sure of. With one last fleeting glance to the back of Jamie's head, she went to the room, grabbing the papers. She found Jamie in the kitchen, downing a glass of juice when she tossed the bundles of papers and notebook on the table.

Jamie swallowed down the last gulp and slowly lowered the empty glass. "What's all that?"

"My work on your biography."

A hint of a smile touched his lips. "You're really…writing it?"

"Yes. At first, I thought it was narcissistic of you to assume your life was worth being written down, but I get it. You…your life has more pain and anguish than most people will ever know. I thought if I wrote down everything I knew, then maybe I could figure out why you are the way you are."

"These are your theories?" he asked, sitting down. He picked up a handful of the papers, thumbing through the pages.

"I don't need theories to understand you."

"Well, I'm touched. I really thought you'd write something mean, but this warms me. You'll show me it when it's done, right?"

"Of course."

He stood up, planting a kiss to her lips before he led her to the living room where they settled in to watch a movie.

Chapter Thirty-Nine

ALEX DIDN'T KNOW when she had fallen asleep. One moment, she was tucked into Jamie's arms, eyes on the movie, and the next, she was asleep. She only knew it was a dream because when her eyes opened, she was back in her apartment in Ponchatoula, sitting with Katrina on her mat in front of the TV.

It wasn't the movie her and Jamie had been watching. *Frozen* played, and Katrina stared, transfixed, as if she had never seen it before. Alex wiped the hair from her daughter's eyes, and the girl turned, face happy and warm. As quickly as it had come, the image distorted, disappearing down a long black tunnel.

As Alex's vision focused, she recognized the white ceiling of Jamie's bedroom.

"You're awake?" Jamie's soft voice filled her ears.

"Yeah," she said, sitting up to wipe her face. She looked around, disoriented. "Didn't we fall asleep on the couch?"

"You did, and I carried you in here. Much more comfortable."

"Thank you," she said, rubbing a phantom pain at the base of her neck.

"You're welcome," Jamie said. "Are you going to tell me what you dreamed about?"

"I-I don't remember," she lied. The twinkle of Katrina's eyes was there every time she closed her eyes, and a hard knot filled her stomach. Losing herself in Jamie's grief had made it easy to forget about her own. Now the pain of her absence was back, sinking into every fiber of her being to the point where she found herself planning out a life with her, Jamie, and Katrina all together.

It could work, an insistent little voice tried to tell her.

How? she countered.

"I thought I've treated you well," Jamie said, sounding hurt for her silence.

Alex wiped her face, focusing on him instead of the voices in her head. "You have."

"Okay, so why do you still feel the need to lie to me?"

Alex wasn't successful in removing all traces of her tears before she met his eyes. "I dreamt about my daughter."

"Ah." Jamie ran his finger along the side of Alex's jaw. "I'm sure she misses you. You're her mother after all."

"Not that it'll do her much good," Alex said, staring down at the blankets. "I can't do anything for her."

Jamie was silent.

Alex pinned him with her stare and said, "You're never going to let me see her again, are you?"

He tilted his head, considering. "We could bring her here."

"W-we can't," Alex said and hated that they'd both had the same idea. She wanted to believe she could have everything she wanted, but it was a foolish wish. It wouldn't work. It *couldn't* work…could it? "I mean to go and get her would reveal where I am, and then you'll be arrested."

"You're thinking about this with a limited mind frame.

Sure, it could all go horribly wrong, but what if it didn't? What if everything went according to plan?" he asked. "I bet I could swipe her right out from under Peter's nose, like I got you, and he'd be none the wiser."

Half of Alex wanted to tell him to go for it, to save her little girl and make them a whole family. The other half of her didn't want him to do anything that could put him in danger. That was the voice that won the fight. "You can't do that!"

"It would make you happy, wouldn't it? Having her here?" Jamie looked surprised she would argue the topic.

"Of course, but it wouldn't be right." Alex rolled over, staring at the wall before she closed her misty eyes, ready to go back to sleep and have the peace of black nothingness take away her pain. "She's there, and I'm here. End of discussion."

Chapter Forty

JAMIE DIDN'T WANT to forget about it, but the steel on Alex's face gave him no choice. She'd made her mind up, and as she drifted back to sleep in his arms, he tried to tell himself she was right. Then she started to cry again, rougher than she had the first time. He tried to wipe the strands of hair away from her face to soothe her, but they stuck to her tears. A handful of thin strands pulled out on accident, and his patience snapped.

Why did she want to *stay* in this turmoil? After everything she had helped him with, why wouldn't she let him do the same for her?

Her daughter?

That was a problem he could fix.

Slowly, he eased himself up off the bed, staring at her in case he woke her. She stirred but didn't open her eyes. He grabbed a piece of paper off the desk and wrote a note, not mentioning where he was going, only that it might be a day or two before he'd return. Before he left, he kissed her on the forehead, keeping the mental image of her in the front of his brain as he went out the door with a bag packed with things similar to the one he'd taken on his original trip to see Alex.

In his head, the plan seemed simple. He'd stalk Alex's apartment, waiting for the moment to snatch Katrina and come home. Based on what he'd seen of Peter during his time in Ponchatoula and the images on television, Jamie was positive he could beat him in a fight if it came to it.

Jamie drove straight there, stopping only once to add gas to his tank. A sense of déjà vu washed over him as he sat in the apartment parking lot, planning out his next move. It was late in the evening, the sky overhead a soft purple. When it turned black with night, he climbed out of the car, pulling his hood up. Crowbar hidden up his sleeve, he climbed the stairs. It was easy enough to find Alex's old apartment. He'd spent so much time staring at the door that he could've found it blindfolded.

With a quick glance to make sure no one was watching, he pressed his ear to the door, listening. Inside came faint murmuring, the sound of a television. Quietly, he moved over to the window beside the door and peered in. It was dark inside, the only light a flickering that could be from the television he heard. He came to two conclusions—Peter and Katrina were either not home or they had already turned in for the night.

Slowly, Jamie breathed out and dropped the crowbar from its hiding place. He wedged it into the window, making as little noise as possible. The screen came out, and he set it aside before slipping into the living room. Heart thudding, he ducked into the shadows behind the couch, preparing himself in case he'd been heard.

No movement.

Jamie tried to get a sense of his surroundings, sitting until his eyes adjusted enough to see the shadowy outlines of the nearby furniture. Crowbar ready, he started to creep down the hallway.

A bedroom sat at the end of the hall with another one closer to him. He tried that one first, and when he pushed open the door, he saw that his guess was right. The room was pink, a nightlight glowing in one corner. The tiny bed was piled high with pillows and stuffed animals. Alex's tiny child was tucked among them, her brown hair splayed across the pillow.

Jamie crept into the room and knelt by her, trying to determine the best way to pick her up. Before he could decide, the tiny girl's eyelids flickered open. When she saw him, she opened her mouth to scream.

Wide-eyed, he clamped his hand over her mouth. "Shh! Shh!" he said. "I-I'm uh…a friend of your Mommy's."

The girl blinked, fear still there, but it was mixed with curiosity as he pulled his hand away. "You know Mommy?"

"That's right. If you come with me, I'll take you to her."

Her eyes sparkled, and she sat up, eyes shining bright as she readied herself to get out of bed. Relief breezed through Jamie until a voice behind him said, "Hands up."

Peter.

Slowly, Jamie stood, hands in the air, and turned, face emotionless. Peter had a gun, and it was aimed straight at Jamie's forehead. In the shadows, he looked bigger than Jamie had anticipated, and the gun wasn't something he had prepared for. Behind him, Alex's child was still seated on the bed, looking back and forth between the two men. He tried to comfort himself by thinking that Peter wouldn't want his child to be exposed to anything as horrible as a person being shot, but he had no way to know for sure.

"You know where Alex is?" Peter asked, tipping his head to the side.

"Y-yes," Jamie replied, wondering if that was information that could help him or hurt him.

Peter cocked the gun. "You're the sick freak who took her, aren't you?"

"She's better with me. And her daughter will be too once you're out of the way."

"I don't think you're in a position to make that call," Peter said, waving the gun for emphasis.

Jamie felt the weight of the crowbar in its hidden spot in his sleeve. It was clear by Peter's tone and stance that Jamie wouldn't be able to walk away without a fight. He counted down from five and lunged.

The last thing he heard was the sound of a gun firing.

Chapter Forty-One

ALEX WOKE UP feeling good until she read Jamie's note. Cold uncertainty spread through her that he had gone and done something stupid. Desperately, she tore through the house, desperate to find him. He was long gone, and she had no way to reach him. The door to his office was locked, and when she looked out the front window, his car was gone.

All she could do was wait, and that wasn't something she could manage with ease. She paced endlessly for hours. Chloe watched her from her safety spot under the couch, helpless. When the day dragged into night, that feeling of dread grew. With no word from Jamie, the uncertainty turned to panic. She curled up in his blankets, picking up a waft of his scent, and sobbed into the pillow. When the knock at the door came, she barely heard it over herself.

The knocks turned to pounding, and she hopped up, racing for the door. She threw it open, smiling. "Jamie, I—"

She stopped.

A handful of police officers stood on the doorstep.

"Alex Alpine?" one of them, an Asian woman maybe a foot taller than herself, asked. She had a serious expression on her face, her body positioned in a way that made it clear she would spring into action if the situation turned dangerous.

Alex nodded slowly.

The officer murmured something to the rest of the policemen who pulled out guns and split up to skirt the house on both sides.

"What's going on?"

"My name is Detective Lang. You're safe now, honey," she said. "We're going to take you home."

Alex took a breath in, stumbling backward. "B-but this is my home."

Detective Lang's bottom lip jutted out. Pity. It was pity that she was watching her with.

"Where's Jamie?"

"Alex," Detective Lang said, setting a hand on her shoulder.

Alex smacked it away, nearly screaming the question. "Where's Jamie!?"

"He's gone."

Alex stared at her, hoping that the scene before her would change. Her heartbeat accelerated, and she no longer saw Detective Lang as her heartbeat accelerated. *It's all another nightmare,* she told herself. When nothing changed, she had no choice but to accept the reality she had somehow stumbled into.

"No!" She tried to push her way past Detective Lang with the assumption that they were hiding him from her.

This was a joke. All a cruel prank, maybe on Peter's part.

"Oh, poor thing," the woman behind her whispered.

She didn't stop try to stop her. Instead, Alex tripped over her own foot. That was the last thing she remembered before her world cut to black.

***

WHEN ALEX CAME back to focus again, she wasn't sure where she was. Whiteness blinded her, and for the smallest fraction of a second, she thought she was dead. She opened her eyes, staring at the ceiling. Gradually, her other senses returned, and she picked up the steady beeping of a machine nearby. Voices murmuring in the distance and the smell of antiseptic.

She was in the hospital.

Groaning in her throat, she tried to sit up and see her surroundings with better clarity. Seated in the one chair in the corner of the room was Peter with Katrina perched on his lap. Both of them stared at her with matching expressions of concern. It had been so long since Alex had seen them that they looked strange, different from how she remembered them.

"Alex?" Peter asked softly. He looked rough. The 5 o'clock shadow turning almost to a thick scruffy beard, and there were dark circles under his eyes. It felt as if an eternity had passed since she'd last seen him. The fight they'd had before Jamie entered her life barely registered. What had it been about?

Alex was confused.

On the news, it hadn't appeared that he'd missed her, so why did he look worse for wear? Was it possible that maybe, just maybe, he'd missed her after all? When her eyes met his, she felt *nothing*. Alex focused on the brown eyes that had once made her feel seen, important.

She stared at him, hoping something would come loose,

even if it was anger or hatred, but the longer she stared, the worse she felt. Peter brought no emotions at all. For as heartwarming as the moment should've been. Alex felt dead inside.

Peter got up, sitting their daughter on the chair, before he crossed the room, wrapping his arms around her and clinging tight. Alex rested her head on his shoulder, drawing in the familiar scent of his cologne, and still felt nothing. He could've been a stranger rather than the father of her child. She wanted it to stop. When he pulled away, she bunched her blankets tighter, hoping he wouldn't do that again any time soon.

"I missed you," Peter said.

Alex let her eyes drop to the white sheets. She was supposed to say she missed him too, and she could *say* that, but it would be a lie. Their marriage had felt like a sham for a while, but she'd never had the confidence to call him out on it.

Now, she wasn't really sure why.

"Momma!" Katrina interjected, running up to the side of Alex's bed with her little arms outstretched.

"Kat, baby. Mommy missed you!" Alex said and hoisted her daughter right up into bed with her.

"Alex, be careful," Peter said, holding a hand out as if she would somehow injure herself by picking up her daughter. She didn't look at him.

"I was so scared you were gone, Mommy," Katrina said, her little arms hugging her back. "Everyone said you went away."

"I would never leave you," Alex said, barely holding in

her tears because she had done exactly that. She'd gotten comfortable in the life where all she had of Katrina were memories. "Never ever."

"C'mon, kid. Let your mom breathe," Peter said and eased Katrina off the bed.

Alex let him do it, but that didn't stop her from glaring at him when he wasn't paying attention. When Katrina's feet were on the ground, he looked up at her, opening his mouth as if he were about to say something else when the door opened.

Detective Lang peered in, gaze moving from Peter to Alex. "Hi there. Hope I'm not interrupting," she said as she moved herself inside the room. "How're you feeling?"

Alex didn't answer. She had the distinct feeling that this woman didn't really care how she felt. This was her job. She *had* to concern herself with it. In Alex's mind, it was this woman's fault that she had been separated from the place and things that made her close to Jamie, the things that made him real.

"I'm glad to see you're doing better," Detective Lang said. "You had us worried."

"What are you doing here?" Alex asked, but she didn't look up from her sheets as she spoke.

"I want to ask you a few questions if that's alright with you."

Alex bit her lip. A few questions made it sound so easy, but she knew what it really was—a police interrogation. "No."

"Can I talk to her privately, please?" Detective Lang asked Peter. "Women who go through the things that Alex has will find it difficult to talk about in front of their loved ones, and it's important I get her statement as soon as I can."

Peter murmured something in response, and a second later, the sound of the door closing told Alex that Peter and Katrina were gone. Only then did she allow herself to look up.

Detective Lang pulled up the chair that Peter had been seated on. She sat down, crossing one long leg over the other before she said, "You've been through a lot, I know, but I need you to walk me through what happened."

Alex looked back down at her fingers. Her skin was almost as pale as her sheets. She didn't want to talk about what had happened. Thinking of Jamie made her want to cry, but the reality of her entire situation was sinking in.

He was really gone.

"Jamie's dead, isn't he?" she asked.

"Yeah."

Alex wiped her face with the heel of her hand, getting rid of any tears that might've found their way free before she peered at Detective Lang from the corner of her eye. "H…how did it happen?"

"He broke into your home. Your husband shot him in self-defense."

Alex let the tears fall, uncertain why she'd felt the need to hide them. She was sad that Jamie was gone, and she was ready to let everyone know it. "He deserved so much better."

"The situation you're in is very complex," Detective Lang said, her face creased in concern. Alex wondered how often she'd had to give similar speeches. "Have you heard of

Stockholm Syndrome? A lot of times when someone is presented with what you've been through, they feel as if they've developed feelings for their captor and—"

"He wasn't my captor," Alex said, tears dripping to her blanket. "I loved him, and he loved me."

Detective Lang's face tightened. It was obvious her next words were a struggle as if she couldn't decide what the best way to break Alex down was. "You may think you did, but it's a biological reaction intended to help you survive. Women who have been in similar situations as you can attest to having the same reactions. In time, they came to realize that those weren't true feelings."

Alex wanted to laugh. She looked the woman over, how pressed and proper she appeared. She had no idea what hell Alex had been through throughout her life. How could she possibly understand all that Jamie had done for her? Alex lifted her chin and said, "No. I'm sure of it. I've never been surer of anything in my life."

Detective Lang uncrossed her legs so that she could lean in closer. "Tell me one thing, Alex."

Alex licked a tear off her lip.

"Did you go with him willingly?"

Alex stared into her eyes, knowing where the conversation was leading. "No," she said at last, voice a shaky whisper.

Detective Lang closed her eyes before she stood up and crossed the room. With her hand on the door, she said, "Then this is officially a crime. I'll have them do your rape kit and let you get a little rest before we take next steps."

"Rape kit?" Alex asked, baffled. "He never raped me."

That sympathetic look was on Detective Lang's face again as she went out into the hall, closing the door.

"He's not a monster!" Alex screamed after her. "He was a good person!"

The door clicked shut, and Alex crumpled into her bedding, thinking of the look on Jamie's face when he'd said, *If anyone ever finds out about that, about you, they're not going to understand. They're going to call me a monster.*

Chapter Forty-Two

PETER DIDN'T COME back into the room, and Alex was glad. She remembered what Detective Lang had told her, that Peter was responsible for Jamie's death, and everything strong left in her drained away. It was just like Peter to snuff out her every ounce of happiness.

More tears bubbled out of her eyes, and she turned over, staring at the wall. She tried to theorize why Peter would leave so soon after getting her back. Most likely, Katrina was beginning to get fussy and needed her dinner and a nap or at least, Alex hoped that was the reason.

It hasn't been a day, and he's already tired of me, she thought and rolled onto her back to stare at the ceiling.

What did it matter if he was? She was tired of herself, tired of the thoughts that kept rolling around the inside of her head. It was as if everything Jamie had kept at bay was back, stronger for the time away.

Jamie's dead. He died for me. She was glad everyone had left because she sobbed into the pillow until her face was raw and the fluffy surface was thoroughly soaked.

Over and over, she pinched her arm, watching the red welts swell up along her unhealthy pale skin, hoping she would wake up from this nightmare. The pain in her flesh and heart was impossible to ignore.

In that state of semi-consciousness, Alex had no idea how much time passed, but the brightness of the room changing in correspondence to the differing levels of light outside gave her a vague idea. When the first of the night stars came out, the door to her room popped open.

Alex had stopped crying by then. Not because she wasn't sad anymore, but because there were simply no more tears to shed. A nurse came in, not Detective Lang who Alex had expected. She was almost grateful except she didn't feel up to human contact in any capacity.

Alex swallowed and winced at the pain in her throat. She was dehydrated—a day of crying could do that—but she didn't want to ask for water. Part of her felt as if she deserved the discomfort. After what she had done to Jamie, she deserved to be uncomfortable every single day for the rest of her life.

"Alex Alpine?" the nurse asked, glancing up from her clipboard.

Alex gave the slightest bob of her head as she waited for the nurse to continue.

"My name is Beverly. I was sent to do your procedure," she said, moving around to the side of Alex's bed to set the clipboard on a nearby table.

Alex forced her gaze to stay on the woman as she asked, "What procedure?"

"A rape kit was ordered for you."

Alex huffed. Earlier, she'd been devastated, but now she was indignant. "I told Detective Lang that wasn't necessary."

"I know you must be scared and feeling vulnerable. After what happened, no one blames you, but this is important. For us to understand what happened—"

"I don't need it. You don't need to understand *anything*," Alex seethed. "Jamie is dead. And even if he wasn't, I wouldn't consent to this."

Beverly simpered. It was a gentle smile, the kind her mother used to give her when she was little and would scrape her knee. In this situation, it didn't feel comforting. It felt patronizing. "They can't force you to comply. I know this is all overwhelming, but you're in charge of yourself. Stick to your guns. For the record, I think you're a brave young woman. What you went through couldn't have been easy. Whatever you do, don't lose that strength."

Beverly patted her foot and left the room. Alex stared at the door long after Beverly was gone, shoulders drooping as she tried to process what had happened. She hoped that would be the end of the issue.

Stick to your guns.

That was a different approach than anyone else had had. They registered her behavior as the result of fear or trauma, but it wasn't. It was so much more and so much less. It was the result of her finally breaking out of the cage that had been built around her for so long, the one constructed of abuse, of neglect, of heartbreak.

For the first time in a while, she told herself she was a person who mattered, and she had Jamie to thank.

Chapter Forty-Three

I T TOOK A few more arguments with different nurses, but Alex didn't back down, and they stopped coming in with tests. With no reason to keep her, she was discharged the next day. One of the nurses had been kind enough to buy her a spare outfit so Alex was fully dressed and waiting in the lobby by the time Peter came to pick her up. Alex had been looking forward to seeing her daughter again, but Katrina wasn't there.

"Where's she at?" Alex asked without greeting Peter first.

Peter had had a half-smile on his face when he stepped through the double doors, but it morphed into a grimace. "I dropped her off at Katherine's for today to give you a chance to get settled in."

"Oh." That would be her luck. An uncomfortable evening and night alone with the person she least wanted to be around.

The smile appeared on Peter's face again. Like always, he hadn't sensed her mood, or he had chosen to ignore it. He set a hand on her shoulder, keeping it there as he said, "It'll be good to spend some time together," and led her through the hallways and out the sliding glass doors downstairs. Outside, they bumped into Detective Lang.

"Alex! Glad I caught you," she said. "Now I know it's been a rough twenty-four hours, but I need you to come down to the station to finish giving your statement, if you don't mind."

"No, thank you," she said, barely looking at the woman. Alex had already said all she could about what had happened without losing it completely. She'd hoped to disappear from the hospital without ever having to see Detective Lang again. Desperately, she glanced to Peter, hoping that for once he'd stand up for her.

Instead, he said, "When do you need her there?"

***

TWENTY MINUTES LATER, Alex was seated in an uncomfortably small interrogation room. It was cold and gray, reminding her of Jamie's basement in a way, except it didn't come with the warmth that Jamie had to offer. Detective Lang sat across from Alex, patient smile on her face as she studied her over.

"I know you don't want to talk to me. After what you've been through, I understand, but I need to know what happened."

"Why?" Alex asked, folding her arms across her chest. She recognized how petulant her own actions were, but she was too deep in her own feelings to decide how else to act.

"As I've already told you, your case went national," Detective Lang said, folding her hands together on the silver table between them. "We spent a lot of time trying to find you. If you ran away with Jamie, that's something we need to know. Bottom line is, we found a dead body, and that's not something we can look the other way on."

Alex's gaze dropped to the table. Jamie had known the truth about Zack would come to surface, and so had she, but she didn't want to think about him. Didn't want to put Jamie in any kind of negative light, but this wasn't a situation that would go away otherwise.

"As far as I know, the search was called off. Why do I have to answer anything when you weren't searching anymore?"

"We had reason to believe that you'd left of your own choice. That you ran away."

"What makes you think that?"

"We monitored your online accounts. When new logins came in from an untraceable IP address, there were some people who thought you'd gone by your own choice."

"But not you?"

Detective Lang's face hardened. "It didn't make sense to me." She carefully watched every fleeting emotion on Alex's face before she added, "So I'll ask you again. How did you and Jamie meet?"

The scene in the bar floated at the front of Alex's brain. Jamie's blue eyes under the light. The laugh they'd shared. The way that he'd made the little ball of tension in the pit of her stomach easier to manage. "I got into a fight with my husband so I went to the bar to cool off. Jamie was there. He bought me a drink. I don't normally drink a lot, but that day I was bad off emotionally. I'd already had three drinks when Jamie approached. I didn't want to be rude when he bought me the fourth, so I drank it. After that, I was so drunk I passed out, and when I woke up, I was tied to a chair in his basement."

"In the house where we found you, correct?"

Alex bobbed her head.

"He kept you there the entire time you've been missing? Didn't take you to any other location?"

Detective Lang wanted to know if he'd held her prisoner at any other house, but all she could think of was the trip to the hospital. The trip to the restaurant. The trip to the cemetery. Yes, he'd taken her places, but they had all been of her own free will. She scanned through all her memories, gauging how far they'd come, and tears misted over her vision.

"Alex?" Detective Lang prompted.

"He...kept me in a shock collar so I couldn't leave the house." She closed her eyes, trying to block out the memory of the blinding pain that had come from her exploration attempt. The more she talked, the worse Jamie sounded. Each story made him sound more and more like the monster he'd been accused of being. What did it truly mean to be a monster? Alex didn't know anymore.

Could a person be both a monster and a godsend?

Detective Lang's face morphed into an expression of pity again as she said, "Were you ever aware of there being other victims in the house?"

Alex could still hear the sound that Zack's body made when Jamie threw him to the ground. Still smell the blood. But she didn't want to tell this woman the truth. To do so would mean spilling Jamie's secrets, and that felt like a betrayal she wanted no part of. "No," she said, but she was sure the evidence would say otherwise. They'd find the bloodstains in the basement, she was sure. They might find hers in the bathroom. Ideally, she wondered what they'd think of that. "During my time there, I did what I thought he wanted to try to get him to let his guard down so I could escape. I wasn't aware that I wasn't alone."

Detective Lang jotted down Alex's every word. Alex tried to read some of it but couldn't make out the messy scribbles. "So that's it. The full story. Am I in trouble or can I go?"

Detective Lang was quiet a moment longer before she looked up. "I suppose we're all set. If we need anything else from you, we'll be in touch."

Chapter Forty-Four

AFTER ALEX WAS dismissed, she found Peter waiting for her in the parking lot.

"How'd it go?" he asked as she climbed in the car.

Alex turned her gaze out the window, watching the world spin past. She didn't want to tell him a thing. It felt wrong.

Peter sighed. "Katherine agreed to take Katrina for a few days so you can get adjusted. I think you'll need more than a day."

Alex turned to him, furious. How dare he make a decision like that without consulting her first? She opened her mouth but changed her mind. She didn't want to admit that he was right. Though Alex wanted nothing more than to curl up with her daughter, Katrina didn't need to see her like this. Didn't need to see *them* like this.

The cold from the glass seeped into Alex's cheek as she stared out the window. It was strange to be alone with Peter after so long. He kept his eyes on the road as if he felt as awkward as she did, but his lip was quirked up at the corner— his irritated expression.

"I could hear you, you know. When you talked to Detective Lang in the hospital."

"Yeah, and?" Alex asked, too tired to feel the anger she would need for the oncoming fight.

"You defended him," he said, voice devoid of emotion.

Alex stared straight ahead. She already knew where the conversation was headed and considered opening the door and jumping out of the car. The crack of her skull against the pavement would hurt a lot less.

"Why would you defend him?" Peter asked. "After everything he did?"

There were a hundred answers that came to mind, but none of them would help her or the conversation at hand. Alex pressed herself closer to the door, focusing on the sensation of the cold. Everything else faded to the background.

Peter shook his head but didn't say anything else as he drove the rest of the way home. He parked and got out of the car without so much as a glance in her direction. Alex trailed him up the stairs and inside the tiny place she used to consider home. Now it felt like the cage she had worked so hard to escape from. For as awkward as it had been seeing Peter again, it was worse standing in the middle of the apartment. She didn't sit down, feeling like a stranger in her own home as she stared down at Katrina's toys scattered around the floor in front of the television.

"You look like you don't want to be here," Peter said, tossing his coat onto the edge of the couch.

Alex sat down beside it, but she didn't deny what he said.

Peter folded his arms as he stared at her, eyebrows drawn together in concern. "You're so…quiet."

Alex said nothing to that either. Jamie would've left her

alone to think, but not Peter. This would continue. He'd poke and jab until she was so frustrated all she'd want to do is cry.

"What did he do to you, Alex?" Peter asked, voice softer than she'd heard in some time.

"He cooked for me," she said, holding back her emotions as she looked up at him. "When was the last time you did something like that? When was the last time you did *anything* that was nice or something small that made my day easier? When was the last time you checked in on me or cared how I felt?"

Peter reached up to scratch the back of his neck. "I know we've been drifting apart for some time, and for that, I'm sorry."

Alex continued to stare at him through half-lidded eyes. If he thought she believed his apology, he was crazy.

"Look," he said, decoding the meaning of her glare. "It's…this is weird for me. You've been gone for so long and to think of what that man did…"

"To you, I was gone long before he ever took me." Rage made her start to shake, and she clenched her hands into fists to quell it. "You were glad for my disappearance, I bet. It's probably why you waited to tell anyone that I was gone."

Peter flinched backward, face contorting as if he had smelled something particularly unpleasant. "What does that mean?"

"Jamie showed me the news. I saw you there except it wasn't just *you*."

"Oh," he said and looked away.

Alex scoffed. "Yeah *oh.* " She sniffled, but felt nothing but anger. Before Jamie, this moment would've wounded her, but now, she doubted she could ever feel pain again. "Who is she?"

"Nobody. I promise you that. She was …she was *there* when you disappeared, and it felt so right that I…"

Alex held up a hand. She didn't want to hear it. Didn't want to hear why he had decided to chase another woman rather than try to find his wife. "Where is she now?"

"I broke it off with her," he said, kneeling beside the couch to take her hand in his.

"When?" she asked, nearly recoiling at the unpleasant feeling of his skin pressed to hers.

Peter looked down at the floor, letting go of her.

"*When?*"

"When the police told me they found you."

Alex stood up, immediately turning her back to him. What an idiot she was for assuming he'd missed her for even a moment. His unkempt appearance wasn't from stress. He'd been living it up, apparently so much so that he'd let his hygiene slip away.

"Alex, I—"

"Where did he die?" she asked, not caring that she cut him off mid-sentence.

A strange expression crossed Peter's face as he stood up. "Who? That man?"

"*That man* has a name. Or he had one," Alex said, biting her lip to keep it from trembling.

"What does it matter where he died?"

"Because Detective Lang said you did it," Alex said, disgusted. "And I want to know what his final moments were like."

Peter was silent for a minute then two. Alex almost thought he left the room when he said, "That man stole you from your life, from your *daughter,* and you want to know what his final moments were like?"

Alex whirled on her heels to face him. "Humor me," she said, pulling back her lip to expose her teeth. "It's the least you can do."

"Fine," Peter said, holding up his hands. "If it'll help you."

It would, but not in the way Peter probably assumed. To see it would mean accepting the fact that Jamie was really gone, that he wasn't secretly waiting somewhere to come in and rescue her again.

"Come on," Peter said, leading her down the hallway.

A sickening lump filled her throat a minute before Peter pushed open the door to Katrina's room. Her white carpet had a giant brown stain near the foot of her bed, and Alex broke down in tears.

There was no way to pretend anymore. Jamie had spent the last minutes of his life doing what he could to make her happy.

Chapter Forty-Five

A LEX WAS A sobbing mess. At first, Peter tried to comfort her, but she pushed him away. She wanted no part of him. Couldn't stand to be in the same room as him.

Alex sat next to the stain, trying to imagine how Jamie's body had fallen. She looked from it to Katrina's bed, and found herself glad that Peter had sent her away. At least this way, she'd have the chance to try to clean it.

Katrina had seen enough violence to last her a lifetime.

Alex went to the kitchen and pulled a bucket out from under the sink. She filled it with hot water and cleaner, watching the white bubbles spring up. With a rag over her shoulder, she made her way back into Katrina's room. The bucket thunked to the floor beside the stain, and Alex dropped to her knees. The chemicals stung her skin when she dipped the rag into the bucket, but she ignored it and went to work scrubbing the carpet.

Midway through her chore came pounding on the front door. Drool had dried to her chin and the chemicals in the rag had made her fingers numb, but she shook it all off as she stood to her feet and rushed toward the door. When it opened, she was surprised to see Detective Lang on the other side. She looked smaller than Alex remembered, as if Alex's case had physically crushed her.

"Hello?" Alex said, more out of annoyance than anything else. She'd told Detective Lang all there was to say.

What else could they possibly need?

"Good afternoon, Alex. I thought I'd stop by, and see how you're settling in."

"I'm fine. It's fine," Alex said, fingers clutching the doorknob tight. "I-I don't want to be rude, but what is it you need?"

"I know you don't like to talk about what happened, but I have to ask a few more questions. Would it be alright for me to come in?"

Alex steeled her shoulders, ready to tell her to get lost when the fight left her. The sooner she cooperated, the sooner it would be that the police would leave her alone. That *everyone* would leave her alone, and she could grieve in peace.

"Yeah," she said, gesturing to the couch.

Detective Lang thanked her and looked around before she sat on the couch. "It's quiet."

Alex closed the door and turned to look at her. "Yeah, Katrina's with her auntie until we get her bedroom cleaned up."

"And your husband?"

Alex frowned, thinking of the night before. The smear in Katrina's carpet, her wail of despair, and Peter's outrage. She didn't know where Peter was, but none of her guesses were kind so she said nothing.

"Okay, well, I'll get to the bottom of this so you can get on with your day. Um." She paused to shift expressions before she said, "It's come to my attention that you denied the rape kit."

Alex plopped down in the armchair. "Yeah, I was told

that I didn't have to take it. It wouldn't help. Jamie and I never had sex."

"I suppose in that case it *wouldn't* help, but I'm curious as to how you're handling all of this emotionally. Everything you've gone through is scarring. Are you...*happy* to be back home with your family?"

Alex crossed her arms over her body, staring at the wall on the other side of the room. "I didn't realize my feelings mattered to the investigation."

Detective Lang looked up at the ceiling, as if considering her words, before she said, "I suppose they don't, but they matter to me. I spent months trying to find you. When everyone else dropped off, I stayed on."

"Well, here I am," Alex said, holding her palms out to either side of herself. "Good job. Jamie's dead, and I'm here."

"You don't seem as if you *want* to be here," she observed. Alex's lip twitched, and she found it increasingly difficult to maintain eye contact. "You're positive that everything is okay?" When Alex didn't speak, she leaned toward her and said, "I've worked with battered women before. If you'd feel more comfortable going to a shelter..."

"I told you what happened, Detective," Alex snapped, unsure she'd be able to handle the rest of her sentence. She knew she didn't qualify for such a place, but she wished there was somewhere women like her *could* go. "I don't know what else I can tell you. What do you *want* me to say?"

Detective Lang clapped her hands together and stood up. "Alright then. I'm sorry to waste your time. If you remember anything else you feel we should know, don't hesitate to call."

"I want his ashes," she told Detective Lang before the woman reached the front door.

The detective turned toward her, confusion flitting across her face before it gave way to sadness and pity. "That's a…strange request, Alex. I don't think…"

"He had no family left. His mother is in prison, and the rest are dead. I want to bury him."

"I don't think—"

"You said you wanted to help. This is what you could do for me."

Detective Lang wanted to argue. Alex could see it in every ounce of her posture so Alex kept her gaze on hers until at last the woman said, "I'll see what I can do."

"Thank you," Alex said.

Detective Lang offered a small smile and left.

The door closed, and Alex wondered about that smile and what it really meant. She didn't have the strength to pull herself out of the armchair so she pulled out her phone, filling her time by Googling urns and cemeteries, and learning all she could about the best way to bury someone.

Peter surprised her a few hours later when he emerged from their room. She'd been so certain he'd gone out that she startled when he leaned over her shoulder and said, "What are you working on?"

He was too close for her to hide her search results, so she held her breath as he scanned the words. His sharp exhale told her exactly how he felt, but he didn't voice it. Instead, he went back to the room and slammed the door.

Detective Lang called back a few hours later. Alex was so lost in her research she almost declined it. "I'm afraid he's already been cremated," she said.

Alex made a choked noise in her throat. "How could this be?"

"Apparently someone made a claim on the body. Said he was Jamie's brother. He had him cremated and the ashes sent to him. I don't know more than that."

Jamie didn't have a brother. She racked her brain, trying to come up with a solution when she realized who it could've been. "Was the brother's name, Damien?"

"I believe so, yes."

"Thank you, Detective." She hung up before the woman could say anything else.

With another glance down the hall toward the closed bedroom door, Alex bundled herself up in winter gear and slipped outside. With her hood up over her head and a scarf wrapped around the lower half of her face, she felt like she was putting on a disguise. The thrum of her blood so loud in her ears that it nearly blocked out everything else.

Reporters crowded the parking lot. Ever since the news had announced she had been found, that she was home, they had been there. Reporters were everywhere, it seemed. She tucked the scarf tighter and hurried past the herd, worried that one of them would recognize her and that would cause the entire gathering to focus on her.

Taking the car was too risky. She looked at it before quickly jogging across the parking lot and down the street. When she was sure she'd gotten away, she slowed to a walk. Walking didn't bother her. She didn't mind being alone with the wind blowing through her clothes, chilling her. The sensation of goosebumps was the closest she could come to feeling anything.

She took bus after bus, filling the four hours between Ponchatoula and Warren with the sounds of bus wheels on pavement and random chatter. Alex tried to take a nap to pass the time, but she kept thinking of what Detective Lang had said and found her brain imagining Jamie in a crematorium, every inch of him reduced to ash. She hated that after everything life had done to him, Jamie didn't have the chance at a proper funeral.

He's at peace now, she tried to tell herself as she stepped off the bus. Things started to look familiar, and that gave her the push to move a little faster.

Frozen, she walked on stiff legs, like a specter. She wasn't sure where she was going until she was already inside the building. Alex was so cold, she collapsed to her hands and knees, out of energy to proceed. Gasps rang around the restaurant, but only one person rushed to her side. He was thin with carefully combed brown hair. His face was plain, but his eyes stood out. They were the color of mud, the way he looked at her showing genuine concern.

His nametag told her he was who she was looking for. "Alex, are you okay?"

Her eyes welled with tears. She didn't need to ask him how he knew who she was. All that mattered was that he did. He was her last link to Jamie, and she wanted to hold onto that, to remember him with someone else who knew he wasn't a monster.

Chapter Forty-Six

WHEN DAMIEN WAS at last able to get Alex to her feet, he sat her down in a booth at the back of the restaurant and brought her a hot cup of coffee before he sat down across from her.

"What are you doing here?" he asked after taking a sip from his mug. "Did you walk here?"

"I-I—" She paused to hold in her tears. It would do no good to cry. Especially since everyone who had seen her enter was still staring at her. "I wanted to say goodbye to Jamie. I asked about burying him, and I was told you...had him cremated."

Damien bobbed his head and took a sip of his drink. "He told me that was what he wanted done if something happened to him."

Alex drew her eyebrows together. "Wait, he made...*plans* for when he died?"

Damien sat forward so that his elbows rested on the table. "He said *in case something happens.*"

"When did you two decide this?"

"A week ago, maybe," Damien said with a shrug. "He told me about his sister and what he wanted me to do if he died. His plot is in the same cemetery as hers."

Alex's eyes stung with betrayal. Jamie had made burial plans and hadn't bothered to tell her? She was hurt, but she couldn't say she was altogether surprised. He'd had regrets toward the end. That much had been clear.

Damien must've caught the expression because he said, "I don't think he knew he'd be using the plans so soon."

He had an idea, she thought and reached up to wipe her eyes.

"He told me about you, you know," Damien admitted.

Alex took a sip of her coffee, letting the hot liquid scald her throat to keep from crying.

"He promised me you were okay so I didn't step in. I took his word for it," he continued. "I'm…sorry."

Alex shook off the apology. "Can we…visit him?" she asked in a soft voice. One so quiet, she hardly heard herself.

"I guess." He slipped from the booth and looked back at Alex. "Give me a minute to clock out."

Alex sipped on her coffee as she waited for him to return.

When he came back, they went out back to the parking lot, and Damien's waiting car. On the outside, his car wasn't much to look at, a rusty gray little sedan, but the inside was modeled with care. The seats were soft and clean, and Alex sank into it, trying to take what comfort she could.

"I guess it's good you asked for this. I figured I'd need to drive you home anyway. You're lucky you didn't get hypothermia," Damien said.

Alex didn't answer. It seemed like in no time at all, the made it to the cemetery. Until then, it had been easy to distance herself from reality, but the cemetery made her face the certainty of Jamie's death.

When Damien parked, he stared at the steering wheel for a long minute before he said, "Want me to come with you?"

She shook her head. This was something she needed to do alone.

"Okay. I'll be waiting here when you're done."

She climbed out of the warmth of the car and tucked her scarf into place. It was soaked with tears that froze to her almost as soon as she pushed her way into the cemetery. The front line of graves consisted of tall lumbering tombstones, most of them cracked or broken in some way. This was a cemetery where people were buried and forgotten.

Alex started to walk forward, reading each name with purpose. Eventually, she found Jamie's grave—a mound of fresh dirt with a tiny rock on top to mark where he had been buried. She sat down, not caring about the cold seeping through her pants.

"Hi," she whispered, staring at the marker as if she expected it to grow lips and respond. She breathed out, wiping away the tears that were freezing beneath her eyes. "I don't know if you can hear me or not, but I had to come see you. It didn't seem right not to after everything."

A pause.

"I miss you, Jamie. Why did you do it? Why didn't you listen?"

She broke down, her sobs echoing around the cemetery. Through her bleary eyes, she stared at the rock, knowing exactly why he had done it. He was selfless, brave. He would've done anything to make her happy.

"It's my fault you're gone."

The silence was deafening in that it echoed her thoughts back at her, and they were anything but kind. Alex didn't know how long she sat there, sobbing, but by the time her tears ran out, her face was raw with the effort. Crescent-moon shaped wounds lined her palms from the places where her nails had cut into the skin. She was so cold, she didn't notice the pain.

If I sit here long enough, will I freeze? she wondered and imagined it would be a peaceful death, to slip into sleep beside Jamie's resting place and never wake up again.

"You'll catch your death out here," Damien's voice said softly from behind her.

She jumped. "How long have you been there?"

"Not long."

She let her eyes drop to the stone again. "He doesn't have a tombstone."

"I know," Damien said. "I'm working on getting one made." He helped her to her feet and said, "Come on."

She didn't argue as he led her back to the car. The warmth blasting through the vent perked her up a bit.

"So, what's the best way to begin this drive?" Damien asked, cranking up the heat. His fingers paused above the GPS, waiting for her address.

Alex wasn't interested in going home. She didn't want to go back to that tiny place with its bland walls and the toxic atmosphere of Peter's unpredictability.

"Can we…can we stop by Jamie's first?" she asked.

Damien drew his eyebrows together. "Why?"

"Chloe…my cat. She's still there. Plus, there's some things I'd like to get. To…remember Jamie by."

"Of course," Damien said, looking almost touched she would make a request.

When they pulled up the winding dirt road that led to Jamie's house, a tiny surge of nostalgia welled in her before being crushed by sorrow. This was the last time she'd ever travel this path. The last time she'd ever see Jamie's house.

Somehow, she held off the tears. Like at the cemetery, Damien volunteered to stay in the car, and she was grateful. There was caution tape over the door, the remains of a thorough crime scene investigation, but she tore it away and went inside.

As soon as the lights went on, Chloe skittered out from under the couch. Eyes wide and mews small, she looked so much more delicate and fragile than Alex remembered. It had been two days since Alex had been here, and she'd guessed no one had bothered to feed the cat.

"I'm so sorry, baby," Alex told her and plopped some food into a bowl.

Chloe went to work devouring the offering while Alex went into the bedroom. There were faint traces of Jamie's scent in the air, and that was what drove Alex to curl up in their bed one more time. She stayed like that for a few minutes, and when she opened her sticky eyes, they landed on the photograph perched on the edge of the dresser. The framed photo of her and Jamie.

Alex scooped it into her arms and looked at her pile of papers beside it. She started to gather it in one pile. She wanted everything. To Hell with the investigation. Desperately, she looked around and found an old backpack of Jamie's in the closet. It would be one more small thing she could use to hold onto him.

She stuffed the papers and her notebook into the bag before tucking the photo into a protective pocket. Confident she had everything, she sealed it and tossed the bag over her shoulder. She walked slowly down the hallway to the front room, that same sensation she'd felt on the road filling her again.

Chloe padded up to her, licking her lips from her meal. Alex grabbed her and opened the front door. She paused, glancing back over her shoulder to whisper "Goodbye, Jamie," before she went out, letting the door clatter shut behind her.

Chapter Forty-Seven

THE DRIVE HOME with Damien brought Alex a tiny sense of peace. She held onto that to keep herself from thinking of what the end of the drive would mean. Chloe struggled in her lap, and she held tight to the cat, petting the tiny thing between the ears until she calmed.

In Ponchatoula, Damien pulled the car to a halt by the curb to keep out of sight of the reporters. "I guess this is where we part ways."

"I guess so."

Damien offered her a soft smile and reached out to pull her into a hug, careful of the bundle of black fur in her lap. "Take care of yourself, okay?"

"You too," she said and broke contact.

She pushed opened the door and stepped out into the cold, wrapping Chloe in the end of the scarf to keep her warm. Damien gave her one more smile through the window and pulled away. Alex waved and watched him go before she trotted up the stairs and into the apartment. When the door closed behind her, she was glad for the silence. Then she turned and realized Peter was standing at the end of the hall, hands on his hips.

"Where the hell have you been?" he demanded. "I thought something happened." His eyes fell to the cat in her hands. Chloe, terrified of the change in scene, fought her way free and scampered for her favorite hiding place—under the couch. "What the hell is this about?"

"Her name is Chloe," Alex said, carefully setting down Jamie's bag before she went to work stripping off her coat and gloves.

Peter held his hands out to either side of him. "So you disappear *all* day and show up again with a cat and expect me not to ask questions?" His eyes went to the bag next. "What is that?"

"It's not really your business," Alex said, kicking off her boots.

"Fine, don't tell me. I'll look through it and see for myself."

"You need to know? Okay," Alex said, balling her hands into fists, angry at the invasion. "I went back to Jamie's and got my things, okay?"

"What?" he asked, nearly breathless as if her words had been a physical hit to the gut.

"I got my *things*. I wanted to say my goodbyes."

"You traveled *alone* to a place four hours away to say goodbye to the man who *kidnapped* you?"

"Yep," Alex said, storming past him. She plopped down on the couch, fingers like icicles. She rubbed her hands together for warmth, thinking about making a cup of tea.

"Alex," Peter said, voice a mix of emotions as he followed her across the room. "You can't...*run off* like that."

"What does it matter? You never cared before."

"I was worried about you," he said, plopping onto the couch beside her. He tried to take one of her hands in his before she dodged the attempt.

She laughed. "I'm sure."

Peter scowled, but before he could needle her with more remarks, the landline hanging on the kitchen wall started to ring. At first, she wasn't sure what the sound was. It had been a long time since someone had called that phone, and she hadn't been sure it was still connected, but she hopped to her feet, wandering into the kitchen to stare at it as if it were a bomb that was about to explode. It didn't have caller ID so picking it up was a risk.

Desperate to stop the thoughts, she picked up the phone. "Hello?"

"Miss Alpine! It's so nice to hear your voice. Mind if I bend your ear for a moment?" a smooth voice said on the other end of the line.

Her instant reaction was to slam the phone down and revert into her shell, but she hesitated. That was what the *old* her would've done, but she didn't want to be that girl anymore. The one boxed in by her traumas, the one who had given up on her life before it had barely begun.

"Yes, this is she. Who am I talking to?" she said, hoping she sounded strong, like a proper adult.

"My name is Eileen Wurniki at the Everlast Tribune," she said. "I was hoping you'd be interested in the possibility of an interview."

Alex said nothing at first, staring down at the faint light coming in through the window above the kitchen. With Zack's discovery, her case was still technically open. The police probably wouldn't be keen about vital information in the case being leaked, but Jamie was dead.

In Alex's opinion, there *was* no case. Every fiber of her being rioted against the idea of having such attention drawn to herself, but this could be her chance to defend Jamie's honor.

He would've done it for her.

Resolved, Alex clutched the phone tight to the side of her face. "I would love to."

Chapter Forty-Eight

ITH THE INTERVIEW scheduled for later in the week, Alex felt a little better about herself. It didn't matter that Peter didn't understand her. She had the chance to potentially make others see what he could not. Alex had been braced for a fight when she told Peter about the opportunity, but he seemed oddly supportive.

The rest of the day, Alex avoided Peter and used her time to plan out the best things to say in the interview. The way to paint Jamie in the best possible light. She wasn't a fool. She knew what the purpose of the interview was—to try and demonize him.

The day after Eileen called, Katherine was supposed to bring Katrina back home. Anxiety nearly overcame Alex as she waited for them to arrive. It was a welcome distraction. The only glimpse she'd had of her daughter had been when she'd woken up in the hospital, and she'd held onto that interaction to keep her going. Alex missed her so much she ached for one normal day with her. Knocking sounded at the door around noon, and Alex hurried to answer it.

"Mommy!" Katrina said at once, rushing across the threshold to wrap her arms around Alex's waist.

"Hi, baby," Alex said, tears in her eyes as she dropped to Katrina's level to pull her into a real hug.

The sweet smell of the chocolate she'd eaten lingered on her breath, and Alex hugged her a little bit tighter. When they broke apart, Alex stood up, and Katrina went into the apartment, calling for Peter.

Katherine smiled as she watched her go then turned her attention to Alex, arms held out for a hug. Alex gave into the gesture, but she wasn't sure what to think. Before everything, they had never been close. They'd been civil the few times they'd talked but had never become anything more than acquaintances.

"I'm so glad you're okay," Katherine said when they broke apart. "You being gone was so hard on her. She barely ate, wouldn't play. It was like she was gone."

A stab of guilt erupted in Alex's stomach when she remembered that last day with Jamie. How she'd told him to leave her daughter alone. How she'd been prepared to stay there with him and never see a hint of her old life again, Katrina included.

Katrina trotted back into the room with a handful of toys, and Alex forced a bitter smile on her face. "I'm glad someone missed me at least," she said. She hadn't expected a warm homecoming, and she hadn't gotten one, but at least, her daughter cared. And that was all that mattered.

Katherine ducked her face to catch Alex's eye. "A lot of people did, Alex. Really."

Did Peter? Alex wanted to ask, but as she went to say the words, they lodged in her throat. What a stupid question. She didn't want to hear what Katherine would say. Peter's confession had been enough. He hadn't missed her. He'd spent his time in the arms of another woman.

"I know you're going through a lot right now, and you're probably tired of people suffocating you, but let me know if there's anything at all I can do to make things easier," Katherine said. "Even if it's just to be someone to vent to about my empty-headed brother, I'm here for you."

"Thank you," Alex said, grateful for the offer. Maybe it would be good to have someone she could talk to. Someone who wouldn't judge her.

A friend.

Alex shot it down, positive that whatever she told her would get back to Peter in some way, shape, or form.

Katherine smiled back and called her goodbyes.

Alex closed the door and turned to Katrina, threading her fingers together. "Want to watch *Frozen*?"

Katrina's face broke into a huge smile, and she clapped excitedly before pressing the buttons on the DVD player. By the time Alex sat down, Katrina had gotten the movie started. Alex rested her back against the couch, holding her daughter in her arms as they watched the movie. The scene was so much like the one from her dream in Jamie's house that it brought tears to her eyes. Her hand reached out to the empty spot beside her, reaching for him.

They would've made the perfect family. He'd been right about that.

Warm tears coursed down her cheeks, and Alex tried to bite back the sob that wanted to come free with them.

Katrina looked up at her through huge eyes. "Are you crying, Mommy?"

"Oh. Yeah," she said and smiled. "These are happy tears. I'm so happy to see you again, sweetheart."

"I missed you," she said, resting her head on Alex's shoulder. "Please don't leave again, Mommy."

"Never again, baby," Alex said and held her tight.

For as warm as the moment made her feel, silent tears continued to soak her face for most of the film. As the movie neared its end, Chloe's fuzzy face peeked out from under the couch, green eyes wide as she sniffed Katrina's foot.

Katrina gasped and sat up, clapping excitedly. "A kitty!"

Alex smiled and reached for Chloe, picking up the small animal to hand to Katrina. "Her name is Chloe."

Chloe mewled softly as Katrina took her, hugging her to her chest. "She's so soft."

"She's a baby, like you," Alex said, scratching Chloe between the eyes until the cat began to relax.

As soon as Katrina let go of Chloe, she cuddled into Katrina's lap, purring. She looked so sweet, so at ease, that Alex felt the smallest pang in her gut. The tiny ball of fluff in the middle of her apartment was the ultimate clash between her life with Peter and the one with Jamie. Chloe was right at home, and Alex envied her that. She wished she had a place where she felt she belonged. Somewhere that brought her a sense of peace.

She'd had that with Jamie.

Chapter Forty-Nine

O N THE DAY of the interview, Peter was more excited about it than Alex was, and for some reason, that annoyed her. This wasn't about him. Not at all, yet he wanted to hold his head high and walk her through the building, holding her hand as if any part of them had been a normal functioning couple for the past few years.

Before they made it to the interview room, Alex ripped her hand from his and walked ahead of him. Independent. Strong. All the things Jamie had believed she was.

Peter was about to ask something when they were intercepted by a woman. She was tall, much taller than Alex was. She had to crane her head back to look into her face. "Miss Alpine, it's good to see you," she said, extending her hand. "My name is Eileen."

Alex returned the handshake, appreciating the woman's professionalism. Most of the people they'd passed had given Alex their own sympathetic looks, but Eileen didn't do that. They were equals.

"Have you ever done anything like this before?" she asked.

"Like an interview or be on TV?" Alex questioned, wincing at her own stupidity.

Eileen laughed, a short musical sound. "Both, I suppose."

"No, I haven't," she said. The decision to do this had

been easy until then. Until she realized she had no idea exactly *what* she was doing.

Eileen gave a reassuring smile that lifted Alex back up. "It's okay. It's real easy. You're gonna sit here, and we're gonna have a conversation. That's all there is to it. After a while, you'll forget the cameras are there."

Alex doubted that, but she would trust her word.

They sat in padded chairs, each of them with a bottle of water on the ridiculously tiny end tables beside them.

The man behind the camera counted down from five, and Eileen began, "Hi, and welcome back. Today, we have an important segment. I'm here with Alex Alpine, America's beloved missing woman. Now tell me, Alex, how are you feeling today?"

Alex took in a breath, unsure how to begin. "I'm good. But I have to say before we get into this, I'm not here to drag Jamie's name through the mud. The news has done a good enough job of that."

"For the record, Jamie is the man charged with kidnapping you, correct?"

Internally, Alex groaned, but on the outside, she made sure she stayed strong. "Yes, but there was so much more to him than that."

"But you can't deny the truth. He kidnapped you. Kept you from your family. There are some reports that say he kept a shock collar on you."

Alex closed her eyes and willed herself not to cry. *Not here, not now.* When she opened them again, she tried to be the newest version of herself. She could do this. And she *would* do this.

She pretended Jamie was sitting in a chair beside her. He'd have his chin propped on his elbow, watching her with stars in his eyes as she worked up an answer. He'd have faith in her, so why couldn't she have any in herself?

"Yes, that is the truth, but a lot of what happened won't be reported because everyone wants to hear stories about monsters. But no one wants to believe that those monsters are people with stories of their own. I know what people think of Jamie, but it's not the truth. Not all of it anyway. He was a good person, but one who faced so much pain he wasn't bound by the same moral guidelines as the rest of us. What he did to me seems wrong, but he had his reasons, good reasons."

"Good reasons?" Eileen asked, drawn-on eyebrows raising dramatically. "What could those be?"

Alex's upper lip twitched with the desire to spill her guts, to scream about how much she loved Jamie until she went red in the face. Instead, she forced herself to stay calm. "I wrote a book about him. Who he was beneath everything he did. You might not believe me, but I didn't see him as anything less than the beautiful person he was. He cared about people. Before him, I was a shell of myself, but he taught me that I have value even when everyone else in the world has given up on me. Yes, he did some things wrong, but don't we all? Who's going to sit here and say that they're perfect? I know I'm not," she said and held up her wrist.

Eileen's eyes were wide as she looked at the scars. They

were red and bright, vibrant in the fluorescent lights almost as if they were fresh again, weeping blood all over the stage. "Where did those come from?"

"I know what you're thinking, that Jamie did it, but the truth is, I did it to myself. Jamie stopped me from making it any worse." She pointed to the wounds, the ones that would've been fatal without Jamie's help. "This should've killed me, but Jamie saved my life."

Eileen looked genuinely impressed as she said, "None of the news stories have mentioned that."

"That goes to prove my point," Alex said and dropped her arms back to her lap. "They want him branded as a monster. They don't want to hear that human nature isn't black and white."

"This is very moving of you to say, but what is your opinion on the man they found buried in Jamie's backyard? The man he's said to have murdered?"

Alex's face went dark as she stared at Eileen. *I killed him for us,* Jamie had said. "I can't speak on that."

Eileen shuffled in her seat looking slightly unsettled at Alex's choice of words. Alex closed her eyes, waiting for a follow-up question. "Now you say you've written a book about your experience?"

Alex let out a breath. "Not just *my* experience, but about Jamie, and why he felt the need to do what he did. I want everyone in the world to look past the label the media has given him to see the person underneath."

"Compelling words," Eileen said, raising her perfect

eyebrows. "Where can interested readers get their hands on your work?"

Alex frowned down at the floor. "I…it's not published."

"Well, considering your circumstances, I'm sure it won't be hard to find it the right home."

Chapter Fifty

L EAVING THE STUDIO and climbing into the car, Alex knew she was in for a bad rest of the day. Peter was icy. Alex had expected that and was almost glad for the change in attitude. The excitement he'd harbored on her behalf hadn't made sense. This felt more like the version of him that Alex was used to.

Alex would've ridden the entire way home at ease with the silence. Tension from the interview sat at the base of her neck, and she wondered how long it would be until it went away.

"You keep defending him," Peter said after a long stretch of silence. It was the first thing he'd said since the interview.

Alex glanced at him, looked at the way his fingers were tightly wrapped around the steering wheel, and disengaged from the situation. If she answered him, he would get angrier, and she didn't want to fight. She wanted to get home.

"Why?" Peter prodded. "Why did you go on television in front of the entire country and defend the man who did this to you? To us?"

Alex stared out the window, vowing to keep her silence. She thought of Katrina waiting for her at home.

Peter must've sensed she wouldn't answer because he took a sharp turn to the left, the speed in the car rising. The brakes squealed and someone honked. Alex gripped the door, her stomach shifting uncomfortably as her entire body rocketed sideways.

"Peter, slow down," she said.

He blew through a red light, nearly avoiding being struck by a blue SUV. "And you're going to write a book about him?" he continued, as if she hadn't spoken, as if they hadn't escaped death by mere seconds.

Another hard turn around a corner that nearly led into a head on collision. The other car stopped in the brink of time, laying on the horn. Peter continued to swerve across two lanes of traffic as if he hadn't heard them.

Alex didn't know quite where they were, but she was ready to take her shot walking home. "Stop the car now!" she hollered.

"How can you do this to me? Do I mean nothing to you?"

"You're crazy!"

Peter laughed, loud and long. "*I'm* crazy?"

"Yes!" Alex spat, tensing as Peter approached another intersection. Thankfully, the light was green. "He never treated me like this! I know now that *this* isn't love. Maybe it never was."

The car started to slow, and Alex risked a glance outside, realizing that he had turned into the parking lot of the apartment complex, the car coming to a halt.

Alex's entire body shook with relief, and she exhaled. "We're over," she said, in a surprisingly calm voice for how much her entire body still shook with adrenaline.

"You're not…*you* anymore," he said, shaking his head as if he were disappointed in her as if he hadn't nearly killed them both. "You're like a ghost of the woman I married."

"I could say the same about you," Alex snapped. "The last day you were the Peter I loved was the day we said *I do.*"

He flinched, his face only momentarily reflecting any sort of emotion before it cleared, and he climbed out of the car, slamming the door behind him.

Alex let him leave and go up the stairs. She stayed in the passenger seat, feeling her heart pound, and trying to get her breathing under control. Rather than focus on how she'd narrowly avoided death, her mind returned to the interview, on the last words out of Eileen's mouth. *It won't be hard to find it the right home.*

The book. Her story. It would be her ticket out of this life.

Her notoriety would no doubt cause publishers and agents to jump over themselves to sign the rights. All she had to do was keep the public reminded of her and Jamie in the meantime and settle only for the highest bid.

Alex worked up the nerve to leave the car and push her way through the reporters to go into the apartment. Katherine sat with Katrina on the living room floor, doll clutched in her hand. She looked at Alex with a smile and stood to grasp her hand gently. "You did great, Alex. I know that couldn't have been easy for you."

"Thank you," Alex said, surprised by her warmth. She didn't want to be rude, but the feeling of Katherine's hand in hers stirred something unsettling. She pulled her hand away as Peter scoffed and crossed to the kitchen.

"You shouldn't encourage her," he called.

Katherine frowned. "What's wrong with him?"

Alex looked at the wall, thinking of the chaotic drive home as she said, "It's hard to explain."

Katherine pursed her lips. "I think I can understand to a point." She looked over her shoulder to see where her brother had gone before she added, "All I can offer is that it's going to be okay. It'll take time for things to get back to normal, but they'll get better. I know Peter can be dumb, but you have to think about this from his point of view. It probably wasn't easy to hear you talk about another man like that. Especially one who did what *he* did to you."

"I know," Alex said, but she didn't. Not really. All she could think of was how long it'd taken Peter to report her missing. How little he had cared about her before she'd become a national tragedy.

Katherine squeezed her shoulder in passing and called goodbye to Peter before she left. Katrina trotted down the hall to her room, and a moment later came the sound of a toy box dumping out.

Peter wandered out of the kitchen, bottle of beer in his hand. "I think we should consider the possibility of therapy."

Alex plopped down on the couch, watching the car commercial playing on the television. "Couples therapy? No. I meant what I said. We're over."

"I don't think you should be so hasty."

"I'm not," Alex said, glaring at him from the side of her eye. She'd never been more certain of anything.

"Look," Peter said. "You've been through a lot. You need to consider talking to a professional before you up and destroy your life."

"No. I don't need therapy. I need to be left alone."

An exasperated blast of air came out of him as he sat beside her. "I know you don't think so, but it could help to talk to someone who knows what they're talking about. Maybe they could...I don't know, help you remember that you don't hate me."

But I do. She frowned, annoyed for his sudden interest.

Things were easier to keep in perspective when he was distant and cold. That was what she had come to know from him, to expect. Anything else confused her. "I don't love you anymore. That drive reminded me of that."

"And that was...unfair of me. This has been hard, Alex. Hell, you're saying you loved the man who took you away from me and your daughter."

Alex said nothing.

"I think the problem isn't that you loved him. The problem is that you haven't processed what's happened. I think he got in your head, and it's gonna take time for you to remember who you are. You were gone for months. Whatever he told you, whatever he did, that's not something you can get over in a week," Peter said. "And it wasn't right of me to think you would."

Alex continued to stare at the television, and Peter took a swig of beer before he reached out and grabbed her knee. Alex glared at his hand and made a show of removing it.

He left the room. Alex stared at the place he'd touched. That was the most warmth he'd had toward her in a long time. *Too little, too late.* Alex ran her finger over her ring finger, suddenly feeling the absence of her band.

In the early days of their marriage, they had been the perfect team. She didn't know what had happened to change them, but part of her missed the easy relationship they'd once shared. When things changed between them, it had been like losing her best friend and soul mate at the same time.

Now it felt like living with a stranger.

Alex wanted to hold onto her hate, her anger, but it wouldn't stay forever. Jamie was gone, and all the wishing in the world wouldn't bring him back. Alex thought of Chloe, how at ease the cat was. If Alex ever truly wanted to feel that kind of peace, she would have to accept that she couldn't go back. All she could do was try to pick up the pieces of her life and move on.

Jamie would've wanted that for her.

She looked to her arm again, at the ugly wounds that were still purple against her porcelain skin. She'd been in the dark for so long she believed she belonged in it. Jamie had been the first person to show her that she could live a life in the warmth of the light, that she could be happy again. That she deserved it.

Alex curled her fingers into a fist, watching the muscles flex under the scars. Maybe therapy could help her after all.

She had always been the type to admit when she was wrong, but going down the hall to tell Peter her decision was probably one of the hardest things she'd ever had to do. By the time she went inside the room, he was asleep. Alex crept toward the bed, studying him for the longest time. She could still remember when his name had been enough to make her giggle and blush. She used to think he was attractive, but she no longer saw it. When she looked at him, she saw ugly memories instead.

Alex closed the door and went back to the living room, sitting in silence. When Peter woke up, she was still in the living room, watching the news, counting how many times she was mentioned an hour. Before he could say a word, she said, "I will agree to go to therapy."

"That's great I—" Peter started to say.

Alex held up a hand to stop him. "I will go, but I'm not doing it for you or for us. I meant what I said. I will go to learn how to deal with what's happened so I can live again. For Katrina."

Chapter Fifty-One

THE NEXT DAY, when Alex found herself sitting in her scheduled therapy session, she wasn't so sure of her choice. She'd assumed it would be hard to find someone who would see her, and she could use that as an excuse to back out of the idea completely, but the interview had left her a public figure. The first office she called was overjoyed for the privilege and scheduled her for as soon as they could.

The office was clinical, the walls seeming to close in on her as she sat there. All she wanted to do was spring from the seat and run far, far away. Dr. Harmon was a nice woman in her fifties. Her long cinnamon colored hair tumbled over her shoulders, highlighting the angles of her pale face. She sat patiently in her chair, hands folded in her lap as she waited for Alex to speak. To share anything about herself.

Alex had no idea where to begin. Hesitantly, she said, "Thank you for agreeing to see me so soon. You...probably know what my issues are from the news."

Dr. Harmon bobbed her head. "I think it'll be quite tough for you to find someone who hasn't heard your story, truth be told."

Alex looked down at her hands. "What's on the news, that's not my story. Not even a little bit."

"Is that what's brought you here to see me today?"

"Sort of," Alex said and crinkled her nose. "It's ...I don't know who I am anymore. I'm home with my family, and

I know that should mean I'm happy and safe, but I'm not. I feel like a stranger in someone else's home. I miss Jamie."

"The man who kidnapped you?"

"Yes, and before you say anything, I already know how messed up it is. Everyone says so, but he...understood me in a way that no one ever has."

"Not even your husband?"

"Not even Peter," Alex echoed. "Jamie was patient, kind. He had his flaws, of course, but for the first time in my life, it felt as if I had someone who really saw me."

"Sounds to me as if your life before that left you feeling unfulfilled."

That was an understatement. "It did, but I love my family. My daughter at least."

"How do you feel about your husband?"

"I love him?" Alex said.

"That's not a statement you should be unsure of," Dr. Harmon said, frowning. "I think you're telling me what you think I want to hear rather than what you actually feel."

Alex looked down at her hands again. She had a habit of that, of saying what other people wanted to hear to end the conversation quicker. She should've known such tactics wouldn't work with someone like this, someone trained to sniff out defense mechanisms.

"I loved him a long time ago," she admitted. "Now? Knowing what he did to Jamie? I don't think I can get over it...that I can go back to living the way I used to. Before Jamie, I used to overlook all Peter's cruelties because I thought that was what love was all about. But now I know, love isn't cruel at all."

Dr. Harmon sat forward in her seat. "People drift apart all the time. Especially when you fall in love at a young age. How old were you when you met Peter?"

"I was in middle school."

"You were kids," Dr. Harmon said.

"And he was my rock for a long time." *As far as I'm concerned, he fulfilled his role in your life,* Jamie had said. It was true, wasn't it? Deep down, Alex had known that for some time, but it never truly processed until then.

"Ending relationships can be difficult," Dr. Harmon said. "But sometimes, it's more painful to hold on to something you know isn't working."

AT THE END of the session, Dr. Harmon told Alex to come back in a week, but she already knew she wouldn't. She'd put too much of herself on display and felt vulnerable. To make matters worse, Peter waited for her in the lobby. He jumped out of his seat as soon as Alex stepped out of Dr. Harmon's office. She'd wanted to come by herself, but he had insisted on tagging along.

Dr. Harmon's words bounced around her head again, *People drift apart all the time. Especially when you fall in love at a young age.*

It was hard to deny that that was exactly what had happened. They had both found comfort in the arms of other people, and pretending they hadn't was foolish. Not only for them, but for Katrina too. She was getting older, and Alex didn't know how much she knew, how much she understood, but she didn't want her to grow up in a dysfunctional home. Alex had barely survived the one she'd come from. Raising another version of herself, flaws and all, made her sick.

Peter didn't sense her need to be left alone. He caught her eye and asked, "How did it go?"

Alex looked away, leading the way out of the office as she tried to decide the best way of telling him everything Dr. Harmon had said. It should be easy to say the words, but it wasn't.

"Alex, talk to me," Peter said, grasping her arm to turn her toward him.

She stared into his eyes, the brown depths that had once been filled with such warmth. The session had done nothing for her except cement the idea that her decision was for the best. She would live the rest of her life missing Jamie. It probably wouldn't matter if she stayed with Peter or not. That ache would always be there. The pain of losing part of her very own soul.

"I can't be fixed," Alex whispered at last.

"What? Of course you can," Peter said, eyes searching hers.

"You don't understand."

"Did the doctor tell you this?" Peter asked, glaring over his shoulder at the building behind them as if he considered going back inside to make a scene.

"No," Alex said, steeling herself for the next words out of her mouth. "It's what I'm saying. I loved Jamie, and time isn't going to make that go away. Call it Stockholm Syndrome, call it whatever you want, but he changed something in me. I'm not the woman I was before him, and I never will be again. I want to be *free,* Peter."

"What are you saying exactly?" he demanded, nostrils flaring with an oncoming surge of anger.

"I'm saying, I think once the media storm dies down, it might be best for us to go our separate ways."

Peter opened his mouth as if he wanted to say something, but his face fell, and he turned away. Alex was glad. She didn't need to hear anything else he had to say. For the moment, she was blissfully numb, but she didn't know how long that would hold up. As soon as it wore off, she'd be vulnerable to any and every emotion. She hoped to be far away from Peter when her mask fell so he couldn't manipulate her, but she had nowhere to go outside of the apartment.

Alex made sure to drive home, keeping silent the entire way. Back at the apartment, Peter was the first inside, rushing down the hallway without saying anything to his sister on the way before he slammed the door behind him.

Katrina watched with furrowed brows. "What's wrong with Daddy?"

Katherine looked at Alex, the same question in her eyes.

"The therapy session didn't go well today," Alex said at last. "We...we have some things we're going to have to figure out. I...is there any way you can watch her for a little while, please? I think me and Peter need to have a talk."

"Of course," Katherine said, holding her hand out to Katrina. "Come on, sweetheart. You wanna go to the park?"

Katrina's bottom lip jutted out into a pout as she looked at Alex. "I want Mommy to come."

Alex stared into her wide innocent eyes, and almost changed her mind. Going to the park with her daughter sounded like a much more fun way to spend the afternoon.

Katherine must've sensed it because she said, "You'll see Mommy later, okay?"

Alex gave Kathrine a grateful nod then looked at her daughter. "Have some fun with your auntie, okay?"

"Okay," Katrina said, mood instantly bright as she gave Alex a hug and followed Katherine out the door.

As soon as the door closed, Alex sank to the couch, letting the swarm of emotions she'd kept at bay sink into her. Somehow, she didn't cry. She stared up at the ceiling, wondering where Jamie was and if he was watching over her. Chloe jumped onto her lap, and Alex looked down into her bright eyes. She petted the cat before she wrapped her arms around it, squeezing her tight. This cat had been a gift from Jamie. One she would cherish more now than when he had initially given it to her. Chloe purred in response, and Alex focused on the happy sound. The idea that there were other people who could love her. Other people who did.

The phone in the kitchen rang, but Alex waited it out, the chirping fading into silence before it started to ring again. Dread sat in her stomach as she looked over the back of the couch, into the kitchen. It rang and rang, and she had the feeling that whoever was on the other end of the line wasn't going to stop until she answered it.

She picked up Chloe and set her back on the couch before she wandered into the kitchen, staring at the device on the wall. With shaking fingers, she scooped up the receiver. "Hello?"

"Can I speak to Miss Alex Alpine please?" a smooth male voice asked.

Alex paused, trying to figure out if she recognized the voice. "Th-this is her."

"My name is Timothy Norris, and I work at Five in One Publishing. I saw your interview, and I wanted to reach out to give my condolences."

"Th-thank you," she whispered, taken aback. No one had given her condolences for her loss besides Damien. Everyone else assumed she was happy, happy to spend every day thinking that it was her fault that the only one who truly made her feel alive was dead because of her.

"You're very welcome," he said. "If you're interested in the possibility of publishing your work, I'd like you to keep my company in mind. We'd love to have you, and we make sure our authors are very involved every step of the way."

Alex took in a breath, unsure what to say. The chance to tell the world her story? To tell the world *Jamie's* story like he had hoped she would do? This couldn't be happening, could it?

"Think about it," he encouraged after a full minute of silence. "No pressure if you're not interested. If you have any questions or concerns, please feel free to call me back at this number."

"O-okay," Alex said. "I will think about it. Thank you."

Alex hung up before she could force out on an awkward goodbye. She buzzed with energy, and all the negativity of the morning was gone. She'd wanted to use the day to start dividing her belongings from Peter's, but the phone call motivated her to put her effort elsewhere.

She grabbed Jamie's bag and sat on the couch, pulling out armfuls of paper. Chloe eyed her as he went to work spreading them out across the couch and floor. The papers parted to reveal the picture of her and Jamie that she had carefully wrapped, and her eyes went glassy. She picked it up and held it to her chest. One tear dripped on the paper beside her, and she wiped it away, leaving a wet smear across her words.

Jamie had helped her once by making her remember who she was. By giving her value and faith in herself. Now he would help her again by giving her the tools she needed to build the foundation of her new life.

Chapter Fifty-Two

ALEX LEAFED THROUGH the pages of her completed book. Delving into the memories of her and Jamie gave her warmth that made it easier to cope with the landslide of her life. It passed the time when Katrina was at Pre-K and Peter was at work.

In the time that she'd been at Jamie's, Peter had had to get a job to pay the bills and deal with the loss of Alex's income. He spent a large amount of time outside the apartment that she doubted was *all* due to his job. Whatever the case, Alex was glad.

Days passed in an uncertain blur. Damien called to check in on her once, and the reminiscing between the two of them had been the highlight of her week. Other than that, she had no sense of time.

Before she knew it, a week had gone by, and it was the day she was scheduled to see Dr. Harmon again. When Peter came home exhausted and dull-eyed, Alex didn't look at him from her place on the couch. She'd hidden away her papers when she heard him clomping up the stairs and waited for him to go on his way to pull them out again.

She didn't know why she felt the need to hide the book from him, especially since he knew she was working on one, but she didn't want him to see it. She feared that if he did, he would destroy it out of spite. Alex tried to keep her face passive, but she could feel his eyes on her, and she turned up the volume on the television, knowing a fight was incoming

"Did you make it to your appointment today?" Peter asked, laying his jacket on the couch beside her.

Alex turned into a statue.

"Alex, you can't shut me out like this," Peter said. "Damn it, you don't have to love me anymore, but you still have to be civil. For God's sake, we have a child together."

Irritated, she said, "No. I didn't go. Happy?"

Peter reached both hands up to rake his fingers through his hair before he let them drop to his side and stared at her. "Why, Alex? *Why*? Dr. Harmon was helping you."

"She did help, but...I don't see what else she can do. What happens next is up to me."

Peter twitched his lip as he waited for her to say something else. When she stayed silent, he said, "You want to get a divorce, and you don't think there's anything else she can do?" He bent toward her. "What happened to you sucks, but you shouldn't destroy your entire life because of it."

Alex lifted her chin to look at him. To make sure *he* looked at her and really *saw* her. "I'm not destroying anything. I'm making a better life for me and our daughter." Alex returned her attention to the television. "I spent a lot of time, a lot of years, hating myself. Thinking that I was utterly weak and useless. But Jamie didn't see that. He saw potential, and he did what he could to bring me up, not down. Jamie fixed me, and I'm not sorry that you don't like this version of myself because I do."

Peter let out a low chuckle that built into a loud bellow echoing around the tiny apartment. "You're insane, don't you see that? Don't you see how much you've *changed*?"

"As if you haven't," Alex said patiently. "Here you are saying that I'm the one who needs therapy, but you have no remorse for what you've done. No care in the world about what kind of effect your actions had on your daughter, on *me*, so stop believing there's anything left to fix."

"Is that what this is about? You're mad at me for killing him? This is your way of getting back at me?"

"Not everything is a conspiracy against you."

"Well, I'm not sorry for protecting our family, Alex," Peter said. "I'm just sorry I didn't protect you sooner."

He stormed out of the room, the bedroom door slamming a minute later. Alex let out a long breath and let herself fall against the couch, staring up at the ceiling. Her eyes burned with the desire to bawl, and she hated that about herself. Hated that she had the desire to *cry* every time she got frustrated.

Chloe wiggled out of her hiding place and rubbed on Alex's leg. She jumped at the contact, relaxing when she looked down at the tiny ball of fluff. Chloe looked back up at her through shining eyes.

"Am I in the wrong, Chloe?" she asked, stroking the cat down its back.

Chloe mewled and nestled against Alex's stomach, settling on her lap.

"Yeah, I didn't think so either."

Chapter Fifty-Three

ALEX DIDN'T TELL Peter about Timothy or his offer. Or the fact she'd taken him up on it. As the next few weeks went by, things with Peter were tense—a standoff to see who would move out first. With no income, Alex couldn't go anywhere, and Peter seemed unwilling to.

During that time, the truth of who Zack was came out. Detective Lang dropped by to let Alex know that the case was officially closed and to wish her good luck with her book. It was funny how much more supportive strangers were to her than her own husband. She used that anger as motivation to work harder.

When the day of her book launch arrived, she didn't tell Peter where she was going. She kissed her still sleeping daughter on the forehead and slipped out of the apartment. The gaggle of reporters that had hung out in the complex when she'd first arrived home had thinned considerably to only a few stubborn vultures.

One called to her, but she ignored them, walking faster to get away. She met up with Timothy outside the town bookstore. He was a stout man in his fifties with tiny glasses perched on the bridge of his nose and a comb-over. He beamed at her, pride on his face that made him look a decade younger. Since that first call, he had flown out exactly twice to see her— this being the second of those times, the first had been to meet her and sign her contract.

"Big day," he said, placing a copy of her book in her hands.

It was the first time she'd seen it in print. It was different than she imagined from the proof Timothy had sent her. Heavier. She stared at the cover, and that same bite of sadness was there, gnawing away at her. The cover was the picture of her and Jamie. She'd insisted. Nothing else felt appropriate.

"I'm excited," she said, looking up.

"Good, because you have a full day ahead of you," Timothy said and led her inside.

The bookstore was bigger on the inside than Alex had guessed it would be from the outside. A counter with the register sat to the left, the walkway going straight to the far wall. Shelves of books filled the building to the right. A table had been set up beneath the windows on the farthest wall. A banner with her picture and a cover of her book sat beside it. Stacks of books were piled on one half of the table, several pens sitting beside them. On reflex, Alex opened one and leafed through the pages, listening to the satisfying crack of the book's spine.

So many times, Alex had imagined what it would be like to have her own book signing. To meet people excited about her work. Now that it was happening, it didn't feel real. She felt like an imposter, like she could be called out at any moment.

"I can't believe I'm here," she said finally.

"Believe it. You've got a story people want to hear."

Alex looked at the cover again. It wasn't *her* they wanted to meet, but Jamie. Timothy took the moment of silence to jump into a rundown of what to expect of the day. Alex knew her social interaction battery would be shot before the first hour was done, but she kept the smile on her face.

"You can do this," Timothy said as the bookstore clerk unlocked the doors.

Alex slipped into the seat. As the first customer walked through the doors, Alex kept her head high. *I did it. This is really happening.*

It seemed as if all she had to do was blink and the lobby was full of readers eager to meet her and read her—*Jamie's*—story. Alex had never felt so *seen* before. So many smiling faces, so many people excited to meet her. Alex didn't know what to feel. She tried to be friendly through the entire thing, but their questions were like fresh wounds across her heart.

Timothy must've noticed. He set a hand on her shoulder and said to those still in line, "Miss Alpine will be taking a little break. She'll be back shortly."

Groans and murmurs filled the store. Alex blocked it all out and slumped against her chair, picking up a copy of her book. She ran her finger over Jamie's face.

"Are you okay?" Timothy asked.

She looked up at him before looking back at the image. "Yeah, I'll be fine. It's…hard."

The doors to the shop opened with a bang as someone forced their way inside. Everyone turned to look, and Alex's stomach hurt when she realized it was Peter. He shouldered people out of his way, storming right up to the table. As hard as he could, he slammed his hands down between her piles of books. When one slipped onto the floor, he picked it up, sneering.

"Are you serious right now? I woke up, and you were

gone. I saw on the news where you were." He tossed the book back down with a thump. "When were you planning on telling me?"

"I wasn't," she said, voice crisp and clear.

Peter let out an ethereal roar of rage and frustration and knocked the entire pile of books to the floor, staring at Alex as if he were ready to lunge across the table and throttle her.

Alex slid out of her chair, and slipped backward, ready for a fight. Timothy stood between her and Peter. "Can we get security over here!"

The security guard descended on Peter, grabbing him by the top of the arm. "Time to go, buddy."

"Let go of me!" Peter snarled before turning to Alex. "You bitch! You owe me answers! Alexxxx!"

Alex kept her eyes on the table as the sounds of his insults grew farther and farther away then disappeared. She kept her focus on the picture of Jamie's face, and closed her eyes, holding that image at the center of her mind.

TIMOTHY TRIED TO get her to put off the rest of the signing until the next day, when both she and the situation had calmed down, but Alex wanted to push through. She sold all the copies he'd brought sooner than either of them expected.

Apparently, the drama had been good for sales.

Timothy let her leave early, but after the scene with Peter, Alex wasn't ready to go home where she'd have to face that anger in private. Instead, she hopped the bus, once again making the journey back to Warren.

In town, the wind blew through Alex's hair, chilling her as she crossed the field. It was warmer than the last time she'd visited, but still colder than any of the days she'd spent with Jamie. Alex crossed through the streets, finding her way to the cemetery. In her hands, she clutched a copy of her book—the first one that had been printed. She focused on the shiny cover as she stepped over the plaques, at last making it to a tiny spot toward the back of the lot. She dropped to her knees, running her hand through the dirt.

The shade from the nearby tree made it cooler here than in the other parts of the graveyard. Was that the only due to the shade or something more? Perhaps Jamie's spirit still lingered nearby. Waiting for her. The plaque that Damien had paid to have constructed had finally come in, the shining surface gleaming up at her.

"I'm here," she whispered, lying beside it. She stretched her fingers out, feeling the dirt.

What she was searching for, she didn't know. Nearby came the chirping of a bird, and she closed her eyes, imagining it was Jamie speaking to her, telling her things he no longer could.

"I did it," she said, setting the book into the dirt. "Or should I say, *we* did it. They all know your story. The *real* story. Just like you wanted."

She turned on her side, staring at the plot as if she expected him to emerge from it and congratulate her. The plastic coating on the book cover shone in the light, and she stared at the picture again. She was glad that he'd forced her to take it because over time, the memories in her head would start to fade. That scared her. Eventually, she wouldn't be able to remember what his voice sounded like, the way he smelled. When she closed her eyes, she found the phenomenon was already starting to happen.

She brought to mind her favorite memories. The smile he'd given her when she'd told him she was working on his book, the way he'd tuck a strand of her hair behind her ear to see her smile back. Lost in her memories, it didn't take long for her to drift away.

Chapter Fifty-Four

DAMIEN WAS THE one to find her. When he roused Alex from her trance, she was so cold, she was sure she had died. In the warmth of Damien's car, memories of the day came back to her. He gave her time to process everything and clean herself up before they went to his restaurant.

Nestled in a booth, Damien took a long swig of his drink and stared at her. "We gotta stop meeting like this."

"How'd you know where to find me?" she asked.

"I didn't. I have a habit of stopping by his grave," Damien said. "Not much else to do in this town."

Alex swallowed a bite of her burger, the warmth settling in her stomach. "The book came out today."

"Jamie's biography?"

Alex looked in her bag then remembered that she left her copy at Jamie's grave. "Yeah, I had my first signing today."

"How'd that go?"

"Fine until my husband showed up and trashed the place. He got carted out by security."

"Oh."

"Yeah, it's…been a day."

"I can imagine," Damien said and tossed a chip in his mouth. "I'd ask how things have been between you two, but that kind of answers that."

"We're separating."

"I'm sorry to hear that."

"Don't be."

Damien leaned on his elbows and looked at her carefully. "Do you have a place to stay?"

Alex thought of the apartment. How cramped and insignificant it made her feel. How stressful it was when Peter was home.

She shrugged.

"You know…Jamie's house is on the market again if you're looking for somewhere to buy. I'd co-sign a loan if you needed me to."

Alex stared at him, stunned by his kindness. "Why would you do that for me?"

"Jamie was my best friend. I'd hate to see his things go to someone who never knew him."

Before Alex could respond, her phone started to ring. She didn't look at it, certain she would see Peter's name on the caller ID. Thinking of the incident in the bookstore made her shiver. She ignored it and took another bite of her burger.

Damien watched her curiously. "Is that your phone?"

"Yeah."

"I think you should get that."

Alex gave in and pulled out the phone. When she saw Katherine's number, she scrambled to answer it. Her sister-in-law rarely, if ever, called her.

It must be an emergency.

"Alex? Where are you?" Katherine asked. Her voice was high, full of something Alex couldn't quite identify. Fear?

"I uh…I went out for a while," Alex said, pulling her

eyebrows together. She didn't want to explain that she'd once again made the four-hour trip out of town. "Why?"

"I need you to come down to the police station as soon as you can and get Katrina. Peter's in custody."

Alex wasn't sure she heard her correctly. "What?"

"He's being charged with a hit and a run. He put a lady in the hospital," Katherine said. She sounded so much older than her twenty-five years.

"Is he going to jail?"

"Looks like it. I'm with Katrina right now, and she needs you. I need to handle Peter's legal stuff so please hurry."

"I'll be there as soon as I can," Alex said and hung up. She stared at the wall for a minute, processing what Katherine had said.

"That sounded important," Damien said, after a minute passed.

"That was my sister-in-law. My ex has been arrested for a hit and run."

Damien looked at her sympathetically. "Seems like your day is far from over."

Alex gathered her bag on her lap. "You can say that again."

"Do you have a ride home?" he asked.

She peered up at him, wincing as she said, "Not exactly."

He smiled in a way that told her he'd already anticipated that answer.

"Anyway you can drive me home?"

Damien looked at the clock on the wall and back at her. He rolled his shoulders, clearly debating his answer before he said, "Yeah, what the hell."

***

ALEX THANKED DAMIEN a thousand times over when he dropped her off at home four hours later. He hadn't asked for a thing in return, but she dug in her bag for any and all loose bills she could give him. She tossed them in the passenger seat and slammed the door before he could protest.

In the apartment, Katherine and Katrina played blocks together as if nothing was amiss.

"Sorry it took me so long," Alex said, panting as she dropped her bag by the door.

Katherine stood and approached Alex as she took off her coat. "Where have you been?"

"I had a book signing today," Alex said, almost surprised Peter hadn't told Katherine since she was sure he'd used his one phone call on his sister. "I was out of town."

"Hell of a day for a trip," Katherine said, hands on her hips. She looked at Katrina. Alex did too. Katherine leaned toward her to keep her voice low as she said, "She doesn't know yet. Thankfully, Peter dropped her off with me before going on his drive."

Katherine stared at her, and Alex guessed she was waiting for her to ask how this could've happened, but Alex wasn't surprised. After all the times he'd trapped her in the car and threatened to crash it, it was no mystery.

It was an eventuality.

"How long is he facing?" Alex asked.

"I don't know yet," Katherine admitted. "He's looking at least at aggravated assault and reckless endangerment. Possibly more charges if the lady gets worse."

"I'm sorry," Alex said, but she didn't really know why. She didn't mean it.

Katherine set her jaw. "I'm not. He's old enough to know better. To *do* better. I'm just glad you two weren't in the car when it happened."

"Thank you," Alex said.

Katherine pulled her into her arms. "Regardless of what happens between you and my brother, for better or worse, we're family. Remember that."

"Will do," Alex said and watched her take her leave.

As soon as she was gone, Alex plopped onto the couch, exhausted. What a day it had been.

"I love you, Mommy," Katrina said, clueless to the weight of their situation.

"I love you too," Alex said and dropped onto the floor to kiss Katrina on the forehead.

The rest of the day passed in seemingly a normal fashion. Katrina didn't ask about Peter, and Alex didn't volunteer any information. She put her daughter to bed and wandered back out to the living room. Without Peter, it was quiet. Alex should've gone to sleep, but she couldn't get her mind to slow down.

She wandered through the apartment, retracing her life step by step. In the kitchen, she looked at the dent in the wall, the chipped paint where Peter had thrown a plate in the midst of an argument. In the living room, one of the cabinet doors hung askew from when he'd slammed it in anger.

It seemed like everywhere Alex looked, there were bad memories.

What happened to the good times? Had there ever been any?

In the bedroom, she pushed open the door and looked at the mess Peter had left. The dirty laundry and the burns in the carpet from dropped cigarette butts and ashes he couldn't be bothered to clean up.

She didn't know how she *should* feel about this place, but there was no way to overlook the fact that it no longer felt like home. It felt like a giant kaleidoscope of the worst time in her life, and she no longer wanted to be surrounded by any of it.

It was time to move on.

Epilogue

S ITTING IN JAMIE'S living room, on his couch with her daughter beside her felt like living in a dream, a mishmash of everything Alex knew.

She ran a hand down her daughter's hair. It was getting long, and Alex would need to find a hairdresser soon who could manage it. There were a few things she still needed to figure out.

Katrina looked up at her, sucking juice from a nearly flat juice box before looking at the television again. Alex couldn't help but think of how many times she and Jamie had sat in this place, watching television. How many times they had watched the broadcasts of her disappearance. The jaunty cartoon currently playing was a jarring contrast.

Knock, knock.

Alex hopped up, running her finger over the frame of the picture perched on the shelf over the television as she passed it. No matter how many times she looked at that photo of her and Jamie, she'd never get tired of it.

On the way to the door, she passed Jamie's bookshelf. His copies of her books were still lined up where he'd left them, but she'd filled the rest of the spaces with extra copies of his biography.

Alex pulled the door open.

Damien smiled at her from the porch. "Good morning, Alex."

"Morning," she said and stepped to the side to allow him

the room to come in. "Thank you for coming over."

"Anything I can do to help."

Alex smiled, knowing he genuinely meant it. She led him into the living room, watching him take a slow look around.

"It looks the same," he said, voice full of wonder.

Alex had left it that way on purpose. She didn't have the heart to change a thing, worried that memories of Jamie would go with it. "I haven't unpacked yet, but it probably won't change much when I do. Doesn't seem right to move things."

"It's your home now," Damien reminded her.

"I know," she said. She would slowly move her things in, but not yet. She wasn't ready.

Damien's attention moved to Katrina, smiling when her wide eyes looked back at him. "Now who do we have here?"

Katrina gulped her juice. "Who're you?"

"I'm Damien," he said and sat on the couch beside her. "I'm a friend of your mom's." He gestured to the television. "What are you watching?"

"*Frozen.*"

Alex smiled at them. "Thank you again for coming over. I know it was kind of short notice."

"No worries."

"I shouldn't be long."

He waved a hand at her. "Take as long as you need."

Alex grabbed her keys and purse. A manilla folder sat on the table by the door, and she grabbed it before pausing. "If you need anything from town, give me a call!" she said and slipped outside.

Spring air filled her lungs, pure and fresh. The budding green trees were a reminder of new life, of second chances. She took it all in and climbed into the car. She'd had it a few weeks, but still hadn't gotten used to the fact that it was *hers*. That she'd been able to buy it with money she'd earned from writing.

Something she'd never believed she could do before she'd met Jamie.

Alex tossed the folder into the passenger seat, the angle knocking the papers loose. *Petition for Divorce* peeked out. Alex picked it up, opening the folder in her lap to straighten the pages.

She stared at the title, her lip twitching. It was hard to imagine how much her relationship with Peter had changed. Strangers, friends, lovers, acquaintances, enemies, and strangers again.

There was no going back.

Alex took in a breath and carefully set the folder into the passenger seat before she started to drive. She backed down the driveway and pulled onto the gravel road. Driving the path alone led her back through her memories.

It was hard to be here and not think of Jamie.

Maybe that was what she liked about living here. It was easy to imagine he was still with her, and she supposed that in a way, he always would be. Without him, nothing in her life would've changed. She would've still been trapped in a gilded cage of her own fear and submission.

She never would've had the confidence to stand up for herself, to pull her life together, and make something of herself for her and her daughter.

"When I first saw pictures of you online, I saw someone who was hurting, someone who deserved a second chance. I couldn't save Lana, but I can save you."

Alex pulled into the parking lot, staring up at the courthouse. She scooped up her belongings and climbed out, ready to turn the page and start the next chapter of her life.